Mary C. Stevens Owens

# Memories of the Professional and Social Life of John E. Owens

Mary C. Stevens Owens

**Memories of the Professional and Social Life of John E. Owens**

ISBN/EAN: 9783337333034

Printed in Europe, USA, Canada, Australia, Japan

Cover: Foto ©Raphael Reischuk / pixelio.de

More available books at **www.hansebooks.com**

# MEMORIES OF THE PROFESSIONAL AND SOCIAL LIFE OF JOHN E. OWENS, BY HIS WIFE

JOHN MURPHY AND COMPANY
BALTIMORE - MDCCCXCII

# PREFACE.

To my husband's memory I dedicate this volume, with the earnest wish that the gift of eloquence had been mine, empowering me to render a more worthy tribute to a well-spent life.

The incentive which led me to write the book is fully designated by its title—" Memories." These imprints of happier days, ever present with me, have sometimes been voiced to our friends; and, observing how heartily they welcomed and enjoyed anecdote or incident of him they knew so well, and the enthusiasm with which his dramatic genius and fame was spoken of, I gradually became impressed with the desire to arrange in readable form the record of my husband's theatrical experience, and combine with it little events of every-day life. Of all this, as his constant companion, I had thorough knowledge, even though my ability to convey it may have proved insufficient. I fully realize that in more competent hands a biography of John E. Owens would have been brilliantly written and ranked as a finished literary work. I am not so presumptuous as to aspire to that standard. It has been a pleasure to me to (mentally) go step by step over the months and years we lived together;

and if my readers will indulgently regard that which I have transcribed as something I might have talked to them about in my own home circle, they will recognize the intent of my true position.　In so doing, their thoughts may, perhaps, dwell more upon the spirit in which my book is written than the manner in which it is rendered.　On this possibility I rest my hope, that happily I shall receive lenient criticism.

BALTIMORE, MD., *December 7th,* 1892.

# CONTENTS.

## CHAPTER VII.



## CHAPTER VIII.



## CHAPTER IX.



## CHAPTER X.



## CHAPTER XI.



## CHAPTER XII.

# ILLUSTRATIONS.

# MEMORIES OF JOHN E. OWENS.

## CHAPTER I.

Birth of *John E. Owens*—English and Welsh ancestors—School days in Philadelphia—Early indications of dramatic talent—Reading play-books—Owens hopelessly stage-struck—He meets a kindred spirit—Hamlet with comic denouement—First visit to a theatre—Supernumerary at the National Theatre—"speaking parts"—Relinquishes theatrical hopes—*William E. Burton*—Encouraging advice—Return to the stage—Pronounced hit—Alexina Fisher—Mr. and Mrs. D. P. Bowers—"I am so confoundedly young"—Astronomical lecture—Transient prosperity—A stampede 1844–45—Season with Peale at Baltimore Museum—Mary Gannon—Mrs. Russell (Mrs. John Hoey)—Wallack—Booth—Mrs. John Drew—Charlotte Cushman—"A bear on the Roof!"—Consequences! Season of 1846–47, with Ludlow & Smith—Début at New Orleans—The pill box dressing case.

THE professional life of an artist belongs to the public. They have a right to discuss and pronounce upon its merits and demerits, however unknown to them may be his personal career. Having, by talent and devotion to his art, achieved fame and position, he invokes deserved admiration; but when in addition to this, he

1

entwines himself about the hearts of people by geniality, integrity, and kind deeds, there is a bond between the artist and the public, rendering a natural sequence that whatever concerns their favorite, will be received with interest. Under this impression I submit my " memories " of a life, whose brilliant histrionic record was only equalled by the goodness and sympathetic tenderness known best to friends in every-day life.

Many of the incidents I shall narrate are personal recollections of my own. Others have been gathered from friends and acquaintances. All are authentic and reliable, which I hope will entitle them to attention, even though I am well aware that an abler pen than mine is required to do justice to the work I have undertaken.

I do not make the faintest claim to literary merit; on the contrary, I deprecate the criticism that would meet my reminiscences on the plane of authorship.

I simply desire to speak of my husband's career and associations, and trust that for his sake I may obtain indulgent hearing.

John Edmond Owens was born in Liverpool, England, April 2d, 1823.

His father, the son of ap Griffith Owen, of Nant, and Annie, his wife, was christened Owen Griffith Owen; but on arriving at manhood added a final s to his last name, for euphony. The family resided at Aberdaron, in the county of Carnarvon, North Wales, until 1809, when they removed to Liverpool; Owen G. Owen was ten years old when he left his native place. Eight years afterwards, he met with John Anderton, a prominent organ builder; the acquaintance ripening into friendship resulted in an introduction to the home circle of the Andertons. They were all musical people; some of them having attained conspicuous proficiency as amateurs. Many pleasant hours were passed there; but gradually the strong attraction to the house for Owen, concentrated in the eldest daughter, Mary Anderton, whose beauty and sweetness of disposition rendered her very loveable. After a somewhat prolonged courtship they were married. Their first-born child was John E. Owens, destined to render famous the name he bore.

During the summer of 1828, Owen G. Owens decided to make a home in America for himself and family. They left Liverpool in a sailing vessel, and after eight weeks voyage landed in Philadelphia. Several relatives had already taken up their residence in that city. Among them, the mother of Owen G. Owens, who, though she had acquired the English language, still spoke in her native tongue to those who understood it. She became prominent and useful in Welsh Societies, and often acted as interpreter to those newly arrived from Wales. Her children and grandchildren being much with the old lady, were familiar with the language; and all his life, John Owens would now and again at home use a Welsh word or sentence with perfect accent.

On the maternal side, John's people were English; some of them being clergymen in the Episcopal church, of which they were all members. His father became a naturalized citizen of America shortly after arriving here.

As soon as the family were settled in their new home, John's education was looked to. He had the advantage of the best schools in Philadelphia, and at an early age gave evidence of aptness for intelligent study. Not content with simply memorizing his lessons, he was always eager to propound questions with a view to deeper insight and clearer knowledge of the subject. On composition and "recitation days" especially he was a favorite scholar. While still a little chap, his teacher would place in his hand a cane, and putting spectacles on his nose have him recite "Pity the sorrows of a poor old man,"—or rather *act it*—for this he did intuitively. Quick of memory, and fond of reciting, the home circle was not free from the boy's bent of "speaking pieces"—*apropos* of which, on one occasion, the baby sister was given to him to hold. Proud of the trust reposed, he kept her tightly clasped, until, through his mind began to run the lines of "Young Norval," to which he immediately gave voice—safely

Cordially Yours
Mrs John E. Owens.

enough till the words—"Rush'd like a torrent down the vale;" impelled him to suit the action to the word, and throw out both arms; when down tumbled the baby sister, whose cries brought John to his senses and his mother to the rescue. Fortunately, no injury beyond fright was sustained.

As he advanced in boyhood, his taste for reading and study increased, but not to the extent of becoming a bookworm. Gifted with a retentive mind, so great was the impression made thereon by his studies, that he could render full justice to them, and yet have leisure for enjoyment of boating, gunning, and like sports to which athletic youths incline. Replete with health and joyous spirits, and lovingly tender-hearted to those at home, he was as the good mother often said, "the sunshine of the house."

When about fourteen years old, he chanced to come into possession of two play-books — "Richard the Third," and "The Spectre Bridegroom." He read, and re-read them, not only at home, but they were smuggled into school. Masking them under cover of a study book, he regaled himself by stealth. This went on unsuspected for awhile, but one day the schoolmaster surprised the deception, and wresting the play-books from young John, severely remarked: "I will settle with you about this, later on." Deprived of his limited, but sole dramatic literature, under the displeasure of Gray, the schoolmaster, of whom he was really fond, the lad was very unhappy. Deeply chagrined, he awaited the expected reprimand and punishment.

Several days elapsed, and then Gray called him aside and returned the books with a mild rebuke for reading them *in school;* adding, after a pause—"If you have any more play-books, my boy, lend them to me." Thus, the dreaded scolding was not only averted, but the schoolmaster and his pupil became great chums.

Years afterwards, while playing a star engagement in Pittsburg, he unexpectedly met his former teacher; now a very old man, and in poverty. Pleased at the rencontre, which brought back the memory of his boyhood, he prevailed upon Gray to adjourn with him to a restaurant, where they had a delightful talk over a good dinner and a bottle of wine. Invigorated in mind and body, the old gentleman's depression vanished, and he was for the nonce happy. Regarding Owens proudly, he exclaimed, "Ah! my boy, your professional success is founded on our reading play-books *together. I* fostered the bent of your taste—and see the result!" He witnessed the performance at night, and was yet more enthused. Waiting at the stage door to say "good-bye," he quite broke down in expressing gratitude for the brightness which Owens had brought into his life, so long an experience of gloom. They met no more, but Gray was always remembered so long as he lived.

Strongly attracted to theatrical life, Owens yet deemed it almost unattainable, as no source however remote, seemed open to him to form the acquaintance of any one connected with a theatre. Despairing of this, his next choice of a future was "going to sea"—the outcome of reading Capt. Cook's voyages, and similar books, that inspire such taste in boys of brave and adventurous nature. He made known this desire to his father, requesting that a position as cabin boy be obtained for him. Both parents gave a decided negative to this request. The father inclined to the medical profession for his son; and to further this intention placed him with Dr. Samuel Jackson, druggist, Tenth Street, Philadelphia.

In the same store was a very bright youth, named James Woodhouse, somewhat John's senior. Soon they discovered to their delight, that they had a mutual taste —I may say longing. Each desired to become an actor. Much "spouting" went on in that store during the proprietor's absence, for Woodhouse was the fortunate owner of many play-books. One day they were essaying a portion of the fifth act of Hamlet. Woodhouse personating Laertes, and Owens, with a table cover draped over him for a cloak, striving to look melancholy, as Hamlet. All went on to their satisfaction, until the " divine afflatus " reached a climax and Owens, with much gesticulation, throwing aside the "inky cloak" —gave the lines "This is I, Hamlet, the Dane" came in violent collision with a shelf of bottles. Crash on crash they tumbled down, and the boys, horror-stricken, viewed the shattered fragments before them. Luckily, their employer was lenient, and the penalty of the accident fell lightly.

By and by, James Woodhouse imparted the startling information, that *he*, had actually stood before the footlights. " How did you get there ? " said the awe-stricken Owens. " How? Why, as a supernumerary ; and so can you." This was the thin edge of the wedge to revive hope in the heart of the young aspirant for histrionic life.

Though unmistakably stage-struck, he had never been in a theatre but twice. The first time, was with his father ; the bill being " *The Mountaineer* " and " *Robinson Crusoe.*" A most blissful evening to the boy, affording him enjoyment which lasted for weeks afterwards. Obtaining a book of the Mountaineer, he read it with avidity, over and over again ; every page being to him, not only entrancing, but illuminated akin to reality, from having seen it enacted. Edmon S. Conner (who played Octavian) he regarded as almost superhuman ; and had the future been then predicted that he would be professionally associated with this hero, such a prophecy could not have been regarded as otherwise than impossible of fulfilment.

On his second visit to a theatre, from the pit of the "Arch Street," he enjoyed the spectacle of "*The Forty Thieves.*" Arriving early, he obtained a seat quite near the stage; and as the play progressed, somewhat regretted his close proximity to the band of robbers. To his youthful and inexperienced eye, they appeared exceedingly fierce, and seemed to threateningly scowl at those near them in the audience; repressing with difficulty a desire to make an attack upon the inoffensive spectators. Long years afterwards, in mentioning this experience, he used to laugh at the thrill inspired by burnt cork moustachios; and a scowl engendered from nervous fright, awkwardness, and a fear of being recognized, and guyed by acquaintances.

But, to return from this digression, to the conference between Woodhouse and Owens, about going on the stage. An advertisement shortly afterwards appeared in the "Ledger," requiring a large number of "supers" for a spectacle about to be produced at the National Theatre, by William E. Burton, the famous comedian, manager, and author. Owens presented himself as an applicant, was accepted; and thus, at the age of seventeen, he began his theatrical life. Night after night, he managed to be on duty unknown to his parents or employer. One evening he had quite a scare. While advancing in a procession of supers, he saw his father with some friends in a box near the stage. Forgetting how much the super's dress and make-up disguised him, he thought the time of discovery had arrived. To use his own words when relating the incident: "I could have sworn that our eyes met, and what astonished me was, that no angry manifestations followed."

Weeks went on and the novelty of being behind the scenes, and before the footlights waned. No prospect of advancement appeared. True, he had now and then a few lines to speak, but the result was not always satisfactory. As, for instance. In a melodrama, being cast for first murderer, and another youth for second murderer, they were much elated with having "speaking parts" assigned them; and ambitious to make the most of the opportunity—*over*studied.

Their first dialogue, informs the audience of intention to commit a murder. During the Third Act, they again appear, and discuss the deed that has been done, and their fear of detection. Owing to excitement, the lines in the Third Act, were spoken *first*. Coming off the stage, they gazed hopelessly at each other. "What shall we say in the Third Act?" was the mutual interrogation.

WILLIAM E. BURTON,

COMEDIAN.

Owens met the emergency, by *striving* to bridge over the dilemma with interpolation; but his efforts were only partially successful. He was fined and severely reprimanded. This, together with the information that "*speaking* parts" would be withheld from him for awhile, was very depressing. Despairing of making progress in the profession, he withdrew, and tried to concentrate his thoughts on the duties of his situation at the drug store.

One day, on his way home to dinner, he heard his name called from the opposite side of the street; looking up, he saw Mr. Burton; he went over and was accosted thus:—"My little Owens, I haven't seen you about the theatre for some time!" "No, Mr. Burton," he replied, "I don't think I'll ever make an actor, so I keep away." "Nonsense," said Burton, "you haven't tried long enough —must learn to walk before you can run—I'd like to have a talk with you. Can you come up to my house?" "Certainly, Mr. Burton; whenever it suits you." An appointment was made, and kept, the result of which was, the return of Owens to the National Theatre; not as a supernumerary, but for speaking parts of a few lines, with promise of advancement.

The Ocean Child was brought out at the National Theatre, September 23, 1841, and Owens cast for Peter Poultice, the first part of importance that had ever been given to him. He made a hit. This prominence being mentioned by the press, revealed to his parents the fact that their son was on the stage. Their surprise was great; but resentment for the concealment was overcome by gratification at his success. Relatives, friends, and neighbors, were invited by the family to go to the National Theatre to see the "Ocean Child," and witness "our John's" performance of Peter Poultice. The piece had a good run, and was revived later in the season. The original cast being as follows:

### THE OCEAN CHILD.

CAPTAIN MANDEVILLE.......................................MR. J. B. ROBERTS.
(of the Windsor Castle).
CAPTAIN STURDY (of the Earl Grosvenor)...... .........MR. SHERMAN.
HARRY HELM.................................................MR. E. S. CONNER.
(an able sailor, on the Windsor Castle).
DENNIS O'TROT (his messmate)..............................MR. E. SHAW.
KOHREK (a Malay sailor)........ ...............................MR. OAKEY.
PETER POULTICE (an apothecary's apprentice)..............MR. OWENS.
JOEL JUNK (otherwise Old Davy Jones)....................MR. ARCHER.
MARY HELM (Harry's wife)..............................MRS. GEO. JONES.
Malays, European Sailors, Midshipmen, &c., &c.

### ACT 2.

(After a lapse of eighteen years).

SIR ARTHUR HAMILTON................................MR. J. B. ROBERTS.
(formerly Captain Mandeville).
CAPTAIN WORTHYMAN................................ .MR. W. THOMPSON.
(of the Antelope).

JACK HELM NEPTUNE........................................MISS ALEXINA FISHER.
LIEUTENANT MANLY...........................................MR. VANSTAVOSEN.
WILL CAPSTAN (a midshipman)...............................MR. BOWERS.
DENNIS O'TROT (landlord of the Shamrock)..............MR. E. SHAW.
DR. POULTICE (Surgeon Dentist)...........................MR. OWENS.
(Man, Horse, and Cow Doctor).
OLD CURIOUS (the steward)....................................MR. ARCHER.
MARY HELM (a maniac)..........................................MRS GEO. JONES.
MARGERY O'TROT.................................................MISS H. SHAW.
KATE (her daughter)............................................MRS. R. CANTOR.

It is a singular coincidence, that his first mark in the profession, should have been made by the personation of an apothecary's apprentice, the position he then occupied in real life. Once having tasted applause, over went the mortar and pestle, and every energy was bent to becoming an actor. Though young, he was not unduly elated by the praise he received, but realized that much study was indispensable. He, therefore, severed his connection with the drug store, and entered with intensity of purpose into the profession—to which, in later years, he was so great an acquisition, so brilliant an ornament.

His course was now onward and upward. The National Theatre, this season, had an excellent stock company; among whom was Miss Alexina Fisher, Edmon S. Conner, Mrs. Rachel Cantor and others.

Alexina Fisher was, perhaps, one of the most polished and attractive juvenile actresses that ever adorned the stage. She afterwards starred successfully, and is best known to the present generation as Mrs. John Lewis Baker. She died in 1887, leaving a son, John Lewis Baker, and a daughter, who is the wife of John Drew. Mrs. Rachel Cantor (then an excellent soubrette) in later years played first old woman acceptably. She travelled with Laura Keene and other prominent stars. At present, she is an inmate of the Forrest Home.

D. P. Bowers, was among the youngsters of the company. He had been popular as a "boy star;" but after retiring from the role of a prodigy, wisely determined to commence at the bottom of the ladder, and strive ·for eminence on a more secure and gradual footing. He became a clever light comedy actor. Graceful, easy, and natural in whatever character he assumed, and was well known throughout the country. He died in 1857 at the age of thirty-five, leaving a widow who has always been a favorite with the public, and for many years a prominent star in the profession she graces. The name of Mrs. D. P. Bowers is familiar to all, and her talent as a great actress thoroughly established.

From 1841 to 1844, Owens played frequently under Burton's management. Mostly in Philadelphia, but occasionally in Baltimore and elsewhere; during which time many brilliant actors were associated with the company, not only as stars, but in the stock. I find a cast of Hamlet in a play-bill of December 16th, 1841; the strength of which, it would be difficult to surpass.

## BURTON'S NATIONAL THEATRE, PHILADELPHIA.

HAMLET ......................................................MR. EDWIN FORREST.
GHOST........................................................MR. J. R. SCOTT.
LAERTES......................................................MR. J. WALLACK.
HORATIO......................................................MR. E. S. CONNER.
CLAUDIUS (King of Denmark)........................MR. J. B. ROBERTS.
POLONIUS. ..................................................MR. W. JONES.
ROSENCRANTZ...............................................MR. HOWARD.
OSRICK ......................................................MR. BECK.
GUILDENSTERN...............................................MR. SHERMAN.
MARCELLUS...................................................MR. WATSON.
FIRST GRAVEDIGGER........................................MR. W. E. BURTON.
SECOND GRAVEDIGGER......................................MR. OWENS.
FRANCISCO...................................................MR. OAKEY.
FIRST ACTOR.................................................MR. BOWERS.
SECOND ACTOR...............................................MR. WATSON.
PRIEST.......................................................MR. VENUA.
GERTRUDE (Queen of Denmark).....................MRS. GEORGE JONES.
OPHELIA......................................................MISS JOSEPHINE CLIFTON.
PLAYER QUEEN...............................................MRS. A. KNIGHT.

Our young aspirant for theatrical fame had every
advantage in daily observation of so much genius; and
the rehearsals as well as performances were closely
watched as a medium of instruction. His ambition was
great, but never o'erleaped itself, for he realized how
very much he had to learn, before he could, in any
degree, approach the position for which he was striving.

One day Mr. Burton said to him: "I think you
would play Zekiel Homespun, well—that is, if you can

speak the dialect—will you try it?" "Let me read the part first, Mr. Burton, and then I can tell you." He took home the book of "*The Heir at Law*" which Mr. Burton lent him, but made no additional remark; for, impressed with the importance of the character assigned him, he was too excited to speak. Past midnight before Zekiel and he parted company, and even when he fell asleep, the lines were in his mind. Next day he asked Mr. Burton to hear him speak a sentence, that his dialect might be tested. "Perfect, my boy," said Burton; "now learn the part." "I have memorized the *words* already," replied Owens, "and I shall study the part and hope to know it too."

He was very nervous when the night for "*The Heir at Law*" arrived. Burton, who played Dr. Pangloss, tried to inspire him with confidence, and thus encouraged he gave a truly excellent performance of *Zekiel*, eliciting warm encomiums. His youthful appearance admirably suited with the hearty, healthy country lad he was representing—albeit, sometimes the bright eyes and boyish face, were obstacles to his make-up.

One night, Mr. Ferris, a mature actor whose dressing room he shared, found him almost crying over unsatisfactory endeavors to effect a resemblance to Bailie Nicol Jarvie, the part in Rob Roy for which he was cast. He confided his woe, thus—"I know the lines, and the business perfectly, but I can't *look* like the character. Oh,

Mr. Ferris, what shall I do; I am so confoundedly young!" With a shrewd dry smile, Ferris replied— "Don't be worried about it, time will cure that, cheer up!"

"*Dr. Ollapod*" in *The Poor Gentleman* was played by Owens at twenty-four hours' notice, and he was dead-letter perfect. True, it did not equal the polished rendition of that character in his riper years; but the performance was creditable.

In the summer vacation of 1840, Owens joined a company which was organized on commonwealth basis, to travel through small towns. Their experience was limited and the treasury even more infinitesimal. Bad business made a short season. In Richmond, Virginia, they disbanded. During the fortnight they played there, Owens became quite a favorite. His clever, though crude, portrayal of the leading comedy, his ready wit, and inexhaustible humor, attracted much attention; and made for him, friends, as well as admirers. One of the prominent citizens, Dr. H—— took a great fancy, and personal liking to the young comedian; and invited him to make a visit to his home on Shockœ Hill. This courtesy was accepted; and Owens became the Doctor's guest, after the disbanding of the company. Not only was the hospitality of the Doctor and his family charmingly agreeable, but access to Dr. H——'s extensive and valuable library was an additional enjoyment. Among

2

other books, were many rare works on Astronomy. This having been a favorite study with Owens, he was glad of the opportunity to increase his knowledge.

By and by, an idea occurred to him. The renewal of theatrical engagement during the summer was impossible. "Why shouldn't he lecture on Astronomy, and earn money to keep him till the fall season began?" He consulted Dr. H——, who much amused, said—"You look far too young for a Professor of Astronomy—moreover, everyone will know you, and laugh, remembering your comicalities. "I can change my name, and wear green spectacles," retorted the youngster;—the Doctor laughed, entered into the matter as a frolic, and promised every assistance in his power;—and so, the writing of the lecture began.

Hard study and the Doctor's library stood Owens good stead. His MS. was soon written. Seeking the companionship of an acquaintance, they joined issue in finances, purchased a magic lantern with astronomical pictures; and arranged a partnership. Owens as lecturer and illustrator, Dawes as door-keeper and general factotum. Off they started to make a tour of the adjacent villages. Sometimes journeying by stage coach, but more frequently on foot for sake of economy. Light-hearted, young, and strong in health, they thoroughly enjoyed the adventurous freedom of the project. Their advertisements and programmes were written in a big round hand, and nailed up in the grocery store, tavern, and blacksmith shop of each village they visited.

At first, the entertainment scored a success with the country people; for (in those days) any public amusement was a novelty to them. Professor Roberts (?) wearing green spectacles and his hair brushed back, was of imposing appearance as a lecturer; and his fluently delivered discourse interested the listeners. His assistant, Mr. Smith (?) was equally acceptable. They made sufficient money to meet expenses, and maintain their dignity by sojourning at the tavern, in each town, and ordering the best it afforded. This pleasant experience was brief. Slim attendance in one or two villages exhausted the exchequer. From bad to worse, they became reduced to hunger.

When referring to this escapade, Owens used to, laughingly, say, that the sorest temptation of his life, was, when standing before the cake stand of an old darkey woman, he offered her his pocket-handkerchief in exchange for a ginger cake. She refused and turned away from him —the cakes were within his reach—hunger gnawing with the intensity of twenty-four hours' fasting—he could scarcely refrain from helping himself; adding, " Indeed, it's a mercy I didn't devour the entire cake stand, old woman included." At New Glasgow, the astronomical enterprise received its death blow. A crowd of rustics gathered in front of the hall, impatient to see " the show," but the owner of the building refused to light candles, and open the door, until a portion of the rent was paid in advance. The Professor and his assistant being penniless, were unable to meet this demand; and deeming discretion the better part of valor, retreated through the back door to the hotel; inasmuch as the prospective audience were becoming noisy at the delay, and murmured threats of violence were heard.

Next day the partners discussed the situation, and agreed that their scheme was a failure; although it had its bright side in the way of " great fun." From the sale of the magic lantern, they realized enough to help them on to Richmond, each having written to their parents for funds to take them thence, home.

For the season of 1844–45, Owens received three offers for the position of first low comedian—a situation which he strongly desired to occupy, and of course, never could in Burton's theatre, as that line of business belonged to Mr. Burton. Moses Kimball of the Boston Museum wrote to him offering an engagement for the position of first comedian—mentioning as an inducement the long duration of the season in his theatre, and detailed its comfortable surroundings; concluding by saying: " I believe the engagement which I propose, would prove mutually agreeable and advantageous. Do me the favor to think the matter over thoroughly before you decide."

Peale of the Baltimore Museum, and William Shires of "Shires' Gardens," Cincinnati, also desired his services for the season. Moses Kimball claimed that greater advantage would accrue from an engagement with him, but did not offer as much salary as Peale; who again was exceeded in terms by Shires. The latter, afterwards became manager of the National Theatre, and Pike's Opera House in Cincinnati, but at the time I refer to he was owner and proprietor of "Shires' Gardens," corner of Third and Vine streets, where the Burnet House now stands. The garden occupied an entire block. It was planted with shade trees, and beautified with flower beds. Interspersed through it, were ice cream booths and places of refreshment. In the centre, stood a pretty frame theatre which was ably managed, with a good stock company supporting stars during the regular season.

In the summer months, *day* as well as night performances were given by the stock company. Here, is marked, the first introduction of *matinées* in this country. The innovation was not a great success with the public, and decidedly unpopular with the profession. In fact, the *matinée* element, caused Owens to decline Shires' offer. For some time he deliberated between Boston and Baltimore, but finally decided in favor of the latter; signing for the season with Peale, at fourteen dollars a week, and two benefits. The position with Moses Kimball, at the Boston Museum, was afterwards accepted by William

Warren; and thus began, as local favorites, the career of two comedians destined to become famous to the world, and brighten many lives. Endeared to hosts of friends, they were most beloved by those who knew them best. As this epoch marked the dawn of Owens' great success in his profession, the little theatre where he attained overwhelming popularity, and from whence he emerged as a` brilliant star, may claim some interest with my readers. I, therefore, give a succinct account of the Baltimore Museum. It was situated on the corner of Calvert and Baltimore streets. Mr. John Clark, a prominent lottery broker, purchased the site, and erected the building in 1829. The lower part was used for a banking house; and the upper part rented to Rembrandt Peale for the exhibition of curiosities, stuffed birds, pictures, &c. Five years later, Edmund Peale assumed the management and inaugurated dramatic entertainments in the Lecture room.

In 1846, P. T. Barnum bought the museum from Edmund Peale, and appointed his uncle, Alonso Taylor, manager. Mr. Taylor lived but six months afterwards. At his death the place was put in charge of Mr. Charles S. Getz, the celebrated scenic artist, whose work and talent is so widely known. Mr. Getz conducted the place until it passed into the possession of Joshua Silsbee (Yankee Comedian) and Albert Hamm—a member of the musical troupe known as the Orphean Family.

On that little stage appeared some of the best talent that ever delighted an audience. Mrs. Russell (Mrs. John Hoey), Mary Gannon, Mrs. Watts, Miss St. Clair, Mrs. D. P. Bowers, Chippendale, Davenport, J. W. Albaugh, and a host of others, won their first laurels here. Among the stars we find James Murdoch, J. B. Booth (the elder), J. W. Wallack, Joe Cowell, J. R. Scott, Charles Burke, Charlotte Cushman, Fanny Wallack, Mrs. Farren, Julia Dean, Eliza Logan, Mr. and Mrs. Barney Williams, Mrs. C. Sinclair Forrest, and many more.

Of John Owens' connection with the Museum, I shall speak more in detail as my narrative progresses. His first season began September 5th, 1844; vaudeville and farce constituted the usual dramatic attraction. Later on, Kate Ludlow joined the company as a feature in "Kate Kearney;" being noted for her singing and dancing. In November Mr. and Mrs. H. Hunt (now Mrs. John Drew) played a star engagement. Mrs. Hunt was a most fascinating and talented comedienne. Her Widow Cheerly in the Soldier's Daughter; Marian, in the Windmill; Fortunio, and all that line of characters, were wonderfully charming.

I always find pleasure in remembering them, and congratulate myself that I had the privilege of seeing her in these exquisite renditions, which will rank with the extremely different character of Mrs. Malaprop that she gives with such perfection to the public of the present day. To descant upon Mrs. John Drew's versatility and excellence as an artist is a work of supererogation—akin to "painting the lily, or gilding refined gold."

The next great attraction at the museum was "Beauty and the Beast," prettily gotten up, with the following strong cast.

### BEAUTY AND THE BEAST.

| | |
|---|---|
| BEAUTY | MRS. J. B. BOOTH. |
| THE BEAST | MR. JAMES L. GALLAGHER. |
| JOHN QUILL | MR. JOHN E. OWENS. |
| SIR ALDGATE PUMP | MR. JOHN SEFTON. |
| DRESSALINDA | MRS. RUSSELL. |
| MARYGOLD | MRS WATTS. |
| THE WILD KING | MR. MACKLIN. |

Not only the talent of the *dramatis personæ*, but considerable musical ability added thereunto, rendered this bill sufficiently attractive to draw full houses.

The Lecture room became Baltimore's fashionable place of resort, and Owens the leading favorite with all. Popular too, among his fellow actors, always bubbling with the mirthfulness which springs from a sunny nature, he found much amusement in his surroundings; though many of them were the reverse of agreeable.

Peale, not content with the inanimate curiosities of the saloon, alone, would from time to time exhibit freaks and monstrosities of various kinds. Owens was antagonistic to this mingling of theatre and menageric; but always saw the ludicrous side of the situation. I have heard him laughingly refer to it thus: "Matters culminated when I read on the bill-boards, a startling advertisement of the performance—headlines in immense letters:

'GREAT ATTRACTION!

JOHN SEFTON!!         JOHN OWENS!!!
*and*

A BEAR ON THE ROOF!!!!'

"I had been reasonably patient, but here I drew the line. Mentally, I ejaculated, 'this association, even in type, is more than I can endure.' I remonstrated with Peale, and suggested that his aim should be to elevate the drama; and *that* certainly could not be effected by placing its representatives on a plane with brute attractions. I made some impression, and he promised to reflect on what I said. Meanwhile, fate intervened. The roof of the museum did not afford congenial atmosphere to the bear. Poor Bruin pined, sickened and died; and thus we were relieved of a mortifying incubus."

Early in the autumn of 1845, W. E. Burton managed the Chestnut Street Theatre in Philadelphia. Mr. and Mrs. Charles Kean being the first stars. To strengthen the support, Owens was engaged to play second comedy to Burton, in some of the pieces, and first comedy in such as

Burton did not care to appear in. Also for the farces; in the latter he was to be made a feature.

During this engagement, Mr. and Mrs. Kean frequently made gracious recognition of the young actor's merit. He was proud of their good opinion, and his gratification was unbounded when Mrs. Kean, after the performance of "*The Stranger*," complimented him by saying, "she had never seen the part of '*Peter*' so well enacted, it being ludicrously comic, yet neat, and withal artistically rendered." In December, Owens played a star engagement of one week at the Baltimore Museum, but the rest of the season he was in Philadelphia and elsewhere, under Burton's management, diligently studying, and all the while advancing in his profession, playing more important parts and with greater finish and force.

Among the offers received for the season 1846–47, was one from Ludlow and Smith, managers of the St. Charles Theatre, New Orleans, for first low comedy business, at a moderate salary, and two benefits. This position was accepted; after signing the contract, Owens arranged to play at various towns on his way down the river to New Orleans. The route mapped out, commenced with an engagement in Pittsburg, under the management of C. S. Porter. The result was satisfactory—he made a hit—and the good impression increased during the fortnight of his stay there. The packed house, and enthusiastic audience which greeted him on his farewell night, not only gratified, but surprised, the young star.

With this inspiring beginning to the journey, he proceeded pleasantly to New Orleans, making his début there as *Sampson Low*, in " *The Windmill*," on the evening of November 21st, 1846. He was received with hearty approbation; and this success, so instantaneously attained, grew and strengthened while he remained in New Orleans. From that time until his last appearance in the dear old city, he was their favorite and beloved comedian. The stock company at the St. Charles Theatre this season was excellent—prominent therein were Sol Smith, Jerry Merryfield and wife (Rose Cline), John Weston, C. F. Adams, Proctor, Rynar, and James Wright.

At this time "The Louisiana Histrionic Association" held exalted position in New Orleans. They owned a pretty theatre on St. Charles street; it was organized and conducted with perfect discipline—each member having his line of business allotted. During the summer the players from the regular theatres were engaged by the Histrionic Association, at high salaries, and many first-class stars appeared. Of course, the amateurs being devotees of the drama were prone to seek companionship with the leading lights thereof. In this way Owens made the acquaintance of Fred N. Thayer, who came of a well known theatrical family; many of his relatives being on the stage—prominently, his uncle, E. N. Thayer, so long a favorite in Philadelphia and elsewhere.

Mr. F. N. Thayer possessed the requisites of an accomplished actor. To attractive personal appearance he added culture and refined taste, a well modulated voice, and strong elocutionary power; these gifts, prominent as an amateur, were fully developed, when, in 1855, he went on the regular stage as leading man in Dion Boucicault's company at the Gaiety Theatre, New Orleans. There, and in other cities he distinguished himself; noticeably in the rôle of Armand Duval; supporting Matilda Heron in her great success of " *Camille.*" Later on, he was chosen by that famous actress to play the part during her New York engagement.

After a few years of theatrical life, Mr. Thayer retired and engaged in mercantile business. The friendship formed between Mr. Owens and Mr. Thayer ripened as time went on and strengthened with frequent intercourse. To the close of Mr. Owens' life none held higher place in our regard than Mr. Thayer and his family. In speaking of the St. Charles Theatre Company, I omitted the names of Mr. and Mrs. George Farren. The latter was leading lady; her talent and popularity so well known, I need not descant upon.

Mr. Farren used to relate an anecdote of Owens which was amusing and also characteristic. The St. Charles Theatre Stock Company having heard that Owens was an immense favorite north, were quite prepared for the manifestation of self-importance on the part of the "New Comic," as they facetiously designated the recent addition to their corps. Mr. Farren said to them, "Well, boys, as the young man dresses with me, I will observe and report any peculiarities that may need subduing." Later in the evening, in reply to their eager questioning he said—"It is quite a mistake; our 'new comic' is by no means arrogant or ostentatious; his deportment is modest and quiet, but he *has* peculiarities, for his dressing-case of paints, &c., consists of *two pill boxes!*" I once heard Mr. Farren tell this story; and here he was interrupted by Mr. Owens good-humoredly ejaculating, "I vow, Farren, that's too rough; I deny the pill boxes;" but Farren, much to our amusement, insisted on the veracity of his story, adding, "The greater credit to you for being able to draw from such limited sources such wonderful make-ups."

# CHAPTER II.



THE facility and rapidity with which Mr. Owens
made up his face for the stage was marvellous.
His preparations, including change of costume, required
but a few moments; my early experience as his dresser
was somewhat fraught with nervousness. As he would
leisurely chat or read the evening newspaper, I could not
refrain from saying, "Do you know how late it is?
The first music has been called." "All right," he would

reply, "I shall be ready," and he invariably was. I soon learned that there was no danger of a stage wait, whether the part chanced to be the merry one of *Joshua Butterby*, or poor old *Caleb Plummer* with his piteous, deeply furrowed face, or the wizen visage of miserly old *Spruggins*. The latter, perhaps, altered Mr. Owens' appearance more than any part he played, and for *that*, I have seen him make up his face in five minutes. He never liked to be entirely dressed until his cue was near, and often said, " I couldn't *feel* the character if I waited—the excitement inspires me." In *Solon Shingle*, he was always putting on his gloves hurriedly, as he spoke the first lines without. But, I have digressed, and must pick up the thread of my narrative by returning to Mr. Owens' season at the St. Charles. Among the stellar attractions, he then had the opportunity of observing, were Mr. and Mrs. James Wallack, Mr. and Mrs. Charles Kean, Anderson, Murdoch; association with whom, could not fail to improve a young and studious actor. In speaking of the jolly and clever manager, Sol Smith, Mr. Owens used to describe his personal appearance as attractive but very remarkable in one respect; the right side of his face had a merry expression; the left, was of serious aspect. Mr. Owens would jokingly add, " the former was invariably turned to whoever he addressed during good business, and the latter when the houses were slim; and this was the only way in which Sol Smith could be double-faced ; "

the usual acceptation of that expression, was the anti-
thesis of his nature.

Owens' engagement in New Orleans closed April 16th,
1847, with a bumper benefit. About this time numerous cases of yellow fever had occurred in the French
quarter of the city. That, being the locality in which
Owens resided, his friends became alarmed for him, though
he did not share their fears. In compliance with much
importunity on the score that he was not acclimated, he
concluded to run no further risk by remaining in New
Orleans; so, made up his mind for the pleasure of a sea
voyage, to terminate with a visit to his relatives in England.

On May the third, he sailed in the bark Emerald, and
though delayed by adverse winds, the trip was very enjoyable. His recollections of England were vague; the most
vivid was that of his mother's sister, Aunt Bessie Orme,
with her sweet face, and gentle ways, and Uncle Orme,
who played and sung so delightfully, and always petted
him. When he arrived in Liverpool, some of his childish
impressions became dispelled; Nelson's monument was
puny, in contrast to his remembrance of it. The big
river Mersey greets his gaze as a mere stream. Proceeding to the home of his relatives, at Aigburth Vale, all
memories of dear Aunt and Uncle Orme were more than
realized. The same warm-hearted loving welcome met
him as in childhood. Many happy days were passed at

the old homestead, and it became so endeared to him that he registered this vow: "If I am ever rich enough to have a country place, I will call it 'Aigburth Vale.'" And so he did, six years later—improving and beautifying an estate which was *home* to us in every sense of the word, so long as he lived.

After adieux to Aunt and Uncle Orme he made a flying visit to Paris, then back to Liverpool, where he took passage in the bark Emerald, bound for the port of Baltimore. There he arrived in September. The Baltimore Museum had been much improved during the summer, the Lecture room having been altered and enlarged into a cosey theatre, with cushioned seats, private boxes, parquette, and gallery. New scenery, and decorations were designed and executed by that well known artist, Charles S. Getz. When completed, the theatre was as pretty a little place as one would wish to see. The Baltimoreans attested their appreciation by crowding the house on the night of September 7th, 1847, when Hamm and Silsbee (new managers) inaugurated the theatre with a good stock company playing *The Honeymoon*, and a farce.

On the 16th Owens began a star engagement, opening in *The Poor Gentleman* and *State Secrets*. His return was warmly welcomed; and so unanimous was the demand of the public for a continuance of his engagement, that the management offered inducements which decided him to remain as a stellar attraction. Apart from business considerations, he was well content in Baltimore, having long inclined to that city with a home feeling. After entering into a permanent agreement with Hamm and Silsbee, for an extended period, he arranged with his father that the entire family should remove from Philadelphia and reside in Baltimore.

At this time, the attractions at the Holliday St. Theatre were mostly Shakespearean (or other) tragedies. Edwin Forrest was playing to enthusiastic audiences. But these performances being so different by reason of their legitimate grandeur, in no way interfered with the cosey Museum's comedy and vaudeville entertainments. In this connection the remark was made after rehearsal, one morning, "our little place is always crowded, notwithstanding Forrest's great success." Whereupon, Owens retorted: "*Apropos* of that, I'll give you a conundrum. Why are we, at the Museum, more fortunate than those at the Holliday St. Theatre?" Several guesses being made, without solving the riddle, the perpetrator was desired to give the answer; which came in this guise: "Because, they have only *one* Forrest, great and grand as he is. While we, have our little *Forrest*, our shady *Bowers*, our green *Fields*, our lovely *Woods*, with *Dawes* pecking about; our beautiful *Rivers*, and always *Wright* with us." Thus, introducing the names of some of the ladies and gentlemen of the company; all of whom, heartily enjoyed the joke, except Mr. Fields, who rather resented the descriptive adjective appended to his name.

Many new plays were given this season, noticeably, "*The Merchant and his Clerks*," which met with great favor from the public. Owens personated *Kit Cockles*, a jolly ne'er-do-well, who among various occupations becomes an organ grinder; whilst his wife, *Betty*, plays upon the tambourine, and collects pennies (more or less— generally *less*) from the street crowd. The part is replete with humor, and was vividly embodied. To make it realistic, Owens obtained from a genuine organ grinder, the use of his organ and monkey; and received instructions how to manage both. He soon found the undertaking beyond accomplishment—so far as the monkey was concerned. The little imp was vicious when transferred to a stranger; though docile enough with his owner, who, standing at the wing, endeavored to control the animal by an admixture of menaces and profanity. Only partially succeeding—as all on the stage were in dread of being bitten by the chattering beast.

To talk of, afterwards, the scene was very funny, but anything else but amusing at the time. Struggling with the hand-organ, and fighting off the monkey in such a way as to prevent the audience from being cognizant of the *contretemps* was, as Mr. Owens said, "the hardest work he ever tackled." When the scene was over, he went up to the Italian, and remarked: "There, my good man, is your property, I gladly relinquish it. Come again to-morrow night; bring the organ, but *not* the monkey. I am convinced that I have no vocation for managing monkeys. The hand-organ alone is a gigantic undertaking. I am sure it weighs a thousand pounds." The fellow stared, scratched his head in a puzzled way, and walked off; not at all understanding the covert humor, for which he had been a target.

The play had a good run, and after its withdrawal, the query was often made of Owens: "Why don't you play Kit Cockles? it's such a funny part." "Yes," he would reply, "very funny to the audience, perhaps, but it's rather *heavy* for me." I never knew him to pass an organ grinder without giving him money; "they earn it," he would say, "for it's hard work carrying an organ. *Kit Cockles* and I, know all about that *weighty* business."

Owens' contract with the managers of the Baltimore Museum, concluded April 22, 1848, and during its seven months' duration he appeared in various characters, too numerous to mention. His versatility has never been excelled. With a voice which embraced every tone in its register, he was equally effective in humor or pathos. Gifted with personal magnetism, he held his audience spellbound; to laugh with him in rollicking merriment, or with misty eyes respond to the tenderness of his pathetic acting. Baltimore was loth to part with so great a favorite even for a short time. A month earlier Owens had signed with Burton to star at the Arch Street Theatre, in "*A Glance at Philadelphia*," a local drama, in which he played Jakey, a volunteer fireman.

Two years previous, he had been cast for a character of the same nature, in "*Change makes Change;*" a play written for Mrs. Mowatt, by Epes Sargent. The part was short and sketchy, but made a hit, and was much talked of. The play, not being a success, was soon withdrawn; but, Owens remembering the "fire laddie," so favorably received, felt confident that he should make a mark as *Jakey*—and he did; far beyond his most sanguine expectations; creating such a furore that the theatre was packed nightly—the sidewalks impassable long before the doors were open. A droll incident happened one evening, as Owens (being rather late) was hurrying along Arch street, striving to elbow his way through the surging crowd, a stout and rather rough man savagely accosted him thus: "Stop a pushing of me; do you think nobody wants to see Owens but yourself?"

The original cast, in Philadelphia, gives John Crocker, as *Harry Gordon;* T. B. Johnson, as *George Petriken;* and Mrs. C. Howard, as *Lize.* After six weeks' run, Burton brought the piece to the Front St. Theatre, Baltimore, where it met with the same enthusiastic reception and crowded houses. Returning to Philadelphia, it was again played at the Arch St. Theatre, supplemented with *Jakey's Marriage;* repeating its original success. Some changes in the cast were made during the run of the piece. Mrs. J. B. Booth, Mrs. Burke, Annie Cruise, alternating as *Lize.*

The character of *Jakey*, given by Owens, was so realistic, so exactly like the "fire boy," seen *then*, in everyday life, that it did not seem at all like *acting*. It was perfect as a type of the volunteer fireman of that period ; and as artistically true to nature in every detail, as the most elaborated Shakespearean part he ever played ; the same powerful conception of character was seen on this lower plane, as he evinced in *Touchstone, Launcelot Gobbo*, and other characters, emanating from the grand master. On the 15th of July, 1848, the season closed, with the same bill still in the meridian of its drawing power. "*Jakey*" brought thousands of dollars into Mr. Burton's treasury ; not only retrieving his losses ; but, additionally, giving him wealth. This engagement furnished Burton with the means to purchase the property in New York, afterwards known as the Chambers Street Theatre. At Burton's request, Mr. Owens went with him to inspect the premises, and give his opinion as to the eligibility of the site for a comedy theatre. They arrived in New York after dark, and Burton proposed that, having had supper, they should wend their way to Chambers street ; saying, "Why should we wait till to-morrow ?—it's a beautiful moonlight night—we can see."

Soon they were on the premises, and having stepped off the ground, discussed its purchase, the probable cost of starting the theatre—in fact, the investment in all its bearings, arriving at the conclusion, that it was in every way desirable. Thus began W. E. Burton's Metropolitan management, which marks an epoch in dramatic history, for the "Chambers Street" rapidly ranked as the leading theatre of New York; superbly producing not only the old comedies, but every new play of merit, and with a company of unsurpassed excellence. Burton played the leading comedy; his name was a tower of strength. He made his first appearance in America as *Dr. Ollapod* in *The Poor Gentleman* at the Arch St. Theatre, Philadelphia, September, 1834. He began his career as an actor in London, appearing at the Pavilion Theatre, Whitechapel, as *Wormwood* in *The Lottery Ticket*. Mr. Burton had much experience as a manager, he was also well known in literature, but his superlative merit was seen on the stage; he was a *great* actor. Captain Cuttle was, perhaps, his best part; but in all that he did, superior talent shone brilliantly attractive. He was coarse at times, but his humor was infectious, and his command over an audience, something marvellous.

But, to return to the inception of the Chambers St. Theatre. Burton appreciated the fact that to Owens, he was indebted for this rapid stride to fortune, and evinced the same at the conclusion of the Philadelphia engagement, by the presentation of a massive silver vase bearing the following inscription :

*Presented by*

WILLIAM E. BURTON

*to*

JOHN E. OWENS

As a memorial of his unprecedented popularity in
the character of *Jakey*, in the local Drama
of *"A Glance at Philadelphia,"* at
the *Arch Street Theatre,*
*Philadelphia,*
1848.

The summer vacation Owens passed in New England, recuperating health and strength, after a long season of over ten months' laborious work. Returning to Baltimore, in September, he again signed with Hamm and Silsbee, for a star engagement, to be renewed if mutually satisfactory. In November, he retired from this contract, in consequence of disagreement with the managers ; he then rented the little theatre at the corner of Charles and Baltimore streets known as "The Howard Athenæum." This he inaugurated with a strong company headed by himself. The public responded to the undertaking by cramming the house nightly.

*En passant,* it was here that Dolly Davenport made his début. He was in the employment of S. Kirk & Sons, jewelers and silversmiths, under his real name, A.

MR. OWENS as JAKEY

In "A Glance at Philadelphia."

D. Hoyt. Becoming stage-struck, he sought an introduction to Owens, and obtained the opportunity to try his power. The experiment was made as *Fred Thornton* in "*The Dead Shot.*" I have heard him say, that the stage fright he experienced, amounted almost to collapse. In the scene where Thornton is brought on, feigning to be dangerously wounded, he has to rise suddenly, and acknowledge the ruse. When the cue came, the unfortunate debutant was too frightened to move, and the whispered promptings of the soubrette were unheeded, until she stealthily stuck a pin in him, and thereby caused a reaction. Dolly Davenport continued under Mr. Owens' management, and improved rapidly; in three months he was playing leading juvenile comedy acceptably.

Under the same management (at the Baltimore Museum) George Jordan, then a printer, made his first appearance on the stage. He was afterwards prominent in the New York theatres; and later on a favorite in New Orleans at La Variete Theatre, while Owens was manager of that famous temple of the drama. George Jordan left New Orleans in 1861, for England; from whence he returned to this country but once; then, in support of Kate Bateman.

As the year 1848 waned, Joshua Silsbee became desirous of retiring from management, and offered to sell his half of the Baltimore Museum to Owens. After some negotiation, the transfer was made. The bright, though brief, season at the Howard Athenæum closed January 1st, 1849. Owens returned to the Old Museum, and took the helm; the management being known as Hamm and Owens; though Hamm's interest was entirely monetary, he being without experience in theatrical affairs. Prosperity smiled on this enterprise, and the winter of 1849 was marked with brilliant performances, both star and stock.

April 19th, 1849, Mr. Owens was married in Baltimore, after an engagement of three years, to Mary C. Stevens, daughter of John G. Stevens, Merchant, Bowly's Wharf. The ceremony was performed by the Rev. Alfred Miller, Rector of Mount Calvary Church. The marriage did not meet with the approbation of Mr. Stevens; he being a member of the primitive Methodist church, and holding prejudices against a profession of which he really *knew* nothing. On the day of the marriage, whilst he was seated in his counting room, brooding over the shock the news had given him, Col. George P. Kane, an intimate friend, came in, and approaching him joyously, said: "Mr. Stevens, I take pleasure in congratulating you on the acquisition of such a son-in-law as John E. Owens. Had I daughters, I would be proud if they were so fortunate in the selection of a husband. *I* know Owens and his reputation, well; he is a man who combines talent with a noble nature and moral integrity."

To this kindly recognition, the young couple owed their restoration to parental favor. Mr. Stevens had great faith in Col. Kane's opinion, and wisely reflected that his personal association with Mr. Owens was likely to be a basis for truer judgment than the inherited prejudices of Methodism. He realized this fully when he became acquainted with his son-in-law. A strong attachment sprang up between them, and increased as time went on. No son could have been more devoted than was John E. Owens to his father-in-law, to whose declining years he was a comfort and a blessing. Daughter and son shared alike, nursing him through his protracted and final illness. The last words spoken were a loving call for "*my* son, John E. Owens."

I refer to these family personalities as briefly as possible, and would not mention them at all, could they be omitted consistently with the continuity of my narrative.

In May, 1849, Owens became lessee of the National Theatre, in Washington, for the purpose of producing Italian Opera on a grand scale. The troupe included Rossi Crossi, Susini, Strini, Amalia Patti, and many other luminaries; together with a full chorus. *Appreciative* audiences attended the excellent performances given; but, unfortunately, the meagreness of numbers gave little encouragement to the manager in his ambitious enterprise. The expenses incurred were heavy; the receipts, disastrously light. After two weeks of ruinous business,

Owens brought the company to the Baltimore Museum, inaugurating "Grand Opera" at cheap prices; thinking thereby to create an excitement and pack the house; but, instead of such a result, dire bad business ensued. As the same ill luck continued in Washington, where the elder Booth had followed the Opera Company, the young manager was losing money right and left—but he was not disheartened. "Buying experience," he called his reverses, and found a humorous side to his misfortune.

One of his stories, in connection with that time, was about Rossi Crossi (director of the Opera Company). With excellent imitation of the Italian artist, Owens would relate the usual Monday interview. The terms of the engagement were: "a certainty, payable weekly." Rossi Crossi with much suavity, would receive a check for the amount and remark: "I am mooch desolate, to to be oblige' to receive dis monish, when ze people do not attendez ze Opera. I can recognize no reason why we not draw; for I do assure you, Monsieur Owens, we are mooch talented." Then, he would fold the check, put it in his pocket and walk away, leaving the perplexed manager to financier for ways and means to meet the requirement of a repetition of the interview, a week later.

It is impossible for me to narrate this, or any other story, with the effect it had when told by Mr. Owens. His graphic and vivid manner of relating an occurrence, merging his individuality into the persons of whom he spoke, gave a reality to circumstances, and life to words, far beyond that obtained when one reads of, or merely listens to a bare recital of an incident.

There is an end to all things; even the intense disagreeableness of losing money with a "mooch talentèd" Opera Troupe. Five weeks closed the Italian speculation, and relieved of this incubus, Owens resolved never again to indulge in operatic ventures. His experience had cost him dearly, but the lesson was salutary. It also recalled a piece of sage advice, which Mr. Burton once gave him : " Don't endeavor to control more than one theatre at a time"—albeit, Burton did not always stick to this rule; for he sometimes directed two or three theatres at once, and invariably regretted so doing.

The dramatic company which had been sent to Washington to support the elder Booth, returned to finish out the Baltimore season. *Jakey*, and other popular plays were revived, and replenished the depleted treasury. The regular dramatic season closed July 4th. A fortnight later, Dr. Fisk rented the little Theatre for the purpose of giving lectures and experiments in Psychology. The Doctor was an enthusiast about the science, and his own wonderful power. He frequently importuned Owens to give him a private sitting, but would receive the laughing reply, "You can't psychologize me. *I* have quite as much power as you possess." Still, he persisted, and the test came unexpectedly. The lectures were over, and in settling up business, there was a slight monetary discrepancy, which each thought his own due. "We will toss up for it," said Owens, taking a half dollar from his pocket. "No, no," replied the Doctor; "suppose we decide it another way! Whichever one of us can psychologize the other, takes the difference." This was agreed upon, and in the presence of witnesses the test was made. The Doctor had no effect whatever upon Owens; but, on the contrary, succumbed to *his* magnetic power, and after sundry satisfactory experiments, was fast asleep.

Owens had frequent applications from persons ambitious to appear on the professional stage; as a rule, he discouraged such aspirations; believing them ofttimes to be inspired by the glitter of a life, whose close study and labor never occurred to stage-struck enthusiasts. Occasionally something out of the usual groove, would transpire, and eventuate in a droll story which Owens would tell with relish. One day an eccentric-looking fellow came to him and said, "Mr. Owens, I've been staying in Baltimore for two weeks on a visit, and all that while I've been haunting the Museum. I never did see such a funny chap as you be. *I* am a *private* play-actor myself, and I want you to hire me, so as I can ketch on to your ways, and astonish the folks when I go back home." "What have you played?" asked Owens (who being at leisure just then, concluded to draw the man out, and be amused). "Well, many things; but my best holt is Temperance dramas. Put me whar' you like, so as I get a chance to learn your tricks." "Won't you be frightened before a *strange* audience?" "Frightened? just you wait till I get top of that staging; and you'll see, I'm middling easy about acting."

By way of a frolic, Owens consented to give him a trial, and entrusted him with three lines to speak. He rehearsed fairly, and with supreme confidence; but, at night failed to take up his cue. The prompter gave him the word; and regardless of his imploring "wait" pushed him on the stage, but not a syllable did he utter. After the fall of the curtain, Owens said to him: "*I* had to speak your lines, you WERE *frightened!*" "No, I wasn't; *I* was all right; but when I got fronting that there proscenery, something frustrated my plans. Frightened? No, sir-ee, not a bit."

The Museum season of 1849–50, began September 5th. Eliza Logan and her father were the first stars. With her name, arises pleasurable recollections of a finished artiste, a genial companion, and a big-hearted woman; whose loving nature and sterling integrity rendered her peerless. During this engagement, Mr. Logan appeared in his great success of "*Aminidab Slocum*" in "*Chloroform, or Baltimore in 1949*," of which play he was the author. The title is suggestive of the intent of the piece. *Aminidab* (under the influence of chloroform) sleeps for a hundred years, and awakes to find his surroundings advanced in science, inventions, and various improvements. His amazement, and the misunderstandings therefrom, gave scope for much humor. The popular book written by Edward Bellamy, "Looking Backward," is founded on the same idea, and though of greater importance as a literary work, it lacks the comic element and wit of "*Chloroform*." After Eliza Logan retired from the stage, she gave Mr. Owens the MS. and sole right of the play. He always intended to include it in his repertoire.

November 19th, 1849, a farce entitled, "*The Live Indian*," had its first representation. It was originally written by W. H. Thompson, a Baltimorean, and submitted to Mr. Owens, with whom it found but little favor. He frankly told the author, that, though the farce had merit, it lacked originality; the motive being the same as "The Mummy." "But, you might write up the dialogue, and make a great difference! Put it in better shape," he added, "and I will play it." Mr. Thompson declined making alterations, wishing to effect an immediate sale of the MS., as he needed money. Taking this view of the matter, Mr. Owens agreed at once to give Thompson the price he named; and thus became owner of "*The Live Indian*." The play was laid aside for awhile, until Owens coming by chance across the dust-covered MS., concluded to give it another reading. After which he re-wrote it, altering the dialogue to make it more effective. Also, introducing another character—*Miss Crinoline*, a dress-maker, whom he personated in addition to *Corporal Tim*, and *The Live Indian*.

*Miss Crinoline* made the farce a success. The quick change (three minutes), from the dress of a gay young man to that of a fashionably costumed lady, was startling; and (at that time) a novelty. With blonde wig, and stylish dress of handsome material, he came on the stage so soon after *Corporal Tim's* exit, that the audience were dazed; and, until they became familiar with the piece, doubted the identity of the two. The dress-maker's scene, with old Brown and his niece, was full of telling points, which evoked roars of laughter. From this to the Indian made another striking contrast, enlivened by Owens' inimitable acting. But *Miss Crinoline* made the farce a hit; without that introduction it would have failed. At its best, Mr. Owens never considered that it possessed merit, otherwise than a funny absurdity to contrast with legitimate pieces. In this light it was immensely attractive and prominent. The minstrel act of " *The Black Statue*," was copied from " *The Live Indian*;" and many other variety acts sprang into existence as popular imitations.

Among the stars of this season, beside Owens himself, came Mr. and Mrs. Barney Williams, James Murdoch, Fanny Wallack, Charles Burke, J. P. Adams, and Oliver Raymond (known as " Toots " Raymond, from having

4

created that part in *Dombey and Son*), Charlotte Cushman, Couldock, Matilda Heron, Bateman children, Julia Dean, &c., &c. With strong stellar attraction at his little theatre, Owens often delegated the management temporarily, while he filled engagements of a week or two in Philadelphia, Pittsburg, Washington and other cities.

January 7th, 1850, Owens became sole owner of the Museum, having bought Hamm's share therein. A noticeable feature of this season was the production of "The Ocean Child," with Owens as *Peter Poultice*, his *first* theatrical hit. Many new pieces were given. *The Serious Family* met with great favor; Owens as *Aminidab Sleek*, Mr. and Mrs. D. P. Bowers, Davenport, Gallagher, the Kembles and Miss Crocker (afterwards Mrs. F. B. Conway) in the cast. This, and other pieces, were played simultaneously with their production in New York. As I look over the play-bills of each week, a bright record of talent meets my eye, and the remembrance of the pleasure of that period is a heritage most valuable. At this time, J. Madison Morton's farces were at the height of popular favor. Those who have seen *Slasher and Crasher, Betsey Baker, Poor Pillicoddy*, &c., &c., know how mirth-provoking was the language, plot and wit which they combined. Owens revelled in the subtlety and unctuousness of their humor, and every farce went off uproariously. One night, during a momentary lull in the laughter, a tall countryman arose in the par-

quette, and with his hands pressed to his sides, called out,
"Stranger, don't make such good fun; I'm weak; for
I've laughed all over." The audience gave the rustic a
round of applause.

In November, an offer was received from John
Brougham, to play at the theatre then being constructed,
corner of Broadway and Broome street, New York, which
was to be inaugurated January, 1851, under the name of
"Brougham's Lyceum," and managed as a stock theatre,
no member being made a feature on the bills, although
most of the company were stars. Mr. Owens accepted
the offer, and this was his début in New York. He
played there two months, and became a leading favorite;
but his crowning success was won in the part of *Uriah
Heep*, for which he was cast when Brougham put *David
Copperfield* on his stage, at the same time it was produced
at Burton's Chambers Street Theatre. The two dramatizations were essentially different. That used by Mr. Burton being arranged by Dr. Northal, and Mr. Brougham's
adaptation being his own work. A strong array of talent
appeared in both. I subjoin the casts:

## BROUGHAM'S LYCEUM.

### JANUARY, 1851.

DAVID COPPERFIELD.............................MR. DAVID PALMER.
URIAH HEEP.................................................MR. JOHN E. OWENS.
WILKINS MICAWBER...............................MR. JOHN BROUGHAM.
DANIEL PEGGOTTY........................................MR. H. LYNNE.

JAMES STEERFORTH.................................................MR. J. DUNN.
BETSY TROTWOOD...............................................MRS. VERNON.
MRS. STEERFORTH..............................................MRS. DUNN.
ROSE DARTLE....................................................MISS KATE HORN.
MRS. MICAWBER................................................MRS. W. R. BLAKE.
LITTLE EM'LY....................................................MRS. GEO. LODER.
AGNES WICKFIELD...........................................MISS MARY TAYLOR.
MARTHA.............................................................MRS. LYNNE.

### BURTON'S CHAMBERS ST. THEATRE.
#### JANUARY, 1851.

DAVID COPPERFIELD.........................................MR. JORDAN.
URIAH HEEP...................................... ...................MR. JOHNSTON.
WILKINS MICAWBER..........................................MR. BURTON.
DANIEL PEGGOTTY...........................................MR. BLAKE.
JAMES STEERFORTH...........................................MR. LESTER.
BETSY TROTWOOD............................................MRS. HUGHES.
MRS. STEERFORTH.............................................MRS. HOLMAN.
ROSE DARTLE....................................................MRS. RUSSELL.
MRS. MICAWBER...............................................MRS. SKERRETT.
LITTLE EM'LY....................................................MISS J. HILL.
MARTHA...........................................................MISS WESTON.

The character of *Uriah Heep* did not belong to the line of business for which Owens was engaged. A villain, and an extremely mean one was *Uriah;* in sharp contrast to the comic portrayals which had made Owens popular in New York. But he determined that *Uriah Heep* should strengthen instead of weaken his hold upon the public. Close study of the "umble" clerk, resulted in a wonderful creation. The make-up was perfect, and so was his manuer and gait. In every detail, he gave artistic rendition of this obnoxious character, which surprised even his warmest admirers.

The press rendered unanimous commendation. Many, and lengthy, were the criticisms, from which I quote only a few lines, to indicate the general tone.

"The slimy, squirming nature of the 'umble clerk was powerfully shown. The stage cannot boast of anything more truthful and effective."

"Owens' embodiment of the part of *Uriah Heep* is sufficient to establish his position as a great and extraordinary actor. It shows the creative power of genius, and is the truest representation of any character in the novel." &c., &c.

During the run of *David Copperfield*, a friend met Owens on the street, and said: "John, I don't like you at all in that part of *Uriah Heep;* not at all!" "I am sorry for that, E——," replied the comedian; "I value your opinion highly. What do you object to?" "Every bit of it; but, principally to the scene where you make love to Agnes Wickfield. When you attempt to take the girl's hand, I hate you so, that I'd like to kill you. Sneaking hypocrite!" "My dear friend," laughingly said Owens, "the entire press of New York has not paid a higher compliment to my acting than you have; by thus identifying me with the character I assume. Thank you very much, for your unconsciously encouraging criticism."

Thomas Hamblen, manager of the Bowery Theatre, came to Owens, after seeing him play Heep, and offered a large certainty or good sharing terms, if he would sign with him, to star in *Shylock*, and *Sir Giles Overreach*. "Drop comedy," he said; "you have struck the keynote of your forte. I've seen nothing to surpass this masterly performance." Though appreciative of approbation so alluring, Owens could not be prevailed upon to forsake comedy. I would here remark that the engagement at Brougham's Lyceum, was the first stock company Owens had joined since he became a recognized star. All through his brilliant career he, afterwards, at times, made these restful breaks from the fatigue of travelling, or tedious rehearsals with new companies; but it was always when surrounded with *prominent* artists, never on any occasion as support to a star. More than once, he made a New England tour in combination with E. L. Davenport, William Wheatly, George Ryer, John Gilbert, and others of eminence. With an equally strong association he played four months in Boston, under the management of Jacob Barrow. When lessee of the Varieties Theatre, in New Orleans, in ante-bellum days, Owens conducted the place on the stock company system, to the exclusion of starring. So it was, in the same theatre, when it was known as the Gaiety, under Dion Boucicault's management; where Owens was regarded as "the highest salaried actor" ever known in this country. I have often heard him say, that the comfort of being surrounded by talent, and certainty that every part would be well played, was indescribable.

The last of his restful departures was made when he joined the Madison Square company, 1882–83. These voluntary releases from care and responsibility, never interfered with his stellar brilliancy, which he resumed at pleasure. Another great comedian had the same method. Charles Matthews, during his last visit to this country, played a stock engagement with Barrow, in Boston, and also with Wallack, in New York; starring in other cities during the interval. Whilst these stock engagements were not so profitable, they were vastly more pleasant, and a luxury worth indulging in by those who could afford it. But, I have wandered from Uriah Heep; however, there is but little more to say. Owens remained in New York two months, following up this great hit with others in legitimate comedy. He returned to his own theatre, well satisfied with his first Metropolitan engagement. During the spring of 1851, *David Copperfield* was presented to the Baltimore public, Owens repeating his success as *Uriah Heep*; and later on playing *Wilkins Micawber*, a part, by the way, which he greatly enjoyed for its unctuous humor, to fully develop it being just to his taste.

Following these Dickens dramatizations, came the spectacle of the *Forty Thieves*, with Owens as *Ali Baba*.

Rather a venturesome production, considering the small-
ness of the Museum stage. That able scenic artist,
Charles S. Getz, did his best in the way of scenery and
effects; but a difficulty arose, which appeared formidable.
There was no space for *forty* thieves on *that* stage! Not
foothold for half the number. To overcome this dilemma,
an additional speech was given to *Abdallah*, captain of
the robbers. Upon his entrance, closely followed by *five*
robbers, he cries, "halt!" and impressively adds, "The
rest of the band will remain in the wood." Happy
thought! which quite reconciled the audience to the
absence of the thirty-five thieves. Owens was intensely
amused at the absurdity of the expression "the rest of the
band will remain in the wood." Ever afterwards, it was
used, *apropos* of any incompleteness that occurred, either
at the theatre, home, or elsewhere. For some weeks
Owens had been importuned by an acquaintance (a young
lawyer of Baltimore) to produce a play written by himself, entitled, "*Gammon and Backgammon.*" Always
ready to lend a helping hand to aspiring youth, Owens
promised to consider the request and if possible comply
with it. He read the manuscript, and realizing that
alterations were indispensable, pruned and shaped the
play to make the most of its resources. A strong cast,
thorough rehearsals, and the concentrated efforts of the
dramatis personæ resulted in *Gammon and Backgammon*
being worked up into a success so far beyond its merits

that everyone thought the author would be delighted. On the contrary, when called before the curtain, instead of making grateful acknowledgments, he denounced Mr. Owens and the company for mutilation of, and general injustice to, his play.

The audience received these remarks in silence, but the moment he concluded called loudly for *"Owens!!"* who immediately appeared and quietly stated, that "the piece had received far better treatment from himself and the company than it deserved. He had omitted the marriage service, and expurged much coarse dialogue, thereby rendering the play admissible for representation. Those who desired to satisfy themselves on these points could do so by inspecting the original manuscript at the Box office on the morrow." All through this explanation, Owens was from time to time interrupted by applause and expressions of approval; subsequently the author's work intact was examined by many citizens, with the result of concurrence in Mr. Owens' opinion, and commendation of his position. Thus ended the dramatic authorship of a gentleman who turning his ambition in another channel, became later on a distinguished lawyer and a leading politician. He frequently said, that he could complacently take a retrospective glance at his career except for *"Gammon and Backgammon,"* the folly of his youth, and of that he was ashamed.

The *first* night having proved also the *last* night of the new play, *The Serious Family* and other attractive pieces held the boards until the date of the next star *Julia Dean.* An even run of prosperity continued until the close of the season, July 5th, 1851 ; and the following year was a repetition of satisfactory management, and successful starring visits to neighboring cities.

# CHAPTER III.



OWENS passed the summer of 1852 in European
travel, most of the time on the continent. While
in Switzerland he made the ascent of Mont Blanc. The
*London Times*, in a long descriptive article about the
achievement, remarked: "Mr. John E. Owens is the
first American who has accomplished that undertaking
for upwards of twenty years." At the present day the
ascent of Mont Blanc is not so infrequent or so hazardous
as it then was. Owens intended his summer tour simply
for recreation, but *en route* he met with so much that was
amusing and characteristic, that he determined to combine

59

these experiences with the greater and grander ones of his tour, and so, form an entertainment, on his return to America, which would prove attractive. On this basis originated his "*Alpine Rambles,*" which met with such great success in 1853; commencing in Baltimore, thence to New York and Philadelphia.

The entertainment was novel, and also one of the cleverest and most effective ever inaugurated; the descriptive monologue being illustrated by superb paintings, copied from drawings taken (under Mr. Owens' direction) at the various localities presented. Some of these pictures were painted by James Hamilton, so celebrated for marine views, others by Hilliard, whose landscapes have rendered his name prominent among artists, but the principal part of the work was executed by Charles S. Getz, in a beautiful and finished style. These, combined with optical illusions, incidental music and songs, rendered the effect entrancingly realistic—not at all like the usual panoramic representation. The tour presented, embraced a rapid journey; starting from New York, per ocean steamer, visiting England, and making brief stops at Dieppe, Paris, Boulogne, and all places of interest in Switzerland; concluding with the perilous ascent of Mont Blanc; then, returning homeward.

No dry description of travel was given, but graphic and vivid delineations, and information delightfully blended with original anecdote and humorous impersonation of his *compagnons du voyage;* characteristics and adventures, of people with whom he travelled, were wittily and brilliantly reproduced : and being woven into a slight plot, interested the auditors, and made them feel that they quite knew these chance acquaintances. The written dissertation is one hundred and fifty pages ; so I give only a condensed account of an entertainment which is something to be remembered through a lifetime, by those who had the privilege of enjoying it. An aggregation of fun, fancy, sublimity, and sentiment, agreeably and skilfully intermingled with dramatic effect.

Peculiar gifts are requisite to hold an audience entranced by *one's* individual efforts through an entire evening; and this was achieved by Owens with his *"Alpine Rambles"*—as attested by the laudations of the daily press in the various cities, and the crowded houses which nightly applauded him. A ludicrous equivoke occurred while Mr. Owens was giving the *"Alpine Rambles"* in Philadelphia. A dear old uncle of mine, born and reared a Quaker, and still continuing to wear the primitive garb and broad brim of that sect, called to see Mr. Owens, and was, of course, cordially welcomed.

After some pleasant converse, he said : " John, I hear that thee has quit play-acting for the present, and are telling folks about thy travels. It is said that thy discourse is very interesting." After modestly replying on the merits of the entertainment, Mr. Owens, briefly, gave the old gentleman an idea of the manner in which it was presented ; adding, " Many people attend, who do not go to theatres, and I would like to see you and your family there. It will give me pleasure to send you tickets." " Thank thee, John, very much, but may I ask thee ; do *many friends* come to see thee?" " Yes, indeed," said Mr. Owens, thinking that uncle took a family interest in his success. Looking pleased, the simple-hearted soul rejoined, " How many does thee think was there, last night?" " Well, about fifteen hundred ; maybe more." " Thee don't say so, John ! Does thee *really* mean it?" " Certainly," replied Mr. Owens, at a loss to account for the astonishment with which his assertion was received. A few minutes later, the old gentleman arose to leave, saying, " I shall be glad to hear thee talk of thy travels, John, and I shall not feel strange in thy public hall."

Pondering on the final words, Mr. Owens was somewhat puzzled to understand them. Afterwards, it occurred to him that uncle used the word "*friends*," as a synonyme for "Quakers." Mr. Owens, understanding it in its literal sense, had unintentionally included an entire audience in the "Society of Friends." He used to say, laughingly, that the gentle old Quaker doubtless considered his new nephew a deliberate falsifier ; or, else inferred that the Quakers of Philadelphia had rushed *en masse* to the entertainment during its early production, and thenceforth given it over to " the world's people."

Descanting upon the *"Alpine Rambles,"* I have gone somewhat in advance of my narrative, as the entertainment was not presented until January, 1853, and Owens returned from Europe, October, 1852, resuming active management of the Baltimore Museum; where the season had commenced a month previous, under delegated supervision. In December, 1852, Henry C. Jarrett expressed a desire to buy the Museum. Owens consented to consider the proposition made; reflecting that, relieved of managerial responsibilities, he would be freer to give ample attention to the " Alpine Rambles " entertainment; and also (later on) to farther extend his professional tours. He was not altogether averse to selling the little Museum, notwithstanding it had been both profitable and pleasant to him. After frequent interviews and discussions, the transfer was made.

In connection with the preliminaries thereof, some amusing episodes occurred. Mr. Jarrett calling one day at Owens' house, was accompanied by a friend—possibly, a *silent* partner in the impending investment; but not in other respects was he mute. Gazing at a portrait of David Garrick, he asked Owens: " Who is that fellow ? " " Garrick, the tragedian," was the reply. " Garrick ! Garrick ! I never heard of him; amount to much ? " " Very celebrated." " Could Harry get him to play at the Museum ? " " No; that would be impossible." Mr. Jarrett, by this time, was covered with confusion, and made wild endeavors to drown the voice of his friend; but soon again he was heard, eagerly saying, "Oh, Harry, don't forget to ask Mr. Owens where you can hire hands to dance." "Yes, yes," responded Jarrett, imploringly, "please don't interrupt us again."

Owens made his final appearance at the Baltimore Museum on the 30th of December, 1852, after having been its manager for four years. His farewell and complimentary benefit packed the house and hundreds were turned away. At the conclusion of the performance, in response to vociferous calls, he appeared before the curtain, and in his speech was frequently interrupted by applause. Adverting to having transferred the Museum to Mr. Jarrett, he asked for that gentleman an extension of the kindness which had so long and so generously been bestowed upon himself, as a manager. A few more words of heartfelt acknowledgment, and the final "good-bye" was spoken. Mr. Jarrett took charge of this prosperous little theatre, January 1st, 1853. In 1856 he sold the Museum to Mr. George Zeigler; but by that time it had lost prestige. The collection of paintings and curiosities were purchased by Mr. Charles S. Getz, who distributed the works of art that were left, among the different public institutions throughout the country.

The amusements henceforth offered at this place, were of the variety show and concert hall order; and were not given continuously. In 1872 the building was totally destroyed by fire, thus obliterating one of the land-marks of Baltimore; for the "old Museum" was fraught with reminiscences inseparable from many remarkable events. During the following year the Directors of the Baltimore and Ohio Railroad purchased the site, together with adjacent ground, and erected a magnificent edifice for the use of the company. I have already recorded Owens' enterprise of "*Mont Blanc*" and "*Alpine Rambles.*"

In February, 1853, he bought Rock Spring farm—198 acres—six and a half miles from Baltimore. He changed the name to "Aigburth Vale;" and, from time to time, added more acres to the original purchase, improving the farm agriculturally, and building a mansion which was surrounded with ornamental shrubbery and grounds designed by exquisite taste in landscape gardening. In fact, he transformed a good plain farm into one of the most beautiful and magnificent estates in Baltimore county. He would often say, "Every man must have his hobby, and mine is harmless. Spending money on my country residence entertains me, and the improvements I make gives work to people who need it." I cannot better convey an impression of the place that was John E. Owens' home for nearly thirty-four years—where he ended his life—than by condensing a description of Aigburth Vale, contained in a letter which appeared in a Washington paper, during August, 1877.

5

"The home of John Owens lies to the north of Baltimore about six miles, on the verge of the little village of Towsontown. You reach it by a lovely road, displaying a mixture of all pictorial ingredients which give such enviable distinction to Maryland scenery. The greatest variety of trees, crowded together with picturesque abandon, variegate the perspective. At last, we reach a broad gate which is pointed out as Mr. Owens' grounds. On the left, as we enter, is a stretch of clear meadow, to the right, a waving cornfield. Nothing more can be seen till we saunter along the avenue of smiling maples, for perhaps four hundred yards, when the road suddenly droops and bends, and we stand in full view of a stately manor house nestling in the valley below. Descending by a winding path, the visitor passes through grounds cultivated with charming skill, and laid off into plats of diamond and semicircle, fringed with loveliest parterres. Dainty bits of country gardening, watched and defended by sentinel elms, make up the immediate surroundings of Aigburth Vale. Around this charming scene, at a respectful distance, is a circle of green hills.

"Mr. Owens has lived here since 1853; loving his country home so well, that he has gradually extended it, until now he is monarch of nearly three hundred acres. Here, from the rare June days, at the close of the season, till the September revival on the boards, Solon Shingle doffs his footlight regalia, and plays farmer. 'My

AIGBURTH VALE (Farm House), 1853.

CAPILLARY

country friends,' says the comedian, with a droll sense of feeling hurt, 'call me a dandy farmer. Bless their sweet souls! they don't realize the struggles I make to become one of their craft!' To indulge in an agricultural metaphor, the tale is rather harrowing. In his early country experience his farm manager came to him one day, and asked for thirty dollars to buy a fertilizer. He got the money, and Mr. Owens made a memorandum of the purchase. On his return from a starring tour his thoughts became violently bucolic. He looked over his books, and took an inventory of his stock and material. Among other things he wanted to know where that thirty-dollar fertilizer was? 'Out in the field, yonder,' was the reply. Out sauntered the bucolic Shingle to inspect the new farm implement. Finding nothing that met his views of a fertilizer, he came back at a quick pace, wondering whether the faithless servant should be shot or hung.

"'James, you want to show me that fertilizer *now* p— d— q—.' 'Lord! Mr. Owens, how can you see it when its all been harrowed into the ground.' The crushed comedian whistled his way back to the house with his thumbs digging into his ribs.

"When his friends call, he sets out milk and champagne, with the tearful request that they will take champagne, because it doesn't cost as much; and he calculates that he swallows a dollar bill with every Royal Trophy tomatoe. The expense of producing his delicious fruits would paralyze the ambition of most people; but he keeps reaching out after the choicest and rarest varieties. When the end of the year comes, and he finds he must enter up the balance on the off side of his Aigburth Vale ledger he is quite content. The pastime is expensive, but delightful. To say that his plodding neighbors refuse encouragement, would be unjust. 'Their sympathies appear to be directed chiefly to my hennery,' says the actor, 'for they often write to me about "Egg-birth."'

"The house is very large, generously constructed with all modern improvements, and is far handsomer than any other in the region around. A piazza runs the entire length of the southern or principal front, and the wings are tastily finished off with gables. The comedian's sanctum, on the right as you enter the wide hall, is a large apartment, and opens into a cozy smoking room. Over the well-filled bookcase is an oil copy of Droeshout's Shakespeare. The walls are entirely covered with paintings and engravings of celebrated actors and authors. One space is filled by the life-size half figure of the comedian as *Solon Shingle,* by the painter, Cross; another, three-quarter figure of *Dr. Ollapod,* by D'Almaine; both, wonderfully realistic pieces of work in expression, drapery and coloring.

"The furniture is rich and solid, not gaudy. Good

taste prevails in all things. The walls of the hall are hung with the portraits of characters once famous on the English and American boards. To one of these the comedian points with especial pride as the only portrait ever taken of Edmund Kean. This dramatic giant (physically he weighed but 110 pounds) had an antipathy to picture makers, and would never grant them a sitting. When Kean was playing an engagement at Philadelphia, the painter Neagle determined to steal a march on the great tragedian. By connivance with Mr. Lee, his manager, the painter was present at a banquet, given privately to Kean. Lee had surreptitiously brought the costume for Richard the Third, and Neagle was, in like manner, supplied with canvas, paints, &c. Under the melting influence of champagne, Kean was persuaded to make an exception *just once*, under promise that it would only take a few minutes. Neagle seized the opportunity and his brush ; and, as a consequence, this vivid likeness of Edmund Kean was created.

" To the right and left of this cherished gem, hang the portraits of Mr. and Mrs. Duff, Macready, Foote, Mrs. Darley, Mr. and Mrs. Francis, and many more ; all being the work of the celebrated artist, Neagle (who, it will be remembered, was the son-in-law of the famous painter, Thomas Sully). A great variety of choice landscapes hang in parlor, sitting-room and dining-room, representing French, Flemish and English art, as well as our own.

Take it all in all, Aigburth Vale is a home which reflects the refined taste and generous nature of its owner.   It is not necessary to tell the members of the theatrical profession that John E. Owens, during his many years of experience and success on the stage, has done very many acts of kindness towards his professional brethren.   They have a grateful realization of the fact; and they will have to let it be known, for he never will.   The vicissitudes he has passed through—for, of course, he has. had his share of them—only give sauce to his quiet charity and relish to his present lot.   At the age of fifty-three he has 'reached the haven of happiness, financial, domestic, and professional; the richest actor in America, and apparently the most contented and jolly man.'"

Speaking of the dramatic portraits in Mr. Owens' library, I am reminded of an incident relative to the bust of Shakespeare, occupying a prominent place in the sanctum.   Within a week of its being placed there, among other guests spending the day at Aigburth Vale was William P. Preston, a distinguished lawyer, of Baltimore; and for many years an intimate friend and neighbor, his country home being near ours.   Mr. Preston was an art connoisseur; and during the after-dinner chat, expressed great admiration for the new acquisition.   Much Shakespearean conversation ensued, whiling away the time delightfully.   A day or two afterwards, Owens received from Mr. Preston the following lines:

### SHAKESPEARE'S BUST AT AIGBURTH VALE.

"In ancient days in good old Rome,
 Each household gave its god a home;
 Then well may Avon's bard divine,
 At Aigburth claim a hallowed shrine.
 Here, when the Thespian fires scarce gleam,
 The world's comedian reigns supreme.
 With health and plenty fully blest,
 Dispensing comfort to his guest;
 At festive board, with dainties crowned,
 Passing the social glasses round;
 And, while the heart with rapture beats,
 Rehearsing Thalia's brilliant feats.
 Long may he reign; and long dispense
 His learning, wit, and common sense.
 While pious cant dare not assail
 The household god of Aigburth Vale."

The autumn of 1854 Owens devoted entirely to farm life, making a visit now and then to the city. Early in 1855 he played in Baltimore, Washington and Philadelphia; cancelling later engagements in New York and other cities, on account of the serious and prolonged illness of his wife. The ensuing summer was passed, partly at the Greenbrier White Sulphur Springs, Va., and finished at his country home. And here I would remark, that his rural life was not only an enjoyment to himself, but productive of good and happiness to many. He was the poor man's friend; administering help in such a delicately adroit manner, that no sense of humilia-

tion was experienced by the recipient of benefits bestowed
by his bountiful hand.   Unobtrusively thoughtful of the
welfare of those who needed work or help, he quietly
relieved want, and sympathetically alleviated suffering.
A contribution, with the loud blast of subscription paper
notoriety, he abhorred; but the same cause he would,
privately, aid largely.   The working people, of Baltimore
county, regarded him as their true friend; and acts of
kindness were as essential to his life as the breath he drew.
At home and abroad, wherever he has sojourned, many
arise and call him blessed.   The brightest stars in his
eternal crown are the good deeds so lavishly and disinter-
estedly done on earth.

The season of 1854–55 finds Owens again a manager
in Baltimore, he having leased the Charles Street Theatre,
corner of Baltimore and Charles streets.   The Company,
headed by himself, comprised much talent—Mrs. D. P.
Bowers, Charles Walcot, Sr., and his wife, Norton, Colin
Stuart, Miss Gaszyneske, &c., &c.   The opening bill was
Tobin's " *Honeymoon*," and " *Turning the Tables*."   Only
moderate encouragement met the new Theatre—full
houses sometimes, but the average was not good.   The
comic interlude " *Villikins and hys Dinah* " (which he
re-wrote), sung inimitably by Owens, created a sensation,
and went far to bring up the business.   The song itself
amounted to nothing, but was made irresistibly funny by
the quaint manner of rendering it.   The mock gravity

attached to the importance of remembering that there was a *front* garden and a *back* garden, and the tragic injunction to the audience *not* to become confused in these localities as the action of the song progressed, together with the comic solemnity of pauses to explain matters clearly, was ludicrous beyond description.

It was at this theatre Edwin Adams made his first histrionic mark as *Edward Mapleton* in " *The Merchant and his Clerks.*" He developed such force and emotional power that Mr. Owens advised him to devote attention to tragedy, feeling sure that his talent was great for that line of the drama. The company was further strengthened by Caroline Richings and her father, " Yankee Locke," and others; new pieces, well staged, were tried, but the desired result—good business—did not ensue.

In March, Mr. and Mrs. G. C. Howard and little Cordelia Howard were announced in " *Fashion and Famine.*" The piece was well gotten up and strongly cast, but proved a failure, drawing only dismally slim houses. " *Hot Corn* " and the " *Lamplighter* " followed, but effected no improvement in the business. Mr. and Mrs. Howard said little Cordelia was sick; no wonder, so was the manager (with depression). The Howards retired for awhile, and Owens, supported by the stock company, filled in the time with the result of better houses for a few nights; but the change was only spasmodic, a cloud of ill-luck seemed to have settled over the theatre, and the manager was losing money hand over hand.

At this crisis Owens thought of the dramatization of "*Uncle Tom's Cabin*," then a great success, north. He purchased the right of the play for Baltimore, and after careful reading of the manuscript, made some alteration in the text and situations. To present to a Baltimore audience the original play intact, would, at that time, have been a hazardous proceeding. When "*Uncle Tom's Cabin*" was underlined, Owens' lawyer (also an intimate friend), William P. Preston, came to him and urgently implored that he would forego the production of the piece, saying : " You will ruin yourself with the 'South,' and get into all sorts of trouble ; the people will tear the theatre down or do you a personal injury." Though holding his friend Preston's judgment in high esteem, Owens was not, in this instance, to be dissuaded from his purpose. Desperate cases require desperate remedies ; and with the consciousness of empty coffers the emergency was a case of "make or break." The dramatization of " *Uncle Tom's Cabin* " was revised ; all that was *glaringly* obnoxious to southern sentiment modified, and some of the parts were re-written.

The role of *Marks*, the Lawyer, was assigned to John Sleeper Clarke, and he made a decided hit ; so pronounced that he started out on his career upon the strength of it. The part was crammed with fun and frolic, and the result was immense; the people laughed so uproariously over Clark's mishaps, as *Marks*, that they lost sight of the more solemn slavery element. Owens played *Uncle Tom* (something not at all in his line). He undertook the part to strengthen the bill, and also to be on the spot should any trouble take place. The following is the initial cast:

### BALTIMORE.

### CHARLES STREET THEATRE.

#### APRIL 16TH, 1855.

| | |
|---|---|
| UNCLE TOM | JOHN E. OWENS. |
| GEORGE HARRIS | COLIN STUART. |
| SIMON LEGREE | EDWIN ADAMS. |
| ST. CLAIR | G. C. HOWARD. |
| MARKS, THE LAWYER | JOHN SLEEPER CLARKE. |
| GUMPTON CUTE | JOHN O'BRIEN (JNO. T. RAYMOND). |
| DEACON PERRY | JOSEPH PARKER. |
| TOPSY | MRS. G. C. HOWARD. |
| AUNT OPHELIA | MRS. JANE GERMON. |
| ELIZA HARRIS | MRS. PARKER. |
| MARIE ST. CLAIR | MISS DE VERE. |
| EVA | LITTLE CORDELIA HOWARD. |

This was the first presentation of *"Uncle Tom's Cabin"* south of Mason and Dixon's line, and I doubt if it has ever been better played. Owens made a tremendous hit as *Uncle Tom*, and the entire play set the town wild with delight and admiration; this success retrieved the heavy losses of the season. Owens had no sectional feeling in regard to the play, and the Baltimoreans accepted it as given, packed the house, and thus filled the hitherto attenuated treasury.

The season of 1855–56 was a restful and delightful one, passed in New Orleans, at the Gaiety Theatre, Dion Boucicault, Manager; this (like "Wallack's" in New York) was conducted solely with a *stock* company, comprising John E. Owens, Dion Boucicault, Agnes Robertson (Mrs. Boucicault), Jessie McLane, James Brown (the original Robert Macaire), Mrs. Place, Johnston, Frazier, Morton, and Fred. N. Thayer; the latter being leading man. The old friendship of 1846, between Thayer and Owens, was revived; and henceforth had no lapse from close intimacy. Nearly ten years had passed, since Owens' first visit to New Orleans; but he now felt quite at home, so cordial was the welcome extended to him. His old friends had kept themselves posted as to his steady advance in histrionic fame, and rejoiced at the position he had attained. At once he achieved general popularity with the public, both in legitimate comedy and lighter drama.

Mr. Boucicault's aim was to give the theatre a brilliant position; the plays were always thoroughly rehearsed and faultlessly produced; he was a strict disciplinarian, and his system produced satisfactory results. Infringement on the rules of the theatre seldom occurred; although the company, among themselves, were much given to having "a bit of fun," which sometimes verged on practical joking. They were a merry set, and derived amusement from slight causes, as is evinced by the following incident: Mr. Thayer, while rehearsing for *"John Dobbs,"* in the farce of that name, remarked: "The business of this part calls for piano playing; *I* am not a musician." "Only a few bars needed," said the Stage Manager. "Stoepel can indicate the keys by having figures pasted on them; strike in rotation as numbered, and there you are, all right!"

The plan worked admirably at first, but on the third night, when Mr. Thayer took his seat at the piano, with self-confident manner, he discovered to his horror that the keys were quite free from numbers. It broke him up, momentarily; but rallying, he picked out "Days of Absence," in faltering tones, and retired ingloriously. For awhile he was uncertain as to the perpetrator of the joke; but reflecting that Owens and himself were wont to play pranks upon each other, he taxed the comedian, who freely confessed, and made the *amende honorable;* so they adjudged it, "give and take," and cried quits.

The Keller Troupe arrived in New Orleans from Havana. At the Tacon Theatre they had created a furore, the fame of which had preceded them, and an engagement was speedily made with Boucicault. Their exquisite tableaux have never been exceeded in beauty, grace and picturesqueness: *"The Birth of the Flowers," "The Battle of the Amazons," "The Shower of Gold,"* and dozens of other dreams of loveliness were charmingly and purely represented. They also reproduced Rubens' great Altar piece; three pictures of the Crucifixion, *Bearing the Cross*, *The Ascent of the Cross*, and *The Last Sigh*. The effect of these representations on the audience was that of intense solemnity. I am sure no irreverent thought intruded, as they gazed with breathless awe, realizing the Bible story with deeper feeling than reading it ever evoked. The tableaux of "The Crucifixion" were given nowhere in America, except New Orleans; when the Kellers went thence on their tour through the country, all other cities protested against what was denounced by the majority of the public as a sacrilegious representation.

While the Keller troupe were at the Gaiety, Mr. Boucicault got up, magnificently, "*Azael, or the Prodigal Son*," which afforded ample opportunity for superb grouping and tableaux. Agnes Robertson, F. N. Thayer, and most of the Company were in the cast; but, being a biblical drama, there was no comic part for Owens, so he, for the nonce, became a gentleman of leisure. After awhile, the manager grew restless under this state of affairs, and "didn't see why the largest salary ever given to an actor should be drawn for naught;" so he decided to have Owens sing *Villikins and hys Dinah*, after the curtain fell on "*Azael.*" I am not certain but what he half inclined to have it sung between the acts. Rather an incongruous entertainment! However, supplementing "*Azael*" may have arisen from a desire to strengthen the attraction, as the biblical drama did not meet with much favor, notwithstanding its magnificent setting, costuming, artistic effect and clever acting.

In those days New Orleans was filled with strangers, during the winter, and "*Azael*" was rather beyond the understanding of some of the audience—if one might judge from remarks overheard. As for instance, after the curtain fell on one of the grandest scenes, "*Temple at Memphis*," a rural party, discussing the play, agreed that it was altogether incorrect. "There is no such building there," said one. "No; nor do they dress that way in Memphis," rejoined another. "We have been there often enough to know something about the town." The school-master was evidently abroad when Egypt and Tennessee could be thus confounded.

At the termination of the "Keller" engagement the management returned to the standard plays and comedies. The public responded to this change with a heartiness which indicated that they had experienced a surfeit of tableaux and spectacular drama. Nothing of marked nature occurred during the remainder of the season, the close of which took place March 12th, 1856.

# CHAPTER IV.



THE ensuing summer was varied by an unpremedi-
tated and brief visit to Europe; a few days being
passed in London, but the greater part of the time in
Paris. Many bright anecdotes and incidents were told on
his return home; among them the following, afterwards
narrated by a friend, in these words: "It is rare fun to
hear John Owens relate his interview with Barney Williams, in Paris. Fancy John having cultivated a formidable suit of facial hair, and attired at every point '*a la
mode de Paris*,' rapping one fine day at the door of a

room eligibly located on the Boulevard des Italiens, and
receiving in response the exclamation from within, 'Entree!'—of course in the purest Parisian (?) accent.  Tip-
ping the rim of his highly polished castor, over his eyes,
till it rests on the bridge of his nose, and assuming something of a swaggering air, John enters; and is received
with the extremest demonstrations of courtesy by Barney,
who is lying off in all the luxury of morning costume,
sipping his *café-au-lait* and reading Galignani.  'Comment vous portez vous, Monsieur?' says Barney, turning
to the visitor without the smallest suspicion, and with all
the politeness and admirable imitation of manner of the
people he was living among; and receiving from his
heavily-bearded caller the usual response.  'Asseyez
vous, Monsieur,' added he, at the same time placing his
guest a chair, and with the most marked French *empresse-
ment* waving him an invitation to sit.  Owens could not
carry on the joke.  The metamorphose of Barney into a
Parisian was too much for his gravity.  Taking off his
hat, and at the same moment clapping his host upon the
back, he exclaimed, in his natural voice and manner:
'How are you, Barney!'  'And is it you, ye divil?'
said Barney, whose first impulse had evidently been to
throw the poker at the head of his visitor, when he found
out to whom he had been airing his French.  'And what
the deuce are you doing in this part of the world?'
'Studying the language, my boy, that's all; and what an

6

"illigant" lesson I have just had; especially in the *accent*
—eh, Barney?'"

Having passed a few weeks pleasantly in Paris, Owens
returned home, and after a swift and agreeable passage
across the Atlantic, arrived at the pier in New York.
As he was leaning on the taffrail, like Juliet in the bal-
cony scene, "his cheek upon his hand," and facilitating
himself that he had reached his native land once more in
safety; one of those amiable gentlemen who signalize
themselves by poking whips in the faces of travellers, by
way of catching their eyes, clambered over the rail, and
giving our friend a gentle slap on the back, said : "Have
a carriage?"  Owens being knocked quite out of his
revery, and nearly out of all the breath in his body, by
this energetic salutation, stood for a moment speechless;
and the Coachee, scanning his costume and the cut of his
whiskers, evidently began to think he was a Frenchman.
Owens perceived this, and immediately determined to
humor the idea, and have some fun out of it.  "Carriazhe!  Vat ees ze carriazhe?"  "Why, the coach—
horses—wheels—things that go round, round, so!  Go
'lang!  Crack!  Take you to hotel!" said the other,
gesticulating all the while, and describing pantomimically
the motion of a carriage, the driving of the horses, and so
on.  "Aha!  Oho!  Oui, oui; je comprend!  To ze hotel.
Tres bien; you sal mak me come to ze hotel Metropolitang, eh?  You know where is ze Metropolitang?"  "The

Meetropolitern? Of course! Take you there in a jiffy. Show your baggage! Come along, Mounseer." "Oui, oui! zat all ver good; but how mosh for take moimême et mon baggazhe to ze hotel Metropolitang?" "Three dollars; that's all." "Tre dollar! Mon Dieu! Zat is too mosh for ze leetle vay to ze hotel." "A little ways! My eyes! Why, do you happen to know, Mounseer, about how fur it is, say? Why," continued Coachee, rising in excitement as he proceeded with his pantomimic description, "there aint no less than three bridges to cross, and ever so much toll to pay before you get there." "What zat, you call ze bridzhe and ze tol, eh?" "The bridge? Why," gesticulating, "high up, so! water running under, so! Cross over; stop! Pay money every time!" "I tell you what it is, Coachee," said Owens, resuming his natural voice, "I'll give you fifty cents."

The scamp was dumbfounded for a second; but seeing that he was "sold," and if he rode rusty, he would find himself in an awkward fix; putting his hand to his mouth and whispering confidentially to Owens, said, with a wink that spoke volumes: "Call it seventy-five, and *say nothing, you know, about the bridges!*"

Owens began the season of 1856–57 in Philadelphia, pleasantly and profitably; thence to the Baltimore Museum, cramming the house with enthusiastic audiences. It was during this engagement that he played *Solon Shingle* for the first time. "*The People's Lawyer*" was then given in two acts; Robert Howard being the prominent part. Owens was pleased with the quaint vein of humor which characterized *Solon;* and later on made a study of the garrulous countryman; cut the Drama to farce length, introduced much new business, and so elaborated the part and altered the piece, that he copyrighted it under the title of "*Solon Shingle.*"

It has been said that Owens imitated Charles Burke in this part. Such an assertion is utterly untrue. Mr. Owens never saw Burke, or anyone else play "*Solon Shingle.*" With equal injustice, the would-be wiseacres assume that Mr. Joseph Jefferson reproduced his brother's portrayal of "*Rip Van Winkle;*" whereas the two performances differ widely. Mr. Burke was a gifted artist—wonderfully so; but the play which Mr. Jefferson has rendered famous has no similarity to that in which Mr. Burke appeared, save that they both are founded on Washington Irving's story. Neither Mr. Owens nor Mr. Jefferson were ever imitative. To each character assumed, they *gave* distinctive expression; original to the degree of inspiration, their genius never required the methods or ideas of others to render perfect those wonderful embodiments which have established their world-wide fame.

In November, 1856, Owens signed with H. L. Bateman to star in Mrs. Sidney Bateman's play of "*Self.*" This Comedy had been produced in New York with Bur-

MR. OWENS as SOLON SHINGLE.

(From a Painting by A. Cross.)

ton as *John Unit*, and in St. Louis with Mark Smith in the same part, and was a failure in both cities. Owens hesitated about undertaking a play already received coldly by the public; but upon reflection, was sanguine of making *John Unit* a character part, and thereby leading up to success for the piece. He took for his model in dress and manner of playing *Unit*, a prominent citizen of Cincinnati, and "like unto a mirror depicted his eccentricities." Those who have seen Owens play *John Unit*, and heard the expression to which he was prone, "It won't pay, sir," need not be told what a natural representation he gave of the crusty old banker; who, beneath his hard exterior had a tender heart for those who really understood him. It was a leaf from life, touching kindred chords in many natures.

*John Unit* proved a valuable addition to Owens' repertoire, winning for him new laurels and establishing success for "*Self*,"—a success so entirely identified with his name that he purchased from H. L. Bateman entire right to the possession of the Comedy. Owens' "*John Unit*" was in fidelity of conception, unsurpassed by anything on the stage. His grasp of the character was perfect, and every light and shade stood forth intensely life-like. Prominent in perfection, the library scene may be considered the gem of the part. The soliloquy, after having made his will, was like the unfolding of the inner nature of the old banker, giving glimpses of its asperity and of its tenderness. The ingenuous retrospection of his life—realization that his methods had brought him to a *lonely* old age, recollections of boyhood and home, yearnings for family ties, were delineated with such depth of sentiment and rugged pathos as to invoke sympathetic response. During Owens' first visit to California, this scene had intense effect upon the rough, red-shirted miners in the galleries. Many of them had been absent from home for years, and the longings for the associations of early life so vividly expressed, found echo in their hearts, and ofttimes caused them to weep like children. The interview with Mary Apex, which follows Unit's soliloquy, where he talks with her in a half-bantering, half-earnest, and entirely affectionate manner, was a type of quaint and hearty wisdom, wonderfully portrayed.

"*Self*" had a prosperous run in Baltimore, and the experience was repeated in Washington. "*Mrs. Apex*" found a strong representative in Mrs. Melinda Jones, "*Mrs. Codliver*" in Mrs. Jane Germon, and "*Mary Apex*" in Miss Mary Devlin (who afterwards became Mrs. Edwin Booth). The latter lady was not only a talented actress, but one of the loveliest and best women in the world. Mary Apex's nature seemed akin to that of the ingenuous girl who personated her.

After Washington, Richmond was the next date to be filled by "*Self.*" The company left Washington in good spirits, not apprehending that the light snow just beginuiug to fall would at all interfere with their journey; but it was destined to culminate in a storm, to be hereafter spoken of as "unparalleled in the memory of the oldest inhabitants." The snow steadily increased, involving frequent stoppages to clear the railroad tracks; and finally the storm became violent. At daybreak, Sunday, the train had been snow-bound for several hours. The engine fires were extinguished, and the snow (already banked up above the car windows) was still rapidly falling. No sign of habitation near; nor could the passengers form an idea of their location, until later on, the church bells of Richmond were heard. "So near, and yet so far," were they.

Having consumed all eatables that were on the train, the situation was growing serious as to ways and means of extrication from this perilous condition. At this crisis a stalwart colored man said, that "he knew all the surrounding country, and would sally forth to seek assistance, if his master would give consent." This was readily obtained, and amidst expressions of gratitude, the passengers made up a purse of fifty dollars, to be given to the man on his return. Additionally incited by this promised reward, he plunged into the snow, which submerged him to his neck; and striking vigorously across country, was soon lost to view. The prospect of relief revived the drooping spirits of the snow-bound passengers; but as hour after hour passed by, without any sign of the return of the adventurous pioneer, hope waned, cold and hunger increased, and the situation became alarming. Towards night the faint tinkle of bells was heard, and then the far-off sound of voices—the listeners were almost afraid to trust their senses, lest disappointment might ensue—but louder and louder came the welcome sounds until, in the distance, they saw a wagon drawn by a team of six oxen, preceded by a snow-plow; the latter driven by their sable deliverer, who had found a farm house, and returned with a relief corps. The hospitable farmer not only brought food for immediate necessity, but insisted on taking all the passengers to his house to stay until the road should be in condition for trains to resume travel.

A merry party were packed away in the long wagon—hunger and cold forgotten, as the farmer started the team, and with a loud "huzza!" and bells jingling, off they drove for "Strawberry Hill," three miles distant. There they remained two days, entertained in true Virginia style by Mr. R. F. Adams and his household. It was a delightful episode to the guests, and also to their host and his family; the former exerted themselves to be agreeable and entertaining; to the latter, this break in their quiet life was a sensational revelation. The evenings were full of mirth and laughter; one source of amusement to the guests being the singing and banjo playing of Mr. Adams' colored people, which was *genuine* plantation minstrelsy; exceeding the best imitations. There was mutual regret when the time came for guests and host to part. The intimation of remuneration for the hospitality extended by Mr. Adams, was rejected by that gentleman, with kindly but dignified firmness. Much hearty hand-shaking, and many cordial wishes attended the leave-taking, and with merry laughter, amidst the babel of many tongues, the party drove off from the old farm-house, which they never forgot.

On their way to Richmond, the passengers held a meeting, organized by John E. Owens and H. L. Bateman, and decided to present a testimonial to Mr. R. F. Adams, expressive of their thanks and appreciation of his kindness and lavish hospitality. Mr. Adams and his family had been invited to visit the theatre towards the close of the engagement of the "*Self*" company; and on their arrival in Richmond, were surprised by the presentation of a handsome silver service and tray, of exquisite workmanship. The largest piece being beautifully wrought with a representation of a snow-bound train in the foreground, a farm-house in the distance; and, in the middle ground, an ox-team wagon coming to the rescue. On the reverse side, the following engraved inscription:

" Presented

by the passengers who were detained by the severe snow storm of January 18th, 1857, on the Virginia Central Railroad, to

R. F. ADAMS

as a token of their gratitude for the true Virginia hospitality extended to them at his house, and for his heroic exertions in releasing them from their perilous and suffering condition."

Mr. Adams was so much overcome by this unexpected token of remembrance, that he could scarcely falter his acknowledgment—grasping Mr. Owens' hand, he said: "Not only do I appreciate this gift, but my children and grandchildren will regard it as an heirloom."

From Richmond "*Self*" wended its triumphal course to Cincinnati, where the prototype of *John Unit* frequently witnessed the play. One of his nephews said to Owens: "My Uncle recognizes himself in the character; and though sensitive about some points you make, he is well pleased at the denouement which elaborates *Unit's* good qualities!" *En passant*, it is rather strange that the likeness should have been admitted, as people are seldom conscious of their own peculiarities. I remember an eminent Italian impressario saying to Mr. Owens: "Mr. Owens, I hear that you have mak' imitate of me; I am mooch distress, and I so speak that you no more do zat same ting." Owens gravely expressed surprise at the accusation, and "really could not imagine *who* had brought such a charge against him;" this response being given with the accent and manner of the impressario, who failed to perceive the imitation; though the bystanders recognized it with infinite amusement.

While in Cincinnati, Owens and Bateman talked over a project of organizing a strong "American Comedy Company," to play through England during the summer months. Something that had not, at that time, been

MR. OWENS as JOHN UNIT

In " Self."

attempted. The more that it was discussed the more feasible the enterprise seemed. Henry C. Jarrett was deputed to ascertain if John Gilbert, William Wheatley and other eminent artists were open to offers; and favorable replies were received. Before making engagements, Mr. Jarrett was dispatched to England, to personally investigate the prospect of securing theatres in different cities, commencing in London. It being understood that a triple partnership, to manage the dramatic enterprise, should be organized on Jarrett's return, if favorable report was brought, justifying the venture. Meanwhile, Owens continued his professional engagements.

After an absence of six weeks, Mr. Jarrett returned, and a meeting of the trio was appointed. Verbal responses and letters from several English managers were most auspicious to the undertaking; consequently, the details of business came under discussion. Owens suggested that each member of the partnership should be allotted separate duties and responsibilities—giving certain views based on his managerial experience; and Jarrett acquiesced in this course, which impressed him as being practical and conducive to their mutual interest; but Bateman fought every opinion, step by step. After considerable talk, Owens remarked: "We are wasting time going over the same ground, Bateman; suppose you give us *your* views of an organization?" "Well, I will," replied Bateman; and after a preliminary remark or two, he summed up the matter by saying: "*I* must be business manager, absolutely; and *I* must have sole control of the entire affair, without dictation from any one. All power and direction must be vested in me, if we want success."

"Oh," said Owens, calmly, "*that* is your idea, is it?" "Yes," said Bateman, "and the only sensible way to carry the thing through." "Then, gentlemen," said Owens quietly (rising), "count *me* out of the enterprise;" and he left the room. So little excitement did he manifest, that Bateman could not believe the affair was closed. Three days later he approached Owens with some question relative to preparation for the "American Comedy Company;" and was quite startled by the unmistakable firmness of the reply given—"I gave my ultimatum, and will not waste further words on the subject."

Speaking of H. L. Bateman—he was a compound of good qualities and objectionable traits. His strong will and love of power inclined him to presumptuous and overbearing conduct. He was ofttimes captious and fault-finding. Mr. Owens, referring to this spirit of discontent, once said to him: "I really think, Bateman, if in the next world you are fortunate enough to be placed with the sheep, you will think it looks pleasanter among the goats." Bateman's indomitable energy and judgment eminently qualified him for a progressive business man. The fame of the celebrated "Bateman Children" (his daughters) extending, as it did, over both continents, was greatly enhanced by his acumen in properly developing their talents. Later on, when Kate Bateman, in early womanhood, achieved fame in " *Leah*," and other parts, her triumphs were much increased by the skilful engineering of her father, who was her indefatigable director.

Matilda Heron, Parepa Rosa, and other illustrious artistes, first appeared in this country under Bateman's management. With Tostee in " *The Grand Duchess*," he inaugurated Opera Bouffe in America. The St. Louis Theatre and others were, at different times, under his management. His latest managerial success was at the Lyceum Theatre, London. Then it was that Henry Irving (now so famous) first came into prominence—with the great run of "Hamlet" and "The Bells," which set all London talking of the rising star. Socially Bateman was companionable and entertaining. An excellent *raconteur*, he also had keen sense of the ludicrous, and appreciated wit and humor in others. He was not free from petty weakness, and this was evinced by his sensitiveness about his christian name, "Hezekiah Linthicum." It was so obnoxious to him, that he invariably made his signature H. L. Bateman, and tacitly permitted his letters to be addressed " *Henry* L. Bateman."

On one occasion, some little business disagreement occurred between Owens and Bateman. A correspondence ensued, and Bateman, as usual, waxed wrathful, and became voluminous in expression. Owens declined further discussion, but Bateman persisted in freighting the mail with reiterative contention. Finally Owens, impressed with the absurdity of this "Much Ado about Nothing," took a comical view of it, and wrote: "If you write to me again on this subject, I will return your letter addressed 'Hezekiah Linthicum Bateman.'" A telegraphic response came — "I will stop." Thus the matter was good-humoredly settled. The next time they met, Bateman, laughingly referring to the ludicrous termination of their difficulty, said: "John, you wouldn't *really* have been so cruel as to direct a letter to me, 'Hezekiah Linthicum?'" "Indeed, I would," said Owens. "I don't believe you capable of such deliberate wickedness," retorted Bateman, "though you frightened me terribly by the threat."

Bateman prided himself, and justly, too, on his admirable tact in extricating himself from a dilemma. His inventive genius seemed inexhaustible. Mr. Owens said he never saw Bateman nonplussed but once, and then not utterly. They were standing on the steps of the Burnet House, Cincinnati, when Bateman exclaimed: "Gracious goodness! here comes a man that I like; a man who entertained me when I was in this city a few months ago, and I have forgotten his name! but I *do remember* he is very sensitive on that point. John, what *is* his confounded name?" "I don't know," said Owens, exasperatingly. By this time the gentleman was ascending

the steps. Bateman rushed to meet him, shaking hands
cordially, and beaming with delight—hoping to gain time
by talking rapidly, and thus recall the name. Failing to
do so, he said: "I've thought of you so often; wanted
to send you a newspaper now and again, but did not know
exactly how to spell your name. How *do* you spell it?"
"s–m–i–t–h," was the response. To any one else this
would have been total discomfiture; but Bateman rallied,
and rejoined: "I was uncertain whether you used an i or
a y, and most people are liable to take offence at an inac-
curacy of the kind."

After the Cincinnati engagement Owens proceeded to
St. Louis where he scored a triumph, thence to Pittsburg
with like result. The remainder of the season was filled
in Washington, Philadelphia and Baltimore. In the
latter city he played several weeks at the Holliday Street
Theatre, and re-appeared there at the commencement of
the next season; after which he made his usual starring
tour through the principal cities, being considered by all
managers a strong drawing attraction. On the 2nd of
March, 1858, Owens appeared for the first time in Boston. *Dr. Ollapod,* in "*The Poor Gentleman,*" was the
part that chronicled his successful début. He was surrounded by a galaxy of talent: George Jordan, James
Bennett, Geo. Ryer, Henry Wallack, Williams, Stuart,
Norton, Julia Bennett, Fanny Morant, Mary Carr, &c.
The performances given by such a company were charm-

ing, so perfectly studied and rendered was every character.

March 24th Owens played *Bob Acres*, in *The Rivals*, for the first time, and made an immense hit. The idiosyncrasies of the character were given with zest and originality. It was a clear-cut picture of the country Squire. His scene in the second act, with *Captain Absolute*, was enthusiastically encored; and all through the Comedy laughter and applause confirmed his success. Mr. Owens' propensity to hurriedly dress for the stage, extended to his preparation of costume for a new part. A few hours before he was to appear as *Bob Acres* he sallied forth to procure some accessory which was required to make his dress complete. Meeting William Warren, he asked *where* he would be most likely to be suited in the article required. "Good gracious!" said Mr. Warren, "you don't mean to say that you haven't every thing ready for a part you play to-night, and a *new* part too! Why, I shouldn't be able to remember my lines if I had to think about a dress. It would upset me to be so hurried." "That very hurry suits me," replied Owens, "the excitement gives me a kind of nervousness which tends to vivacity, and brightens my wits."

Many old comedies were played at this time, but "*The Road to Ruin*" was perhaps the one in which Owens gave the greatest surprise to even his most ardent admirers. "*Silky*" is so entirely *un*-comic that much comment was made when Mr. Owens was announced for the part. But, having made a study of it, he knew he could do justice to its portrayal. The delineation he gave was a gem, and by its excellence became *the* feature of the comedy. His make-up was perfect. The angularity of limbs, the stooping shoulders, the semi-palsied appearance of hands, and the wizen face were all marvellous personalities of the miserly usurer. The shrewd avaricious glance which gave way to servile obsequiousness, in change of situation, the piping voice and cackling laugh were each and all masterly points.

Owens simulated age with extraordinary accuracy, but he was not unmindful that age has many phases and personal distinctive traits; hence, of the numerous old men he played, no one resembled the other. In *Solon Shingle* his voice ruralized into eccentricity, and in *Caleb Plummer* it sobered into pathos. His versatility was wonderful; he could be a young man, a romping lad, or a centenarian with equal fidelity to nature. "*Silky*" and "*Gillman*" (the youthful bridegroom) constituted an evening's entertainment which, in their contrast, vividly displayed these remarkable gifts; so did "*Tony Lumpkin*" and "*Spruggins*," and numerous other equally astonishing and delightful performances. During this Boston engagement, among other novelties produced, was "*The Queen's Heart*," by Dr. John W. Palmer, of Baltimore. Dr. Palmer was well known in literary circles as the author

7

of many able and brilliant works in prose and poetry. One of his specialties in poetry is the never-to-be-forgotten and thrilling poem of "Stonewall Jackson's Way."

The comedy of the *Queen's Heart* possessed self-asserting merit; inasmuch as the plot and action were original, and the dramatis personæ different from the stereotyped pattern so often found in plays. *Madame Mondieu*, created by Miss Fanny Morant, was a superb piece of acting. I say *acting*, for though true to nature, no other word can express how much this talented artiste made of the part by *look and gesture*. The text became eloquent by the inimitable shrug of the shoulders with which she emphasized its meaning. Owens as *Napoleon Bonaparte Aravier*, a French comedian, made a decided hit, and strongly depicted the eccentricities of the loquacious comedian, who, under the guise of flippant bombast, plots to defeat wicked designs and bring help to the deserving. His rendering of the semi-inebriated song, "*The Little Brown Man*," was nightly encored. The "*Queen's Heart*" won deserved popularity. Later on Dr. Palmer gave the play to Mr. Owens, who intended to include it in his repertoire, but always found it difficult to secure a competent *Madame Mondieu*.

The first theatrical performance ever given on Saturday *night* in Boston took place May 1st, 1858. The play-bills for more than a week previous having the preliminary announcement, by this heading:

## "SPECIAL NOTICE.

"The Legislature of Massachusetts during the last session, having abrogated an old law, which prevented Dramatic Representations from taking place on Saturday evenings, and the Board of Aldermen also having granted the petition of Mr. Barrow to open this Theatre on Saturday evenings, he purposes testing

### Public Opinion

by giving a *Dramatic Performance of a High Order* on Saturday evening next."

The public did not respond cordially to the innovation. Slim attendance being the rule for many Saturday nights; but gradually business increased, and before the season was over, Boston made no distinction between Saturday and other *night* performances. Owens remained in Boston several months. The favorable impression he made at first strengthened as his engagement became prolonged. Much social enjoyment brightened the time. With his professional associates, and many friends, he found congenial companionship. Many pleasant hours were spent in the society of William Warren. Occasionally a charming re-union and supper in Miss Amelia Fisher's renowned and picturesque kitchen made a red letter day.

One of the warmest friendships formed at this time was with Henry A. M'Glenen, now business manager of the Boston Theatre. It strengthened as time went on, and to the end of his life Mr. Owens esteemed " Harry

M'Glenen" with deep regard, and knew it to be sincerely reciprocated. No truer friend mourned his loss, or rendered tenderer tribute to his memory.

The evening previous to leaving Boston, Mr. Owens entertained a few friends at the Parker House. As they were about separating, one of the guests (a jolly but impecunious individual) said: "By the way, Owens, I owe you three hundred dollars—perhaps more." "Don't mention it," answered the comedian, who, liking the man personally and knowing his irresponsibility, mentally regarded the money as a gift, not a debt. "Ah! my boy, that won't do; business is business, and I prefer to settle the matter before you leave the city." Then taking from his pocket a slip of paper, he said: "Here is my I. O. U., that will secure you." At this Micawberish adjustment, a covert smile pervaded the company, but Owens gravely received the note, and held it in his hand while they stood chatting, ere they separated. Finally, with affected unconsciousness, he twisted the paper and used it to light his cigar. A horrified remonstrance arose from the giver of the note. "My dear boy, see what you are doing! Don't be so absent-minded!" "That's all right, B——, such a lighter must needs give my cigar a good flavor, and at the same time relieve you from the shadow of responsibility."

October, 1858, finds Owens again in Boston, but only for a short engagement, as he had signed for the season with Thomas Placide, Manager of the "Varieties Thea-tre," New Orleans. The original Varieties Theatre, erected 1849, was managed by Thomas Placide until 1854; during that year it was destroyed by fire. When the theatre was rebuilt, Dion Boucicault assumed the management and changed the name to "Gaieté Theatre—it was so known for two years. When in 1858, Placide again became manager, he restored the old and more popular title. This theatre was situated on Gravier street, and owned by the "Varieties Club," an exclusive, aristo-cratic and wealthy association. The name was suggested by "La Varieté" in Paris. The theatre ranked as the most fashionable in New Orleans. At that time song and dance and specialty performances were limited to music halls, and not termed "variety shows;" but later on, when thus designated, it became necessary to change the name of New Orleans' famous theatre, least the origi-nal title, "Varieties," might give a wrong impression in regard to its dramatic position.

The season of 1858–59 was conducted on the stock system; a superb company having been engaged. The sterling old comedies were given, varied with the new pieces, then being played in London and New York. As usual with New Orleans seasons, Owens found this one delightful as well as profitable. At its close, Pla-cide's lease having terminated, Owens was solicited by the stockholders to become the next manager, and accepted a four years' lease, beginning 1859–60.  Upon the conclusion of the present season, Owens took the company to St. Louis and Cincinnati, and gave six performances in each city; so great was the furore created, that the houses were packed and many unable to obtain even standing room.

Perhaps there can be found no more brilliant dramatic record than the New Orleans season of 1859–60.  The stockholders gave Owens *carte blanche* in respect to beautifying and furnishing the Varieties Theatre ; and this unlimited power, guided by his judgment and exquisite taste, resulted in the Theatre being a model of elegance in regard to auditorium, stage setting and general effect. The dramatic corps selected was second to none in the country, and the splendor of the season was unparalleled. The wealth, beauty and fashion congregated in New Orleans, this winter, was never exceeded in that notably gay city; the "Varieties" nightly thronged with pleasure seekers ; and Owens, both as an actor and manager, considered peerless.

Among the new comedies produced this season was "*Everybody's Friend.*"  It was put on the boards simultaneously with its production in New York.  E. F. Sothern as *Featherley*, Sara Stevens as *Mrs. Swandown*, and Owens as *Major Wellington DeBoots*.  To the latter character Owens brought original conception, and played perfectly ; making so great a mark that ever afterwards

MR. OWENS as MAJOR WELLINGTON DeBOOTS

In "Everybody's Friend."

it was included in his starring repertoire. Owens' conception of *DeBoots* was not as an eccentric braggart, only to be laughed at, but a man of excessive vanity, weak character and infirm purpose. The self-satisfied catchy little laugh or chuckle, which he originated in this part, has often been imitated, but never reproduced with the vitality and infectious mirth wherewith Owens invested it. The business introduced was irresistibly droll, but neat, and, with an occasional interpolating line, made the bombastic *Major's* character vividly life-like.

And here I would remark, that a tendency to gag has been attributed to Mr. Owens which he did not deserve in the actual sense of the word; it is true he was prone now and then to introduce a sentence not set down in the text, but it always fitted so perfectly with the character he was representing that it seemed exactly what the author would have consistently written. Exuberance of spirits never led Mr. Owens to the objectionable habit of making topical jokes, or allusion to those surrounding him. He was far too conscientious an artist to sacrifice the integrity and illusion of a play to raise a laugh, or create merriment at variance with principle and taste.

Sara Stevens made a charming *Mrs. Swandown,* and E. S. Sothern was admirably suited to *Felix Featherley,* which he played in his usual graceful, mercurial and polished manner. Each of the cast seemed to have a part that might have been written for their especial abilities;

and this insured a favorable reception for the comedy. The first and second nights of its representation there was a bit of amusement not set down in the bill. For the scene where *Featherley* presents *Mrs. Swandown* with an Angora cat (supposed to be sleeping peacefully in the covered basket which he carries), Sothern insisted upon being realistic, to the extent of having a *live* cat. Of course, puss became frightened when the cover was removed, jumped out, and having made a bewildered plunge here and there, scampered off the stage amid the laughter of the audience. For the next night, Sothern suggested a small guinea pig as being less nimble, and sure to remain quiet, but the same exhibition of stage fright (?) occurred, except that the pig dived awkwardly into the orchestra. The general impression prevailed that these innovations were not actuated so much by Sothern's desire to be realistic as by his propensity for practical joking.

" *The American Cousin*," in which Sothern had made a hit at Laura Keene's New York Theatre, the previous season, was strongly cast, but met with only moderate favor from the public, and less from the press. It was at this time that Sothern originated the " *Brother Sam* " letter which he introduced into the part of *Dundreary*, and afterwards rendered so celebrated. *The American Cousin* held the boards for two weeks. On the night of final representation Sothern (as *Dundreary*) read a witty letter conveying a request from the company for permission to testify their admiration by crowning him with an appropriate wreath. His lordship having expressed gratification and given consent, the imposing ceremony was performed, and the renowned *Dundreary* crowned with a chaste wreath of "*woathed chestnutzs*," beautifully relieved by "*Oythter Theltz*" and "*Shwimp Think*." "My Lord" made a brilliant acknowledgment, replete with stammerings and hops. The audience and the artists evidently enjoyed the joke intensely, and the majority of them quite understood that it was a good-humored rebuke to the overdone gush of floral presentations which had become rather tiresome during the season.

Sothern's *Dundreary* is so much a part of stage history that everybody knows he continued to elaborate and improve the character, until it became identified with his name, placing him on a pinnacle of prominence which he had failed to reach through his equally clever and more legitimate personations.

The great sensation of season 1859–60 was "*Dot*," Boucicault's dramatization of *The Cricket on the Hearth*, in which Owens played *Caleb Plummer* for the first time. Careful rehearsals were given, and also every attention to the stage setting and transformation scene. The Fairy Prologue was charming. The initial performance took place on Christmas night with the following cast:

CALEB PLUMMER.................... ..................MR. JOHN E. OWENS.
JOHN PEERYBINGLE..........................MR. C. W. COULDOCK.
TACKLETON............................................MR. M. LEFFINGWELL.
EDWARD PLUMMER....................................MR. H. A. COPLAND.

DOT.......................................MISS CHARLOTTE THOMPSON.
BERTHA............. ...............................MISS SARA STEVENS.
MRS. FIELDING......................................MRS. W. A. CHAPMAN.
TILLY SLOWBOY...................................MISS POLLY MARSHALL.
MAY FIELDING.......................................MISS ELIZA COULDOCK.

Polly Marshall, the soubrette, was much dissatisfied with having the part of *Tilly Slowboy* assigned to her. The lady was an English actress who had been a favorite at Burton's Theatre, New York, and it was expected she would be equally popular in New Orleans, but a mild liking was the extent of approbation she inspired; sensitively aware of this fact, she entreated Mr. Owens to substitute some one else for *Tilly,* assuring him that the part was utterly out of her style, and to attempt it would culminate her unpopularity. Mr. Owens thought differently, and courteously but firmly declined to change the cast; whereupon the lady retired from the interview in a distressed and tearful condition. Short-sighted mortals we are. *Tilly Slowboy* proved to be the first hit of Miss Marshall's engagement; she took the audience by storm, and afterwards every part she played was favorably received. No soubrette, in New Orleans, ever held greater sway over an audience than did Polly Marshall.

Owens' personation of *Caleb Plummer* belongs to the annals of the stage. It stands unrivalled and crowned with well-earned glory. The public, the press and his fellow artists have conceded to him the perfection of finished art in this character, and ranked him as incomparable. His great charm was unaffected adherence to nature. He took *Caleb Plummer* bodily from the word-painting of Dickens, and made him flesh and blood. There was no attempt at heroism in depicting this affectionate-hearted old man who had suffered so long with cheerful resignation ; it was simple nature in all its purity and goodness, and the illusion perfect in delicate blending of pathos and quaint humor.

The " God bless us all " of old *Caleb* lingered in sweet influence with the audience, and found echo in the hearts of all who saw and felt his nature as embodied by John E. Owens. It was a poem, a comedy and a sermon. No description can do justice to his bits of by-play—the quick transition from distress to cheerfulness, for the blind daughter's sake, caused the auditor to break into laughter while yet the eyes were moist.

When depicting tender emotion Mr. Owens had what the French term " tears in the voice " (as well as in his heart), and the effect was magnetic. It has been said of Owens' personation of *Caleb Plummer*, that " it compares with *Solon Shingle* as an oil painting does with a crayon sketch."

ished, farm and country life were forgotten, and he became absorbed in dear old *Caleb*.

"*Dot*" was immensely popular in New Orleans, and was played for two months—an unprecedented run for that city, no piece having previously had such a hold on public enthusiasm. It was withdrawn in the height of success, and given at intervals later in the season. Having made so great a mark as *Caleb Plummer*, Owens purchased from Boucicault the sole right and possession of his adaptation of *Cricket on the Hearth*, entitled "*Dot.*"

A very sad event occurred towards the spring. Harry Copland (juvenile man of the company) had some difficulty with Mr. Overall, dramatic critic of the *True Delta*, arising from adverse and personal criticism. The quarrel eventuated in a rencontre, during which Copland was shot. The arrest of Overall followed, but he was released on bail, pending Copland's treatment at the hospital where he had been taken for amputation of his leg. The symptoms were serious from the first. Copland was a manly ingenuous young fellow, and a great favorite with Mr. Owens, who was devoted to him during his illness. Copland craved this constant presence, and found much comfort in his friendly ministration. At the final hour Owens was with him, and afterwards drove immediately to the Mayor's office and gave notification of the fatal result of the affray. Overall's re-arrest ensued. He was tried for murder, but acquitted on the plea of self-defence.

The prosecution made a strong effort to secure conviction on the charge of *premeditated* malice on the part of Overall; the evidence was powerful, but was rendered ineffectual by reason of a peculiar defence. It was proved that Copland died of lock-jaw, resulting from gangrene caused by verdigris on the pistol ball. The defense maintained that this could not have been the case had the pistol been *freshly* loaded by Overall, with murderous intent; hence the shooting had *not* been premeditated, but the pistol picked up hurriedly when needed for self-defence. On this plea Overall was acquitted.

After the regular season a supplementary summer one was inaugurated by the engagement of Mrs. John Wood, who fascinated the New Orleans people, as " *Pochahontas*," and with many equally charming bits of acting. The company included much musical talent, which was a desirable element in the production of " *Pochahontas;*" and to render it yet more attractive, Owens introduced a drill and march of forty female Zouaves. Requiring appropriate music, he was difficult to please, as he wanted something spirited and yet not too martial. Carlo Patti (brother of Adelina Patti), the leader of the orchestra, was called upon for suggestions. He ran over various airs, all of which were rejected, and was growing hopeless, when he struck the chords of *Dixie*, then a minstrel song but little sung. " *That* suits," said Owens, " it is exactly what I want. We will have a song and chorus with the drill and march." It was thoroughly rehearsed, and the Zouave drill with *Dixie* chorus took the town by storm. Soon the air was whistled in the streets, played by the bands, hummed by everyone; in fine, became the sensation of the times. And thus originated the popularity of "Dixie's land," which resulted in its adoption as a southern war song.

In May the theatre closed, and Owens returned to Aigburth Vale, his Maryland farm; passing the summer months pleasantly there, except for an occasional sojourn in New York to make preparations for the ensuing New Orleans season.

# CHAPTER V.



MR. OWENS took great pride in his theatre, and having now become a stockholder, determined that it should exceed its former record for elegance and attractiveness. He therefore did not limit himself to the liberal amount authorized by the board of directors for the renovation of the theatre, but expended much of his private means for costly furniture, carpets, &c. When the "Varieties" opened November, 1860, with a strong dramatic corps in keeping with its surroundings, the manager was satisfied with his preliminary labor, and the public amazed and delighted with the magnificence and brilliancy presented for their patronage.

112

Legitimate comedy and all the new plays were produced with that close attention to correct costume and appropriate scenery which ever marked the management of John E. Owens. These he held secondary to dramatic force, but he considered them indispensable to the presentation of a play, and his *personal* attention was always given to the superintendence of every detail in the theatre. From the paint room to the stage he was present and directed the veriest minutiæ. Thus executive ability combined with judgment and refined taste rendered his success as a manager Napoleonic. "*Dot*" was revived and warmly welcomed in 1860–61—"*The Romance of a Poor Young Man*" and "*Playing with Fire*" were among the novelties. The casting of the pieces was simply perfect, embracing such talent as George Jordan, Mark Smith, Charles Bass, Dolly Davenport, Charles Thorne, Jr., Myron Leffingwell, C. H. Morton, F. Maeder, Geo. Wallack, Charlotte Thompson, Annie Graham, Mrs. W. H. Chapman, Mrs. Leighton and a host of others. The most important new production was "*Jeannie Deans*" (or *Heart of Mid Lothian*), for which the entire resources of the theatre, in scenic painting and mechanical effects, were brought into requisition, and the strength of the company included. The famous pictures of the trial, &c., were represented in tableaux effect with exquisite accuracy, and were nightly encored. The storming of the Tolbooth was exciting and impressive. This representation

8

was appreciated by crowded houses for nine consecutive weeks.

Towards the close of the winter much restlessness prevailed through the community, and the "States' rights" question was increasedly agitated.    Opinions, at first quietly expressed, developed until the "cloud no bigger than a man's hand," grew ominously threatening.    The gay crowd in New Orleans, hitherto on pleasure bent, became thoughtful, and gave less time to amusement and more to the impending crisis; and the topic oftenest discussed was "Secession."

My narrative has no connection with the Civil War, except to mention it as it affected Mr. Owens.    He was a Southern sympathizer, but never took up arms against the United States.    Had the seat of war been in Maryland he would have defended his home.    No honorable nature can censure him for standing firm to his honest convictions.    It was a matter of principle with him, involving the sacrifice of prosperity, for he not only lost his property in New Orleans but forfeited the three years' lease of the theatre, which proved an El Dorado to the Northern manager who used the theatre and its expensive appointments.

A course dictated by policy was foreign to Mr. Owens' nature, hence he was willing to endanger his popularity rather than express views which he did not entertain. Quietly resolved, but never aggressive, no one can truly say that he was ever treacherous to the government. He played a short engagement in Washington and in Baltimore—a long interval between these, on account of serious illness in the family. Then followed the Pittsburg date, rendered memorable from the fact that he was not permitted to play. So great was the antagonism against him, for alleged Southern sentiments, that threats of personal violence were rife, and Mr. Owens' friends prevailed upon him to quietly leave town without making any attempt to fulfil his engagement.

A fortnight later he was due in Boston, where he nightly packed the large auditorium of the Boston Theatre; his friends and the public *there* not lessening one whit of their cordiality because his opinions did not coincide with theirs. He came before them as an *artist*, not as a politician, and they knew full well that he was incapable of dishonorable conduct, and respected him for his moral courage and dignified course which increased their admiration and regard.

After the War was over, an amusing incident occurred one election day, when Owens presented himself at the polls to vote. An effort was made to interfere with his right of suffrage—the time was past when such a thing could be done on the ground of Southern sympathy. Owens' vote was challenged under charge of "non-residence." The animus was patent; but taking the matter coolly, Owens said: "I beg your pardon, I don't quite understand the objection." "Non-residence, *where* do you live?" "Well, I live in London, Paris, Boston, New York and many other places, but my home is *here* in Baltimore County, and *here* I vote."

At this juncture a half-tipsy loafer, with unkempt hair and soiled attire, lounged in front of Owens and said: "Where d'ye get your washing done? *There's* where a feller votes." "In that case, my friend," responded Owens, "I should say *you* never had a vote in all your life." A roar of laughter followed this sally, which put even the antagonistic element in a good humor. The challenger laughingly said: "Go on and vote, Owens; we give in." October, 1861, Owens was drafted in the Union army; he received the notice in Washington, just as he was coming off the stage, and meeting one of the actors, while passing to his dressing room, remarked: "There is a very disagreeable draft here." The literal young man called to some of the stage hands: "Shut that door; Mr. Owens complains of the draft." Whereupon Owens laughed heartily, and explained the misapprehension.

He speedily obtained a substitute, but on the way to Baltimore the man vanished. A few days afterwards another was secured, a regular vagabond specimen. Determined to hold possession this time, Owens fitted the man out with good clothing, took him to the farm and lodged him in an upper room of one of the cottages on the place; keeping him under close surveillance for three days, until the papers, &c., were arranged. The fellow was more than satisfied with his quarters, and having his meals served to him three times a day; loudly asserting, that "he wished it might continue, as he never before lived so well." After his examination and acceptance, he was taken to camp; where he pocketed his $400, and Mr. Owens gladly received his release.

Next morning, about dawn, Mr. Owens (as was his frequent custom) sallied forth with his dogs and gun, for an hour or two's shooting before breakfast. While standing on the portico, he saw a carriage driving rapidly down the road. When within a few yards of the house, it stopped under a huge oak tree; the driver got down, opened the door of the vehicle, and lifted out something like a large bundle which he placed under the tree. By this time Owens had reached the spot. He recognized the driver as an employé at Barnum's Hotel, and said: "Hello! Michael, what's all this about?" "Sure, sir, and the young man has been on a bit of a spree; he says he's your nephew, and told me to bring him out home; and I didn't like to wake the family up before sunrise, so I thought I'd lave him quiet *here*.

Turning his eyes to the supposed bundle, Owens saw his substitute huddled up in a drunken stupor. "Michael," said he, solemnly, "that person is *not* my relative, he is a deserter; take him to the camp. If he escapes, you are liable to be arrested as an accessory." Michael needed no second bidding.  Picking up the ninety-pound substitute, he deposited him in the carriage, and drove off to the camp; where he was given into custody.

Owens played in Cincinnati, St. Louis, and Nashville and Memphis this winter.  Later on in Boston, from thence a return date in Cincinnati.  The Burnet House was military headquarters, and Owens, who stopped there, was thrown into daily intercourse with the commanders, who sought him socially, and admired him professionally; not concerning themselves about his Southern sentiments.  In Cincinnati he closed his season, but before retiring for the summer to his farm, consented to play for the benefit of a friend connected with Wood's Theatre.  This necessitated remaining over a few days in Cincinnati, which he was quite willing to do.  The decision having been made, I was astonished when he returned from rehearsal and said to me: "I want you to pack up, so that we can leave here to-night."  Noting my look of amazement, he continued: "I can't tell you *why*, but on my way to the theatre an overwhelming impression possessed me to start for home; I could not shake it off.  I told my friend that I was called home, and asked him to say what my name on the bill was worth to him, and oblige me by accepting a check instead of my services; so that is all arranged."

Presentiments and forebodings were so utterly inconsistent with Mr. Owens' nature that I could not realize that he was actually altering his plans on that basis, and queried: "Have you bad news from home which you intend to break to me gradually?" He assured me to the contrary.

We left by the midnight train. Mr. Owens did not appear at all depressed, but bright and cheerful all the journey. We were not expected at home till several days later, therefore no carriage was at the County station to meet us. Mr. Owens procured a wagon, and we jolted slowly along. Our arrival was a joyful surprise. The family, at that time, consisted of Mr. Owens' father and mother. They were both seated on the portico, as we drove up, and greeted us with exclamations of delight.

I don't think four happier people existed that charming summer afternoon, as we chatted together with the blessed sensation of homefelt rest and peace. A few hours later Mr. Owens said to me: "Just see the absurdity of presentiments! If we had found sickness or trouble at home, my strong impression to return would have been regarded as a warning. On the contrary, 'all is well' to the full extent of that comprehensive phrase."

The next morning, at ten o'clock, Mr. Owens' mother died suddenly of heart failure. He was standing beside her, when she fell back in his arms and expired with loving gaze fixed upon him, but powerless to speak. I do not say that this sad event was foreshadowed; I only tell the facts.

The loss of Mr. Owens' mother was the first grief of his hitherto sunny life. He loved her with a devotion and tenderness which only a pure and noble nature is capable of. Thoughtful and attentive to her comfort, his every word seemed to convey a caress which her warm heart cherished and responded to. They were alike in nature, and worthy of each other. For months after her death Mr. Owens did not resume his profession. Most of the time was passed on his farm. He bore his affliction bravely, but he suffered intensely.

His first engagement of 1863 was in Boston, from thence (as oft before) a tour of the New England towns. The company at this time was superb, including E. L. Davenport, Wm. Wheatley, John Gilbert, and other famous names. In fact the cast was a galaxy of stars. Old comedies were the leading attraction: *"Heir at Law," "Poor Gentleman," "She Stoops to Conquer,"* &c. One of the most pronounced events was the production of *" Money,"* brilliantly performed throughout. The impression Owens made as *Graves* was immense; he not only elicited triple calls, but encores after the most effective scenes.

A return engagement was played in Boston by this grand combination of talent, with results even greater than that of a few weeks previous. Boston was one of the cities which Owens especially loved. He had there many warm and congenial personal friends, and as an actor was ever *en rapport* with his audience. He was a favorite with Longfellow, Holmes, Agassiz, Felton, and others of that wonderful literary coterie. The public of Boston claimed him for their own, as also did Baltimore and some other cities. Though born in England, Owens belonged to America. Through all the length and breadth of this country the mention of his name will cause a twinkle of the eye and a joyous remembrance of his mirth-provoking genius.

Leaving Boston he returned to Baltimore, appearing there in a round of his popular characters, which he repeated the following week in Washington. Much of this season was passed quietly on the farm, restfully and pleasantly affording an opportunity to indulge in reading and study, of which Mr. Owens was very fond. An enthusiastic lover of Shakespeare, he was a close student of the immortal bard; always discovering fresh beauties and new points of interest in the most familiar passages. He delighted to read over and over again a favorite speech, and discuss its intricate yet clear significance.

In the copy of Shakespeare, which he read oftenest, I find on the fly-leaf the following quotation from Dr. Johnson: "Time which is continually washing away the dissoluble fabrics of other poets, passes without injury by the adamant of Shakespeare." Mr. Owens was not only cultured and refined, but scholarly in his taste. As a comedian his Shakespearean characters held exalted position. "*Touchstone*," "*The First Grave-digger*," "*Dromio of Syracuse*," "*Launcelot Gobbo*," and others were enacted with the full quantum of humor, and yet legitimately and entirely free from coarseness. He would have considered it akin to sacrilege to render them otherwise than in their integrity.

About the middle of June, 1864, Owens received a letter from George Wood, formerly manager in Cincinnati and St. Louis, stating that he intended to open the theatre, corner of Broadway and Broome street, New York, originally known as "Brougham's," and afterwards as "Wallack's." He purposed making it a comedy theatre, and desired to have Owens inaugurate it by being the first star. This place of amusement had deteriorated from a first class position, having verged on entertainments of the variety show species.

Owens hesitated about entering into negotiations, though excellent terms were offered. Upon stating his objection to Mr. Wood, he was met by the argument that "the reputation of John Owens would elevate any theatre, and stamp its position as equal to the best." He was not so sanguine as the manager, but at length upon the promise of Mr. Wood to provide for support, "a company capable of playing the old comedies in a manner acceptable to a New York audience," Owens signed a contract for six weeks, renewable if mutually satisfactory.

MR. OWENS as LAUNCELOT GOBBO

In " The Merchant of Venice."

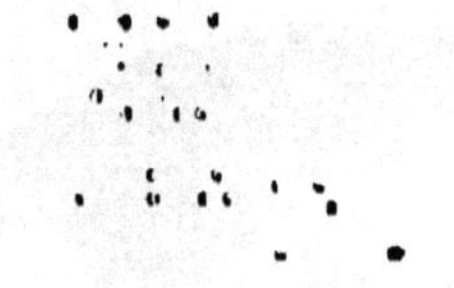

This he did with the consciousness that the circumstances of his re-entree before the New York public were inauspicious, as he would have to overcome prejudice against the theatre in order to draw the class of audience to which he was entitled. That he accomplished this in a superlative degree, and won continued fame and enthusiasm, marks a well-earned histrionic triumph which has never been excelled.

August 29th, 1865, Owens commenced his engagement at the Broadway Theatre, where thirteen years previous he had made his first success in New York. The opening bill was "*Married Life*" and "*Solon Shingle.*" In both pieces he made a favorable impression, but in the latter an overwhelming hit; a hit which grew into a sensation, and culminated in a furore. Crowds packed the theatre nightly, and before the rise of the curtain, "standing room" was unattainable. Owens' marvelous delineation of the old farmer became the leading attraction of New York.

"*Solon Shingle*" was the theme everywhere. "The apple sass case," "Jesso, Jesso," and other quotations were heard on the streets, in the cars. Acquaintances meeting, facetiously greeted each other with: "Why, Mr. Winslow, how *do* you do?" On all sides "*Solon*" was the reigning excitement. "*Married Life*" was withdrawn after the first week, and "*Victims*" substituted. In this piece Owens won high encomiums. It was played eleven consecutive weeks; then "*The Poor Gentleman*" was produced, and afterwards other comedies; but all the while *Solon Shingle* kept steadily on increasing in popularity, and achieved the longest run hitherto known in New York, or any city in America.

Noting the hundredth performance of Solon Shingle, one of the leading papers drew attention to many wonderful things history records to have taken place in that given space of time; and terminated with the following paragraph: "In one hundred days France passed through the throes of two revolutions—lost a king, gained an emperor, and again bowed to a king. In one hundred days Napoleon left Elba, marched to the throne of France, fought Waterloo, and was conquered. In one hundred nights '*John Owens*' fought a fight for popularity single-handed against the hordes of New York theatre-goers, and conquered them. In one hundred nights the Broadway Theatre passed from the position of a concert hall to the height of fashion. We take pleasure in chronicling such great victories. *Solon Shingle* will run additional hundreds of nights, if this great artist so chooses."

A true prophecy, for it would have continued uninterruptedly the whole season, had not Owens, at the end of six months, become weary with the monotonous repetition of Solon, and suggested to Mr. Wood an entire change of bill. "What!" said the manager, "take a piece off in the full tide of success, while we are turning people away, and actually filling other theatres with our overflow!" "Well, all the easier to pick up '*Solon*' again, when I have had a little rest from him," replied Owens. Mr. Wood finally yielded, when to these importunities others were added from friends of Mr. Owens who had seen him play "*Caleb Plummer*," and were desirous that New York should enjoy this masterpiece. "*Dot*" was produced early in March, and Owens' *Caleb Plummer* proved to be a dramatic sensation.

The encomiums lavished upon it were quite as numerous as those elicited by *Solon Shingle*, with the additional tribute that the artist had "mounted into an atmosphere rarer and more delicate than that which surrounds Solon Shingle." The piece was played a month to immense business, and universally conceded to be the most exquisite embodiment of *Caleb Plummer* ever witnessed.

During this month Mr. and Mrs. Charles Kean arrived in New York. Mr. Owens had known them in England, and the pleasant acquaintance was now renewed. They remembered Owens as a young actor in Burton's Theatre, and many courteous references were made to his embryo talent in those days, and much pleasure expressed congratulatory of his present fame.

The Keans came frequently to see *Caleb Plummer*. After their first evening's enjoyment of it Mrs. Kean wrote the following letter to Mr. Owens:

"METROPOLITAN HOTEL, March 23d.

"JOHN E. OWENS:

"*My Dear Sir*,—Accept the best thanks of Mr. Kean and myself for the great pleasure you gave us on Saturday evening. We laughed and wept like children, over the amusing and touching simplicity of old *Caleb*; and we both agreed that we had not for a long time seen such *admirable* acting.

"You were very well supported, for the drama was well done throughout. Your Bertha was *very* blind and *very* handsome. Wishing you a great success in London. Believe me, my dear sir,

"Yours truly,

"ELLEN KEAN."

Mr. Owens always prized this letter.

Mr. Kean was equally enthusiastic about the performance, and was also much impressed with Owens' make-up. "Why, my dear boy," he said, "not only does your face simulate age, but your figure is shrivelled, your neck and hands are withered, and your eyes are dim! What do you do with your sparkling eyes, and doesn't it take you a long time to accomplish this metamorphosis?" Owens laughingly replied: "I allow myself fifteen or twenty minutes to dress and make up." Mr. Kean asked if it would be admissable for him to witness the process, and received a cordial assent. An appointment was made, and Kean looked on while Owens, quietly chatting, got old *Caleb* ready for the stage. When finished, Kean expressed amazement and thanks for what he termed "an artistic revelation."

Mr. and Mrs. Charles Kean came to New York without an engagement, but with firm belief that an opening would be made for them in one of the leading theatres. No disposition was evinced to meet their views. Unfortunately all dates were filled for the season; and the indications were that they would have to abandon the idea of playing in New York. Mr. Owens thought that these famous artists should not be permitted to return to England without receiving the honor and attention to which they were entitled—and additionally conferring upon their many admirers the pleasure of enjoying their performances. He spoke to Mr. Wood, expressing his desire to relinquish a fortnight of his engagement, the time to be placed at the disposal of the Keans. Mr. Wood complied with this solicitation to make a special opening for the Keans; and offered them a fortnight engagement, which they accepted.

Mr. and Mrs. C. Kean were appreciative of this courtesy extended to them by Mr. Owens, and cordially expressed acknowledgment. They played to full houses for the two weeks; at the end of which time Owens resumed his engagement, appearing in "*The Live Indian*" and "*Solon Shingle*." This bill continued to be strong attraction until the close of the season. *Solon Shingle* became identified with Owens' name, so much so that he received many letters facetiously directed to "*Solon Shingle Owens*," and "John E. Owens, *care of Solon Shingle*,"

&c.  I have in my possession many humorous epistles of the kind, two of them very wittily written by Howard Paul, in England, but as they are of a social and somewhat confidential nature, I do not incorporate them in my narrative.

Owens' *Solon Shingle* was a finished piece of character acting, perfect in detail, and yet free from exaggeration. The power of the artist is prominent from the fact that this great success was evolved from a mere sketch, which his own genius elaborated and clothed with vitality. This marvellous portrayal has formed the basis for many rural dramas, wherein the central figure is a palpable imitation of Owens' *original* conception and manner of playing *Solon Shingle*; but their light is a borrowed one, relatively as bright as the moon compared to the sun.

One performance was given in Brooklyn for the benefit of the Orphans' Asylum there.  A crowded house brought large pecuniary aid to the orphans, and their presence secured for them an unusual enjoyment, if one might judge by the silvery peals of childish laughter.

Several portraits of *Solon* have been taken, prominent among which are two oil paintings—a full-length figure, by Constant Meyer, and a life-size three-quarter length, by A. Cross, of Louisville, Kentucky.  The former excelled in artistic merit and finish, but the latter was equally striking as a likeness, and perhaps more characteristic.  Constant Meyer's picture was on exhibition in

MR. OWENS as SOLON SHINGLE.

(From a Painting by Constant Meyer.)

New York for some time, and attracted much attention. It was subsequently purchased by a wealthy French gentleman, and is now in his private collection in Paris. The painting by Cross was taken for Mr. Owens, who considered it admirable. It found place in his library, the position it still maintains among other treasures.

The celebrity attained by *Solon Shingle* rendered it thereafter inseparable from Owens' repertoire, but it was by no means his favorite. I think he best loved *Caleb Plummer*, and he was devoted to the old comedies. He gave conscientious work to all he did, but in some characters he especially delighted. He revelled in the unctuous humor of *Perkyn Middlewick*, and played that jolly butter-man with power unexcelled. A slight touch of dialect conduced to the naturalness with which he invested the part. He was peculiarly gifted in rendering dialect, not only of nationalities, but the delicate shading of localities. The Lancashire, Yorkshire and others were spoken with a nicety of accent that would delight those whose ear and taste were attuned to the accurateness of tones.

May 27th, 1865, Owens sailed per steamer City of Boston, for England, to fulfil an engagement of six weeks, for which he had signed with Benjamin Webster, to play *Solon Shingle* at the Theatre Royal Adelphi, London. He had hoped for a week or two of leisure before leaving America, wishing to pass a few days at

9

home on the farm, and also to have time for enjoying the
social companionship of his friends in New York.  To
his surprise Mr. Wood refused to release him from any
portion of the engagement for which he had contracted.
In vain was monetary remuneration offered, and the
surety of supplying a star to fill the unexpired time
pleadingly urged.

Mr. Wood was inexorable; no inducement could alter
his determination that "Owens must play continuously
up to the time of his departure."  So the curtain fell on
his final performance within ten hours of the sailing of
the steamer.  He had not the opportunity of even a
hurried adieu to his friends.  Naturally he felt vexed
and distressed at being obliged to leave in this abrupt
manner.  Conduct seemingly so discourteous was incompatible with his nature; and to extricate himself from a
false position he wrote (on the eve of his departure) the
following card for publication in the *New York Herald:*

"A CARD FROM JOHN E. OWENS TO THE PUBLIC.

"The lengthy period of my twice-extended engagement at the
Broadway Theatre has now closed, and I am left free personally to
express, in terms of unconstrained sincerity, my grateful appreciation
of the cordial favor and unvarying kindness, and generous consideration with which my professional efforts have been received by the
public of New York.

"Success does not at all times appeal to the same emotions; and
though in my long and varied professional experience it has been

my proud fortune to receive many flattering and cherished marks
of popular favor and esteem, yet never before has my pride as an
artist and my gratitude as a man been more deeply stirred than
by the kindnesses here lavished upon me; and I can but say that
the thanks which now I seek to convey spring from the most earnest
and warmest impulses of my nature.

"To the gentlemen of the critical press, whose impartial sense of
justice and of the true requirements of art, have pointed alike their
praises and their censure, I rest under many courteous obligations
which will be as pleasantly remembered as they are now warmly
acknowledged.

"In a few hours I shall bid adieu to the citizens of New York, to
gratify in a distant land those ambitious longings which their favor
has intensified and stimulated anew. But in the comparatively brief
period of my absence my heart will still be linked to them by the
proudest and happiest recollections, and by the cherished hope that
their esteem may prove as enduring as the gratitude of

"The Public's obedient servant,

"John E. Owens.

"New York, May 27th, 1865."

The engagement thus terminated had been of nine
months' duration, and for length, brilliancy and success
was unprecedented in the record of New York theatricals.
The overflowing house which greeted the star on the
closing night attested his unabated popularity. Financi-
ally it was phenomenal in results; Mr. Owens' personal
emolument being $65,891.39.

# CHAPTER VI.



SHORTLY after Owens arrived in London "*Solon
Shingle*" was put in rehearsal. Benjamin Webster,
manager of the Adelphi, received the American comedian with cordiality, and manifested every disposition to
render his surroundings in the theatre agreeable; and
many warm friends welcomed him to London. Whatever coldness he encountered arose from professional
antagonism. To this phase of feeling there were pleasing
exceptions; but the theatrical atmosphere was largely
charged with the unuttered thunder of " we don't want
you here," and " we hope you will be a failure." For-

132

tunately this stormy and disagreeable element did not possess the public.

From the first night of Owens' appearance in London he made a favorable impression, which steadily increased as his engagement progressed. The house that welcomed him was full, and not only fashionable, but intellectual and discriminating. Among the audience were Charlotte Cushman, Hon. B. F. Moran, American Minister, Charles Dickens, and other famous people, distinguished in literary and social life. From Dickens, Miss Cushman, and many others present, Mr. Owens afterwards received warm congratulations, and pleasantly written notes of commendation, which with his innate modest unobtrusiveness he refrained from making public. But he prized these kindly words from such illustrious sources, and always kept them. They are now in my possession, and regarded as an invaluable heritage.

The English public were not familiar with the special type of individuality embodied in *Solon Shingle*, but they recognized it as a magnificent piece of *character-acting;* and rendered homage to Mr. Owens' talent in the verdict: "The worst play we have had from America, but the best comedian. The piece a failure, but *Solon Shingle* a great hit."

Everybody was enthusiastic over Owens' wonderful powers of delineation, and irresistible humor. The theatre was thronged by an audience delighted with the power of an actor who could win unqualified praise, when handicapped with such a poor piece as *"Solon Shingle."* Universally the *play* was condemned; but the voice of the public was forcibly given in one of the leading papers, in speaking of Solon Shingle as being the ruling sensation: "The man who found a diamond amongst a heap of rubbish is not reported to have talked much about the rubbish. The play-goers will find Owens' *Solon Shingle* the diamond in the dust-heap; the piece is not worthy a second thought. The diamond has a bad setting; but anything more brilliant than the gem itself we have never seen."

Owens not only made a success in London, but a triumphant one. The fact that the English public did not accept the piece with favor, in no way deteriorated from the artist's celebrity, but on the contrary added thereto. Before the six weeks of his original contract with Benjamin Webster had expired, an offer was made to extend the engagement until September. This Mr. Owens consented to do; continuing to draw large and appreciative audiences, and being complimented by enthusiastic calls nightly, encores of scenes, &c.

The London engagement having been concluded, Owens played a fortnight at "The Prince of Wales Theatre," Liverpool. From the opening to the closing night was a series of well-earned triumphs, responded to by a hearty jovial audience who gave vent to their approval with a cordiality that warms an actor's heart, and stimulates him to his best work. While in London, and afterwards, Owens received flattering offers from several leading theatres in the provinces. These he declined, as he had already prolonged his absence from home far beyond the time allotted.

Some weeks previous George Wood wrote reminding Owens of the offer for the following season at the "Broadway," New York, which had been made before his departure for England. Mr. Wood urged that favorable consideration and an early reply be given to this offer; and suggested opening in November with "*Victims*" and "*Solon Shingle.*" Mr. Owens accepted the offer conditionally, but declined to commence at so early a date; naming January 8th as the time which would suit him. For this delay he had more than one reason. He desired to have a few days' relaxation at home; and he was averse to reappearing in New York with insufficient rehearsals. Moreover he intended, before playing *Solon* again, to reconstruct the piece.

The English opinion of its flimsiness turned his thoughts to the advisability of introducing the same old *Solon* to the public with improved surroundings. Though not blindly swayed by criticism, Mr. Owens always gave it consideration; and was quite willing to acknowledge any imperfection pointed to, if it was apparent to him, and improvement suggested could be made.  His reflections on the play of Solon Shingle resulted in the creation of a three-act drama, entitled *"Uncle Solon Shingle."*  This was formulated by Mr. Owens, Clifton Tayleure, and others; and finally revised by Mr. Owens.

In November, 1865, Mr. Owens returned from England, having been absent six months instead of less than half that time, as originally intended.  He proposed indulging in a home-rest on his farm until his presence was required in New York.  But hosts of friends and admirers in Baltimore were so importunate for him to play in that city, that he consented to do so for a few nights.  Opening in *Caleb Plummer* and *Happiest Day of My Life*, November 26th, he received a glowing welcome.  This appreciation continued for the entire two weeks, during which time he appeared in various characters.

January 8th, 1866, Owens made his re-entree at the Broadway Theatre, New York, producing *"Uncle Solon Shingle."*  He was greeted with a hearty reception, the house being jammed, notwithstanding bitterly cold weather—the coldest night ever known in that locality; thermometer twenty degrees below zero.  This chilliness did not seem to pervade the sentiments of the audience.  The enthusiasm of the former season had in no wise abated, but appeared to increase as they renewed their acquaintance with *"Solon Shingle."*

The new comedy, though it was poorly cast, met with approval; nothing being lost of *Solon's* eccentricities and amusing peculiarities. Increased interest was added to the old man's movements from the fact that he had strong motives for every action in *this play*, which had a plot to sustain it. A month's run of "*Uncle Solon Shingle*" was given to crowded houses; and so it would have continued, but urgent requests being made for "*Caleb Plummer*," Owens, ever inclined to play that part, changed the bill. After a pleasing episode of "*Caleb Plummer*," the public clamoring again for "*Solon Shingle*," he concluded to play the one-act piece, that he might give the younger characters with it as a contrast; this being impossible with the three-act "*Uncle Solon Shingle*," as its length precluded a double bill. Unabated prosperity continued until the closing night at the Broadway, April 28th, 1866.

The comedian's next engagement was at the Boston Theatre, beginning May 12th. "*Uncle Solon Shingle*" held the boards the entire twelve performances, and gave promise of cramming the house indefinitely had he been able to prolong his stay in Boston, but he was under contract for Providence, and other New England towns. These dates satisfactorily filled completed the professional labors of 1865–66. This sojourn in Boston recalls an incident which occurred at that time.

Mr. Owens was ultra-progressive—always kept abreast of the times, and availed himself of every facility to expedite business. His telegraphic correspondence was in excess of that by mail. All labor-saving inventions received investigation from him; and those possessing merit were added to his already numerous agricultural implements. Reapers, binders, &c., of the most approved patents, abounded at Aigburth Vale. Jocosely he would say to me: "*You* are *non*-progressive, or your housekeeping would be better supplied with modern inventions; but I won't censure your 'grandmother's' system while the results are so satisfactory. All the same you *are* non-progressive." While in Boston we made our usual tour of inspection in Cornhill. After persuading me to purchase sundry labor-saving kitchen utensils, Mr. Owens had his attention called to a patent cow-milker, which being explained to him, found favor in his sight; and the dealer was instructed to pack it with the numerous articles to be expressed to Aigburth Vale.

Shortly after our arrival at home, Mr. Owens observed to me: "I think I will personally test that cow-milker before giving it in charge of the milking boy; my best opportunity to do so will be while the farm people are away at dinner. I might as well experiment to-day!" Laughing and joking, he sallied forth at noon, and wended his way to the cow-house; but in less than half an hour he returned, looking much discouraged, and bearing upon his coat evidence of contact with dust. I refrained from questioning, but soon he remarked: "I can't manage this machine alone. The 'sarned cows switch their tails so viciously." I suggested that we should make a combined effort to prove the utility of the milker; he assented, and the next day at noon we went to the cow-house.

Mr. Owens selected a mild-looking Alderney, placed the milking stool and pail for me, adjusted the patent milker, and then holding the cow's tail in one hand, with the other turned the crank. The cow kicked (literally and figuratively) against the machine. I was precipitated to one end of the cow-house, and Mr. Owens to the other. Regaining our feet, we gazed a second at each other, and then broke forth into peals of hearty laughter.

Clearing away all traces of our discomfiture, we returned somewhat crestfallen to the house. With a merry twinkle of the eye, Mr. Owens said: "I suppose *you* think this wonderful invention is a failure! Nothing of the kind. The blame rests entirely with the cows. They are *non*-progressive—like—like—yourself!" Whereupon we had another hearty laugh.

The cow-milker was never again tested. Some time afterwards I came across it in a trunk, the contents of which Mr. Owens had desired me to catalogue; but this article *he* had already classified by placing upon it a tag labelled: "Owens' folly."

The summer vacation of 1866 was passed at Aigburth Vale, except a month at the Virginia Springs. September 24th Owens began his season in Philadelphia, at the New Chestnut Theatre, W. E. Sinn, manager; *Caleb Plummer* being the initial character. As usual, much praise was lavished on this exquisite and beautiful piece of acting; so perfect that no trace of *acting* was visible, for nature and art were so charmingly mingled that the illusion was complete in consistency and naturalness.

No one ever thought of Owens; he was merged into *Caleb Plummer*—his personality entirely lost. One of his greatest charms was, that he was never obtrusive; he had mastered the great art of repose, and in everything he did, the thorough rendering of the play was his object. At no time did he subordinate the supporting cast to himself, that he might be elevated higher; on the contrary he was always desirous for even the smallest part to be well played, and receive deserved praise. To this end, he was careful at rehearsal to be as helpful as possible in promoting opportunities for developing good points for each and every one in the cast.

When any of the company (especially the younger people) played a part meritoriously, Mr. Owens took pleasure in seeking them after performance, and to his commendation adding thanks for the support they had given him. I have heard many persons (who now have assured prominence in the profession) refer to the encouragement and kindly words thus given them by Mr. Owens, in their early career. They valued his praise, for he was equally quick to detect incompetence or carelessness, and did not hesitate to speak *forcibly* of these shortcomings.

"*Solon Shingle*" and the "*Live Indian*" were given the second week at the Chestnut Street Theatre; "*Solon Shingle*" and "*John Dobbs*," the third week. "*Victims*" and the "*Live Indian*" constituted attractions for the fourth week, which concluded a satisfactory engagement.

On the 12th of November Owens appeared at the National Theatre, Cincinnati, in "*Self*" and "*Happiest Day of My Life*," to what was pronounced by the manager "the biggest crowd ever in that *very big* theatre." The bill was unchanged for two weeks, then succeeded by other pieces for a fortnight. One week in Buffalo, another in Troy, filled the time to December 17th, for which date he was booked to begin an engagement of four weeks at the Broadway Theatre, New York. The opening attraction was *Solon Shingle*, of whom the public never seemed to weary. *Solon* was supplemented by *The Live Indian, Forty Winks*, and other short plays. The houses kept up to Owens' original standard at the Broadway Theatre, and that announcement, so pleasing to a manager's eye, "standing room only," was nightly indispensable.

From New York Owens went to Newark, playing with D. W. Waller, who was managing the Opera House with a first class company. Four nights were pleasantly filled there. January 28th inaugurated a satisfactory week in Louisville, Ky. As it drew to a close the manager made a request, at the instigation of the citizens of New Albany, that Owens would play one night in that town. At the same time promising to arrange all details of company, scenery, &c. Owens consented, and directed *"Solon Shingle"* and *"Live Indian"* to be announced for performance.

The night arrived, and brought all one could wish in the way of numbers and enthusiasm. Many cultured people were present, but the crowd included considerable rough element. The town had been lavishly billed by the manager. Some of the posters of *"The Live Indian"* being very showy, attracted much attention, which led up to somewhat of a mistaken impression. This inadvertently came to the ears of the star. As he and his agent were taking supper in a restaurant, two men who occupied a table near by began to discuss the play. One of them seemed jubilant, and declared "the show was chock full of fun." The other disagreed, and remarked: "Well, to tell the truth, *I* was terribly disapinted." "You laughed tarnation much," rejoined his friend. "Yes, I s'pose I did, and enjoyed the feats, but still I warn't satisfied with the show. From them thar Indian picters I 'lowed the feller was going to throw knives or do juggling tricks. I tell you I was misled—it warn't a square show."

It was in this same town that a gawky individual came to the box-office, and stated that "he wanted to see Mr. Owens' diploma." The bewildered treasurer was about to ask for an explanation, when the man added: "I want to get some seats." With this flood of light upon his meaning, the diagram of seats was courteously submitted for inspection.

The next date to be filled was February 18th, in New Orleans. Six years had elapsed since Owens played there. The Civil War which devastated the South, had made marked changes during the interval; but some of the old families yet remained. Their cordial welcome was extended to our comedian as a favorite actor and a cherished friend. In the new element of the community were numbers with whom he had established popularity in other sections of the country.

This visit to New Orleans was at the solicitation of Ben DeBar, manager of the St. Charles Theatre, and it was the only departure Owens ever made from being located at the "Varieties Theatre," when playing in the Crescent City. DeBar knew that the re-entree of New Orleans' favorite comedian would create a sensation, and asked on the basis of old acquaintance, that the éclat should be given to his theatre in preference to the new management at the " Varieties." Owens consented, and opened his engagement at the St. Charles in *"Solon Shingle"* and *"The Live Indian."*

The New Orleans public had, years before, given full meed of praise to *Solon Shingle,* as played by John E. Owens; and the press *now* plumed itself on having discerned and dilated on this merit in advance of the furore which its performance had created in New York. The two weeks at the St. Charles Theatre bore no novel record. I should but tautologize were I to speak of the crowded houses, and manifestations of approval and delight. After a short rest at home, an engagement was filled at the Holliday Street Theatre, Baltimore, with John T. Ford as manager; beginning with *Victims* and *Solon Shingle*—followed by *The Rivals, Heir at Law, Sweethearts and Wives, Ticket-of-Leave-Man,* and other comedies of his repertoire. The attendance and success was nightly in accord with Owens' great popularity. It was during this engagement that an old acquaintance (Judge S——) came up to the comedian one morning at Barnum's, while he was breakfasting, and said : " John, I saw you play Solon Shingle, Monday night—funny old man. I laughed all the time—always do. But you play another old fellow, quite different, but even funnier—that miserly chap who hunts for a bed, and tries to steal a nap from the tavern keeper ! What is *his* name?" "'Spruggins,' in *Forty Winks,*" replied Owens. " Yes,

MR. OWENS as FRANK OATLAND

In "A Cure for the Heartache."

yes; that's it. Say, John, why don't you play *him?*" "I played the piece LAST NIGHT." "Well, why don't you play him *again?*" "Just give me time." "Yes, yes! John, play him *again.*" Moving off to the door, the Judge called back: "Play him *again* John, keep on playing him. I want to see him *often.*" Whereupon the guests at the table were much amused, and Owens rather embarrassed by this conspicuousness forced upon him.

While professionally engaged in Baltimore, Mr. Owens always went out to the farm (if only for an hour or two), on such days as no rehearsal occurred. In one of these visits he had occasion to inspect some work recently done, and to direct future employment. He found that the work had, through carelessness, been badly botched. Of course he was indignant, and proceeded to set forth to the men their shortcomings, and his consequent displeasure.

Instead of excuses, or looks of contrition which usually responded to such rebukes, the men seemed to find difficulty in suppressing laughter. Some of them turned their backs and walked off a few paces, and all appeared demoralized. This conduct enraged Mr. Owens, and he was about to discharge the entire party; when one of them stepped forward, and exerting much self-control, said apologetically: "Indeed, Mr. Owens, we are sorry the work is wrong, and we beg your pardon for laughing;

10

but we couldn't help it. We saw you act *Solon Shingle* last night, and was a-talking it over when you comed up, and—and (here another smothered laugh)—and—please excuse us, sir; we hadn't got over the funniness, and couldn't listen just right when you began talking serious."

Owens called up his gravest demeanor, and bade them " in working hours to keep their minds on work;" turned away, and walked to the house, pursued by subdued giggling. He used to, laughingly, say that the moral of this incident was: " Never allow your servants to see you play a comic part if you wish to maintain dignified authority."

From Baltimore Owens went to Washington, playing a varied round of characters at the National Theatre, under the management of Spalding and Rapley; then short engagements in Albany, Utica, and other New York towns; after which he filled three weeks in Boston. The record of the time I have thus condensed was satisfactorily monotonous, being an experience of professional success, and pleasant social intercourse with friends; agreeably rendering a fitting termination to the season of 1866–67.

A portion of the ensuing vacation was passed at Brattleboro, Vermont, and the remainder in the repose of home comfort at Aigburth Vale; where, as usual, friends from time to time enjoyed the hospitality of "*Farmer Owens*," and added to the pleasure of his home by their presence under his roof. Guests he dearly loved to have, when they would be informally of the family circle; but *company* requiring frigid conventionality did not at all accord with his idea of companionship.

He liked to have his friends sally forth with him, and inspect stock, fields of growing grain, vineyard and orchards; and would wax eloquently in praise of country life. I have known guests to catch the enthusiasm, and express desire to buy a farm. Then Mr. Owens would look solemn, and warn them against such a step; invoking the amazed query: "Why not? *You* find everything delightful here, and such stock, such crops must bring you in a good return for the investment!" "Delightful? yes; but revenue? no. Honestly I tell you that if it were not for John Owens the actor, John Owens the farmer would starve. I don't want it on my conscience that I have led another man to assume the responsibility (though enjoyable in some respects) of supporting a farm."

No one thoroughly knew the true inwardness of Mr. Owens' broad nature until they associated with him in his own house. *There* the sunshine of his presence was experienced to its full extent, making each visitor feel "this is *my home* while I am here." Mr. Owens was essentially jovial, and had ever a pleasant greeting for acquaintances even casually met. I have heard many say that ofttimes when depressed, passing moodily along the street, the sight of Owens' bright face and merry smile would dispel the clouds, and make them cheerful again.

During August of this home-rest, much excitement pervaded the adjacent village of Towsontown, anent the arrival of old John Robinson's Circus. Mr. Owens insisted on our household attending the afternoon performance; and as we had at that time a young relative, of seven years old, staying with us, we all consented to go, "just to please the child." (Strange! how often *children* are the *alleged* cause of grown-up people visiting a circus.) Mr. Owens took charge of the party; we clambered over the rough benches, and were comfortably seated before the orchestra heralded the "grand entree" into the ring. In less than ten minutes some of the circus people had recognized Mr. Owens, and communicated the fact of his presence in the audience; thereafter, from the clown to the ring-master, the dialogue was spoken *at* him. Gradually this dawned upon the congregated multitude, and afforded them much enjoyment.

Our friends and neighbors seemed intensely amused at sundry personal and local hits, and even more so at the increasing embarrassment of Mr. Owens. His confusion culminated when, between two acts of horsemanship, the door-keeper came in breathlessly, and casting a searching glance around the tent, discovered Mr. Owens. He made straightway for him, and in a wheezing (but alas! *audible*) voice said: "Mr. Owens, here's your money back. You hadn't oughter pay to come in here; Mr. Robinson would feel 'urt if we took pay from a big light in *our perfesh*! So here's your money, Mr. Owens." Mr. Owens declined to be reimbursed, but was met with persistent remonstrance in pleading tones: "Now, I just ask you to please consider Mr. Robinson's feelings, *cully!*"

By this time the discussion had attracted concentrated attention; and to avoid further conspicuousness, Mr. Owens was obliged to receive the money. The amount being speedily invested in peanuts, pink lemonade, &c., for the child, gorged that youngster to his temporary delight and subsequent illness. When the first half of the programme was over Mr. Owens escaped from the tent, and returned no more until he came to escort the party home. At night he sent all the house servants and every farm laborer on the place to the circus. When I jestingly asked, "Are *you* going to-night?" he replied: "*Never* again to a circus in my own neighborhood. No, not for a herd of Alderneys as a reward."

Mr. Owens dearly loved a good story, and if the point of it was against himself he seemed to derive the greater pleasure from telling it. Adjoining the boundaries of Aigburth Vale, a German owned an acre or two of land, upon which stood the little home he had built. The man had but slight command of English, and Owens having some knowledge of German endeavored to communicate with him through that language; and managed to be understood so long as the subject of discourse was lending a horse, plough, or aught else to the German. The same intelligibility was not apparent about a matter upon which it was necessary to speak *often*, viz., the breaking down of fences by the German's cow, hogs, or boys.

Many mild exhortations proving ineffectual, Owens discovering one day a fine field of grain trampled down through repetition of the offence, lost all command of patience and temper. Giving full vent to his indignation, he roundly berated the man with forcible expletives in *strongest* English. The countenance of the Teutonic cottager remained placid until Mr. Owens paused for lack of breath; when he stolidly remarked: "Mr. Owens, dot ish not de *Sharman* language." The effect was like a douche bath. Mr. Owens calmed down, regretting that "so much good rage had been wasted."

The season of 1867–68 commenced in quite a different locality from any previous one. September 19th, the comedian appeared at the Opera House, Leavenworth, Kansas, under the management of Miss Susan Denin. Many persons will remember Susan Denin as a beautiful woman and clever actress. The fame of the lovely "Denin sisters" extended throughout the country. Susan, a perfect type of brunette beauty, and Kate, equally enchanting in blonde loveliness. Both of them were charming in manner, and made hosts of friends, who admired them for their manifold attractions and their devotion to each other. To this popularity Susan Denin added the qualification of a competent business woman, which was evinced by her theatrical management at Leavenworth; and there, aided by G. D. Chaplin, the lessee, she achieved for the Opera House position and success.

Leavenworth at that time was a very different place from the enterprising city it now is. No unusual occurrence then to meet in one's daily walks Indians attired in their native costume, and gay with painted faces; still many cultured people resided in the town and suburbs. At Fort Leavenworth, the military post, quite a number of distinguished officers were stationed, who together with their families were a valuable acquisition to the refined society of the town. Thus the audience which greeted the comedian, was not entirely of the typical " far west " aspect. Many of the leading citizens called upon him to renew acquaintance pleasantly made elsewhere, and introduced friends of theirs.

Among the strangers presented was one whose gentleness of manner and physical beauty rendered him conspicuous. He was clad in huntsman attire, which well became his graceful and athletic figure. The golden hair worn in ringlets had no appearance of effeminacy, for the manly bearing and honest blue eyes invested him with quiet dignity.  Mr. Owens did not clearly hear the name at the time of introduction, but being strongly impressed with the stranger, he questioned Mr. Chaplin next day.  Great was his surprise at the reply : "J. B. Hickock, known as 'Wild Bill,' the most famous scout of the West."  Having knowledge of this hero of the plains, he seemed incompatible with the quiet-mannered gentleman who had conversed so courteously for the pleasant quarter of an hour.

The terror of the country round to those who had incurred his animosity, "Wild Bill" was chivalrous in his nature, and as honorable and generous-hearted as man could be; and without qualification he hated *all* Indians.  For that matter so did many people in and around Leavenworth—apropos of which an incident. Owens innocently proposed to play *"The Live Indian;"* the suggestion was received with much laughter. "Good gracious," said Mr. Chaplin, "the sight of you in an *Indian* dress would end your popularity *here,* perhaps your life.  In fact I don't think we would get further than putting out the printing; for the pictures of the Indian (as an attraction) would most likely create a riot, and result in an attack on the theatre.  No, my dear boy, this atmosphere is not favorable for the delineation of Indians; for that "go east; go east, young man."

Leaving Leavenworth, Owens was next due at the Crosby Opera House, Chicago. Before starting for that city considerable chaffing went on at the theatre relative to the coming engagement, based on Mr. Owens' assertion that he expected to open to immense business or a disgustingly small house. "It is sure to be one or the other," said he. "Chicago is a city I can never reckon upon; I am always at extremes there." The chronic joking continued until his departure, when he promised to telegraph them the amount of the gross receipts of the first night. On the 30th of September he appeared at the Crosby Opera House in *Solon Shingle* and *The Live Indian*, and the next day telegraphed the result to his friends in Leavenworth: "*House*, $1,548.90;" quickly receiving from the manageress the facetious response: "We don't believe there is so much money in the world." The opening bill continued unchanged for a week, and was followed by *Caleb Plummer, Heir-at-Law, Everybody's Friend, Victims,* &c.; securing appreciation commensurate with Owens' genius and talent.

The next date, October 21st, was at the Louisville Opera House, under the management of George F. Fuller; from thence to Cincinnati to fill an engagement of four weeks with Samuel Colville. *Solon Shingle, Victims, She Stoops to Conquer, Rivals,* &c., being represented in a manner which multiplied the laurels of this famous comedian. The last week of the engagement was rendered memorable by the production of "*Grimaldi; or, The Life of an Actress;*" Owens having some time previous bought the sole right of that play from Dion Boucicault.

The character of *Grimaldi*, the old French actor, is difficult to portray with discrimination and delicacy of touch, owing to its admixture of qualities. The triumphant hit which Owens made was another proof of his great versatility. His accent was faultless, and his bearing entirely natural. Voice and gesture, though not inspiration, are an actor's symbols; and he used these gifts to intensify a graphic picture.

The divers phases in the life of the poor artist, step by step until he is seen as the rich nobleman, were sympathetically rendered, and a distinctive personation given of the tender-hearted old man who was merry, pathetic, ambitious, affectionate and proud, which held the audience spellbound, and by its realism invoked the tribute of alternate smiles and tears.

December 9th Owens returned to the Holliday Street Theatre, Baltimore, for twelve nights, appearing in his usual round of characters; from thence to Washington for a few nights. December 14th, 1866, he played for the "Benefit of the Association for the Education of Southern Children." The free use of the Holliday Street Theatre, Baltimore, being tendered by Mr. John T. Ford (the company and attachés having volunteered their services), the *entire* gross receipts were given to the cause. "*All that Glitters is not Gold*" and "*The Happiest Day of My Life*," with Owens in both pieces, constituted the bill. The immense audience was one of the most fashionable which ever filled the theatre, and the performance went off with éclat.

Mr. Owens afterwards received a courteous letter from Mrs. Wm. H. Brune, President of the Association, conveying her thanks, and those of the ladies of the Board, for the aid extended to the cause. Mrs. Brune's manner of appreciating this offering, and the good wishes which she expressed, were so charmingly conveyed, that her letter was not only highly prized by Mr. Owens at the time, but found place among the mementoes he ever retained of sunshiny events in his professional life.

January 20th inaugurated an engagement of two weeks in Philadelphia. Commencing with *Caleb Plummer*, he found that the dear old toy-maker had lost none of his attraction, nor yet his power to draw smiles and tears from those who had often before laughed and wept with him. From Philadelphia brief visits were made to Trenton, Newark and Brooklyn; thence to Boston for three weeks, where he repeated the old comedies "*Self*" and "*Caleb Plummer*," the greater part of the time being filled with the latter attraction, which was always a great favorite in Boston.

After a tour of the New England towns Owens returned to Baltimore, appearing at the Holliday Street Theatre in an entirely new character: *"Farmer Allen,"* in Charles Reade's dramatization of Tennyson's poem of *"Dora."* His conception and portrayal of *Farmer Allen* was equal in finish and dramatic power to anything he ever did. The imperative nature which veils (and even *hardens*) a loving heart, which endures self-torture while asserting "my will is law," was graphically drawn. The father's affection for his son, subordinated to maintain parental authority at all risks, was so forcibly personified as to render *"Farmer Allen"* one of Owens' masterpieces. The variety of emotions depicted—rage, grief, remorse and affection—require extraordinary power to convey them fully, and yet free from exaggeration; and this Owens was equal to, blending and harmonizing these emotions perfectly.

*"Dora"* was superbly staged; the exquisite painting, scenic effects and stage setting being the work of Mr. Charles S. Getz. Three scenes were given: Winter, Spring and Summer. All were gems of art, but the last act was super-excellent—a wheat-field radiant in the glow of the setting sun, with the gleaners picturesquely grouped. The incidental music to *"Dora"* was effectively rendered, especially the Christmas Carols which, with fine voices and choruses, were a feature of the play. A western tour, including St. Louis, Cincin-

nati, Indianapolis and Cleveland, closed the season of
1867–68.

The summer vacation was passed at Aigburth Vale in
luxurious restfulness—with two breaks therein of a professional nature. On these two occasions Mr. Owens
played in Baltimore. Appearing in June as "*Aminidab
Sleek*" and "*Paul Pry*," for the annual benefit of James
L. Gallagher, an intimate friend of "Auld Lang Syne;"
and on July 29th for a benefit for the sufferers from a
flood, which had occurred in East Baltimore, causing
much affliction and destitution.

October 12th, 1868, he began his season at Pittsburg
as "*Major DeBoots*" and "*Solon Shingle.*" Eight years
had elapsed since he played in that city. Listening to
the prolonged plaudits of the audience, no one could
realize that aught like animosity had ever existed in that
city against the comedian whom they thus delighted to
honor. Mistaken and blinded prejudices, engendered by
the excitement of the war, had long since passed away,
and the Pittsburg people now placed Owens in the position he originally held as their favorite comedian. From
Pittsburg he went to Cincinnati ; and while there produced "*The Lancashire Lass*," appearing in a new rôle—
"*A Party by the name of Johnson.*"

This character was of a different type from those he
usually essayed, and strongly evinced his illimitable
histrionic power. The cool villainy and imperturbable

sangfroid of "*The Party by the name of Johnson*," and
the vindictiveness and depth of feeling underlying these
qualities being thrillingly depicted. The scene where he
exposes the hypocritical character of *Danville* was masterly; the intense and electrifying tones of his voice, the
eloquence of his expressive eyes, conduced to culminate
an effect which produced not only a storm of applause,
but most frequently a persistent encore.

I remember at the time he was playing this part, com-
ments upon the perfection with which he rendered the
denunciatory scenes, so rife with hatred and desire for
revenge, called forth a revival of an old report that Mr.
Owens was originally ambitious of becoming a tragedian.
The story runs that even his early success in comedy
failed to eradicate this aspiration; his final cure could
not be effected until he attempted and failed to play
*Richard the Third.*

This *mis*-statement has the shadow of foundation. At
the close of a season in Baltimore Mr. Owens announced,
among other attractions for his benefit, "the *5th Act of
Richard the Third*," knowing it would be a sensational
advertisement. As he expected, the house was packed.
He *affected* to play the part seriously until full attention
was gained; and then gradually burlesqued, increasing
in fun until the combat scene at the close, for which he
had provided (and rehearsed with) a basket horse—in
other words it was a hoax, for he never intended to enact

the character tragically. The whole thing was arranged as a novelty for his benefit—understood by some of the audience, and laughed at by all.

Later on it was repeated elsewhere with the same rollicking fun. With his power of pathos, and strong well-modulated voice, Owens could have shown in tragedy, had he so elected; but he preferred that jollity should predominate, and thus developed into a peerless comedian.

After "*The Lancashire Lass*" was played in Cincinnati, "*Dora*" was put on the boards with exquisite stage setting. "*Farmer Allen*" won his deserved position, and was thoroughly appreciated. A pleasant week in Louisville followed; from thence to St. Louis, opening November 30th at the Olympic Theatre, with Spalding and Albaugh. Legitimate comedy was given, in which the star was strongly supported by Mr. and Mrs. John W. Albaugh. Then came "*The Lancashire Lass*," well cast. Mrs. Albaugh (Miss Mary Mitchell), as *Kate Garstone*, invested the character with strength and depth which could not be excelled. Mr. Albaugh was the author's ideal of *Robert Redburn*.

Of Mrs. Albaugh's support during this engagement nothing was more acceptable than her "*Mary Apex*," in "*Self*." That part Mr. Owens often found difficult to fitly cast. It required a good actress, but one who had judgment and taste to avoid the appearance of acting.

"*Mary Apex's*" genuine simplicity rendered any *seeming* effort utter destruction to the correct impersonation of her sweet guilelessness. Mrs. Albaugh brought out all the salient points, and yet with delicacy and ease which gave to *Mary Apex* just the gentle nature and firm principle that so endeared her to her crusty old god-father—and to the audience. Mrs. Albaugh ranked in this part as one of the very few whom Mr. Owens pronounced entirely satisfactory to him.

Two weeks in Chicago was the next booking; after which followed a short engagement at the Broadway Theatre, New York, on the eve of his departure for California. Opening January 22d in "*Victims*" and "*Solon Shingle*," which had been a favorite bill with the New York public two years previous, Owens had the gratification of realizing that its attraction had not decreased. A succession of crowded and fashionable houses continued through the engagement.

# CHAPTER VII.



FEBRUARY 12th, 1869, Owens started for California by the Aspinwall and Panama route. He was always fond of a sea voyage, and this one proved to be especially delightful. From the time of arrival at Aspinwall (or Colon, as the inhabitants call it), to the hour of entering the harbor of San Francisco by the Golden Gate, was an enjoyable experience. Intermediately, the tropical gorgeousness of the Isthmus of Panama, the quaint town itself, the charming exploration of Acapulco and other Mexican towns, all combined to render the voyage a holiday excursion, rather than business travel.

11

Subsequent journeys to California (after completion of the railroad) were made by that speedier transit; but, though fraught with many advantages, could not compare in comfort and enjoyment with the steamer route. The latter was often referred to, and dilated upon, by Mr. Owens as a red-letter reminiscence. After twenty-three days of the pleasurable travel, we arrived on a gloriously bright morning at San Francisco—having been met in the harbor by Lawrence Barrett and other friends.

The engagement which he came to fulfil was with Barrett and McCullough, at the New California Theatre, the first star appearing at that theatre under their management. The initial bill, March 15th ("*Everybody's Friend*" and "*Solon Shingle*"), included the following strong cast:

### EVERYBODY'S FRIEND.

MAJOR DEBOOTS......................................MR. JOHN E. OWENS.
MR. ICEBROOK....................................MR. JOHN McCULLOUGH.
FELIX FEATHERLEY...............................MR. W. F. BURROUGHS.
MRS. FEATHERLEY..............................MISS EMILY MELVILLE.
MRS. SWANDOWN.................................MISS FANNY MARSH.
MRS. DEBOOTS....................................MRS. C. R. SAUNDERS.

### SOLON SHINGLE.

SOLON SHINGLE.................................MR. JOHN E. OWENS.
ROBERT HOWARD..................................MR. W. MESTAYER.
CHARLES OTIS.................................MR. W. F. BURROUGHS.
JOHN ELLSLEY................................MR. JOHN WILSON.

HUGH WINSLOW..........................................................MR. E. B. HOLMES.
TRIPPER..................................................................MR E. J. BUCKLEY.
TIMID......................................................................MR. G. MATTHEWS.
CLERK OF THE COURT.......................................MR. EDWARD MARBLE.
JUDGE....................................................................MR. S. W. LEACH.
THOMPSON..............................................................MR. F. ROBINSON.
JOHN.....................................................................MR. J. TORRANCE.
MRS. OTIS..............................................................MISS WETHERILL.
GRACE OTIS............................................................MISS K. LYNCH.


(Many other strong casts followed this, notably that
of "*The Poor Gentleman*," combining brilliancy of talent
seldom equalled.)

## CALIFORNIA THEATRE.

### APRIL 15TH, 1869.

### THE POOR GENTLEMAN.

DOCTOR OLLAPOD........................................MR. JOHN E. OWENS.
LIEUTENANT WORTHINGTON...................MR. JOHN MCCULLOUGH.
SIR ROBERT BRAMBLE.........................MR. W. H. SEDLEY SMITH.
FREDERICK BRAMBLE..........................MR. LAWRENCE BARRETT.
CORPORAL FOSS.....................................MR. HARRY EDWARDS.
HUMPHREY DOBBINS..............................MR. JOHN T. RAYMOND.
SIR CHARLES CROPLAND.......................MR. W. F. BURROUGHS.
EMILY WORTHINGTON...........................MISS EMILIE MELVILLE.
LUCRETIA MACTAB.................................MRS. JUDAH.
MARY HARROWBY.................................MISS MINNIE WALTON.


Owens was received by a crowded house, and cordially
welcomed.  Through his six weeks at the California Theatre, he continued to win golden opinions, and maintain

his exalted position as an artist. He played numerous parts with his usual effectiveness; but of the many encomiums bestowed upon him, those elicited by his *"Caleb Plummer"* and *"Grimaldi"* took precedence in unani- . mously pronouncing him peerless in these characters.

Mr. Owens lingered in San Francisco awhile, after his professional duties ceased, for he found his surroundings very pleasant. In addition to the approbation of the public for his histrionic merit, he had also gained many congenial friends. Prominent among these was Lawrence Barrett, with whom a friendship, founded on esteem, was formed, which grew and strengthened into affection as time went on; being mutually cherished and prized. To the last of his life Mr. Owens spoke of Barrett with admiration, and in the faith of warm regard.

An offer from Virginia City, Nevada, for twelve nights was accepted. The citizens were well pleased with every performance, and the comedian found entertainment in this town and other mining districts quite equal to that which he afforded the public by his dramatic talents. The Pacific Slope, and its peculiarities, revealed a new experience to him. The country *then* was exceedingly primitive, and daily observation of various types of humanity, with whom he met, formed an interesting and ofttimes amusing study; and the grandeur of the country—exploring its resources, and gaining information thereof, was a matter of delightful investigation to him.

MR OWENS as DR. OLLAPOD

In " The Poor Gentleman."

(From a Painting by D'Almaine.)

The theatres in the mining districts were decidedly incligible to the correct production of a play. The resident managers deemed but one thing necessary for their prosperity—securing a *star*; the supporting company, and other accessories, they considered of little importance. Unacquainted with these local opinions, Owens was astonished at a first rehearsal to find the company so limited as to render the casting of his pieces impossible.

Appealing to the manager, he said: "I sent you my manuscripts and books, and was assured of full support. You know the number of people required; why are they not here?" "No use getting mad about it," replied the imperturbable manager. "I didn't read no books or things you sent. I knowed we could pick up people when we wanted 'em. They'll be on time, you bet!" Determined to reconcile himself to this novel situation, Owens viewed it in its amusing originality, and refrained from further irritation. The "pick-up" people came, and though eccentric in some respects, had the merit of good memories and strong voices; so the first night's performance was given to the satisfaction of a jolly crowd.

The manager had heard some one from San Francisco speak of *"The Poor Gentleman"* having made a hit there, and was urgent to have that comedy announced for the third night. "It is impossible," was the response. "We can't cast it; our company is too short and weak for such a play. And especially, we lack a man strong enough for Sir Robert Bramble." "If that's all that stands in the way," retorted the manager, "I can get the right sort of people."

While Mr. Owens was smoking his after-dinner cigar at the hotel, the manager came up to him, accompanied by a six-foot Hercules miner, whom he introduced thus: "Here's your 'Robert Bramblers,' and" surveying his friend with pride, "I'd like to know where you'd find a *stronger* man than big Jake H——! I told you I'd fetch the right party." Owens, suppressing a smile at this *literal* acceptation of his objections, received big Jake affably; and entering into conversation with him, learned that the stalwart miner had at times been transiently connected with strolling companies, and was still theatrically inclined.

An appointment was made to meet at the theatre next day, from which arrangement resulted the engagement of the miner for the part of Sir Robert Bramble. He frankly admitted that he had not the "proper fixings" to dress in; but he would do the best he could. Nothing more dreadful in the way of costume can be imagined than what "the best" proved to be. Coarse pantaloons stuffed into long rough boots, questionable coat and slouched hat were the equipments in which the "Baronet of the old school" appeared before the audience; and worse yet, his pronunciation was equally startling. The line, "Had I the patience of a Job," was given with stentorian force; but alas! for misconception, it was rendered " had I the patience of a *job*," thus utterly obliterating all analogy with the scriptural character noted for endurance.

Fortunately the audience were good-natured enough to be indulgent to this and other inaccuracies, and the comedy went off mirthfully. Some of those present were unaware of errors; and the cultured portion of the audience put up with the inevitable weakness of the cast, as they came to the theatre to see the star, and expected no enjoyment in addition thereto.

Concluding his provincial engagements, Owens remained some weeks longer in California, that he might indulge in a pleasure tour; beginning with a flying visit to Sacramento and other towns, thence to the Geysers in Sonoma County. The stage-coach ride, to the latter place, was ever one of the brightest memories of that charming holiday jaunt. The novelty of the mode of conveyance, the characteristic stage driver " Foss," who had attained celebrity in his way, was a revelation; and these specialties, together with sundry incidentals of the trip, concentrated more than the usual excitement and pleasure in what, to most people, would have been an ordinary ride.

The drive from Calistoga Springs was the customary, exhilarating summer-morning bowling over a beautiful country—the effect being blithesome, and giving to one the "glad I am alive" feeling. The distinctive episode of the journey began when the Calistoga stage came to its terminus at the house of "Foss," and the passengers were transferred to the care of that famous whip. Mr. Owens always liked to recall his first meeting with Foss, and their subsequent fellowship.

Standing on the porch, awaiting the summons to lunch (the delicious fragrance of its preparation whetting one's appetite with promise of good cheer), Mr. Owens was contemplating the grand scenery around him; when a tall broad-shouldered man passed him, and stopped before a state-room trunk, a few steps distant, which he eyed with unfavorable glance. Giving it a slight kick, he asked in a gruff voice, "What's this?" "Looks like a small trunk," said Owens, calmly. "Whose is it?" "Mine." "What's it here for?" "Going to the Geysers." "Oh *no!* guess not; don't take trunks to the Geysers. If you want to put on style, better stay at Calistoga Springs—Geysers too rough for frills." "Just suits me," said Owens, laughingly, "and I am going *there;* so is that trunk."

Foss looked searchingly at him, but seeing that no offense was meant, weakened in his determination, and rejoined: "If I take that trunk, I shall have to put on six mustangs, and I intended to drive only four, to-day!" "I have no objection to six; I am sure *you* are equal to managing a dozen," was the response. Just then lunch was announced, and the discussion dropped; entire attention being given to the delicious chicken, rich cream, and other dainties, for which Foss' meals were as justly famed as for the appetizing manner in which they were served at his beautiful cottage.

When the coach was in readiness and the passengers called to take their places, Owens noticed, admiringly, the team of *six* mustangs, and also the fact that the objectionable little trunk was safely stowed away, to bear him company. As he passed along, Foss inquired: "Do you care to ride on the box-seat with me?" "Very glad to do so, if I don't inconvenience you," was the ready response. "Like to have you; jump up." Needing no second bidding for this opportunity to see the country to the best advantage, and cultivate further acquaintance with the eccentric Foss, he was speedily seated; and off went the team. No reference whatever was made to "*that* trunk." Foss, at first taciturn, gradually relaxed, and finally thawed entirely under the influence of agreeable conversation. Anecdotes and incidents were narrated, and the antagonism of the first meeting was magnetically dispelled, resolving itself into pleasant companionship.

Owens delighted in the rough-and-tumble ride, the magnificent scenery, and the masterly control which this wonderful driver held over his horses. Foss quickly perceived this admiration of his skill, and was pleased with the appreciation of an accomplishment upon which he prided himself.　Much of the road to the Geysers is steep, narrow and apparently dangerous.　While cross-that portion of it known as "the Hog's back" (a mere ridge overhanging precipices on either side), some of the passengers became nervous, and made exclamations of fear.　Foss, looking over his shoulder, glanced at them, and remarked: "No, you *wont* be upset; though I des'say you felt the motion of the wagon a leetle."　Scant comfort, when one's breath was nearly jolted out of one's body.

Some one asked: "Has there *ever* been an accident on this road?"　"Not when *I* drive," said Foss, "nor with my men.　A smash-up did happen about a year ago. A Sacramento galoot was handling the reins; but that fellow wasn't a regular—only a substitute; *he* don't count.　What could you expect from a driver who wore gloves and blacked his boots?　Bah!" and Foss touched up his leader with an imperative "g'lang!" to give vent to his feelings.

As the afternoon lengthened its shadows, the stage stopped at a wayside spring to water the horses.　Foss then tethered them to rest awhile, and signalling Mr. Owens, walked away a pace or two, saying as he did so: "There is a cooler spring a few steps off, if you'd like to refresh yourself."　By a turn in the chapparel, they quickly reached the place; and from a hidden nook, behind the spring, Foss produced a bottle and glasses, tersely asking: "Do you ever drink?" "Sometimes," replied Owens. "Well, try that; the Occidental Hotel never set anything better before you." After the recommendation had been proved true, in the pledging of "good health," he remarked: "*This* is whiskey spring, number 1. On the way to the Geysers, there is number 2 and number 3, just like it. I don't invite anyone here, unless I feel that they are of the right stripe."

Owens was attracted by the mixture of trustfulness and reticence, kindly manner and curtness, in the demeanor of this singular man. The remainder of the drive was replete with interest. Alighting at the Geyser Hotel, Owens unexpectedly met with some acquaintances, who immediately set up a shout of welcome. After exchanging salutations, he went in-doors to register; and Foss took the opportunity to inquire: "Who *is* that man?" "Why, don't you know him?" replied Col. G——, of San Francisco, "that is John E. Owens, the comedian." "Well," said Foss, "I ain't often wrong in taking a man's measure, and this time I hit it mighty straight. I froze to him from the first ten minutes. I haven't been as well pleased since I drove Forrest." And this, by the way, was a superlative compliment. Forrest was the standard of perfection for Foss; the pride of his life being, that it had been said he bore a physical resemblance to the great tragedian, whose manner he was ambitious of imitating.

The sojourn at the Geysers was fraught with such enjoyment and content to Owens, that his intended stay of two days was prolonged to as many weeks. The guests were refined and agreeable people; and the daily life, and its environments, was fascinatingly wild and rough, with the charm of novelty. The primitive hotel was supplied with delicious fish and game, captured by "Fritz," the hunter, and upon his good or ill luck depended the dinner hour; the time varying anywhere from two until eight, P. M. If the supplies came in early, the guests dined accordingly; but no one thought of being dissatisfied when an improvised lunch was served, and dinner delayed indefinitely.

Of the Geysers as a wonder of nature, everybody is now aware. In 1869 it was more difficult of access, and excited greater astonishment with its two hundred mineral springs, including every variety that can be named, and every temperature also; for side by side are boiling springs and icy cold ones, only a few inches apart. Exploring the canyons was a never-failing source of interest; equestrian parties to the Indian Spring, trout-fishing, an occasional bear hunt, for the gentlemen, the daily arrival of the stage (including a chat with Foss when he was not too grumpy), constituted varied and pleasant entertainment from sunrise until sunset.

The Geyser Hotel of to-day is an imposing building, elegantly appointed; but I doubt if it resounds with as much genuine mirth as did the old wooden structure, with its canvass walls, whose unconventional guests enjoyed to the utmost, the "camping-out style" of living, which characterized the place at that time. Leaving the Geysers, Owens' route lay through Santa Rosa Valley, which gave him further opportunity of stage-coach riding. The exhilaration of these new scenes was indescribable; on every side bloomed flowers in rank luxuriousness, and orchards of oranges, pomegranates and other fruits abounded. Stopping now and again at an inn, to refresh man and beast, a lovely panorama met the eye at every turn.

The name Santa *Rosa* speaks for itself, but no words can describe the roses it denotes. In size, fragrance and profusion they are incomparable. All these delights were of the long ago, when California was less frequently visited by Eastern people. Mr. Owens always liked to talk over this episode in his life, and would recount many incidents thereof, long after stage-coaches and their noted drivers—Foss, Hank Monk, Yuba Bill and others, had passed away; and the railroad rendered the trip to California of small moment, instead of the undertaking it was considered when much time was required, and novelty attended the journey.

En route home, a stoppage of two days was made at Salt Lake City. The honors of the beautiful town

were courteously extended by Elder Claussen, who acted
as cicerone to all places of interest.  The Tabernacle,
President Young's house, Masonic Temple, Theatre
and other buildings were thoroughly shown, with many
pleasant words of information respecting them.  Endeavors were made to prevail upon Mr. Owens to play
a week or two at Salt Lake City; but he declined these
flattering offers, having already been absent from home
much longer than he originally intended.

It was the middle of July when he arrived at " Aigburth Vale," but he did not feel as if his summer vacation
only began *then*.  The pleasure tour in California had
been delightful recreation, and the rural life strongly
recuperative.

Shortly after this return home, Mr. Wm. R. Floyd
came to the farm, partly on a friendly visit, and (as
afterwards transpired) with a view to effect a plan
which he thought might not be accomplished by correspondence.  It was to obtain Mr. Owens' consent to play
a short engagement at Wallack's Theatre, New York, in
August; "*Self*" being the comedy suggested.  This scheme
was broached the day after Mr. Floyd's arrival, and at first
found no favor; but persuasion and strong inducements
finally resulted in acceptance of the offer.  Supported
by the full strength of Wallack's company, he began
his engagement August the 2d, and had every reason to
be satisfied with its artistic and financial success.

The season of 1869–70 commenced with a Western tour, including Pittsburg, Cincinnati, Indianapolis, Louisville and St. Louis, during which time good business and the full meed of appreciation greeted our comedian. Many interesting incidents of the sojourn in these cities find place in his diary; but as they are in the main a record of social intercourse, I refrain from giving the witty and pleasant jottings, lest in being made public, they might be regarded as an infringement on personality.

A disastrous finale marked the close of the Western tour, in St. Louis. The weather there was bitterly cold —almost beyond thermometer register; and Mr. Owens, while playing "*Caleb Plummer*," was so placed on the stage as to be exposed to the many draughts for which DeBar's theatre was (among other *dis*comforts) renowned. The thin dress worn for "*Caleb*" intensified the ill effects; and a heavy cold and severe cough were contracted. Finding that the exertion of playing increased these ailments, he endeavored to cancel the last week of his engagement, but the manager declined to release him; so night after night he continued to play, at the risk of permanent loss of voice and health.

His strong will power enabled him, despite physical suffering, to keep up to the degree of his usual performance; but when the engagement was over, this tension gave way, he succumbed to illness, and was obliged to remain in St. Louis several days, under medical care.

This inevitable delay fretted him exceedingly, as he was due at the Varieties Theatre, New Orleans, November 22d, and naturally desirous to be there in advance, for the purpose of thorough rehearsals. The manager, Mr. W. R. Floyd, having been informed of Mr. Owens' illness, kindly telegraphed him to refrain from uneasiness, as the plays would be put in preliminary rehearsal, and all would be right. He recuperated rapidly, though still a very sick man when he started for New Orleans; but on his arrival there, signified his intention of commencing the engagement on time, Mr. Floyd positively refused to allow an exertion which might cause not only suffering but a relapse to illness—adding: " I have arranged stock performances for next week, that you may be entirely relieved, and as a friend I insist upon your taking care of your health."

Mr. Owens gladly availed himself of such considerate forethought; and appreciating this regard for his health, he could not forbear reflecting that his illness would not have occurred had his previous manager been as humane as Mr. Floyd. A week under the care of Dr. Chopin proved effectual in making a permanent cure.

November 29th Owens appeared at the Varieties Theatre, after nine years' absence from that stage—a stage associated with his theatrical management (the most brilliant ever known in New Orleans) and with some of his greatest professional triumphs. In fact *"John Owens"* and "*the Varieties*" were so inseparable in the minds of play-goers that the mention of one suggested the other. He had reason to be proud of his reception. Despite a pelting rain-storm, the house was crowded in every part; and deafening applause, together with uproarious laughter, proved that the comedian had not lost the hold upon the habitués of the old " Varieties " which he maintained in former years.

The engagement extended over four weeks, and included many of his most renowned personations. The closing week was marked by the production of "*Dot*" —always a favorite play with New Orleans people, who inclined to think they had a special right to Owens' *Caleb Plummer*, as it was on the Varieties' stage he first played the part, and won the hearts of all by this dramatic inspiration.

Opening in Mobile, on the 27th of December, Owens gave seven performances to full and fashionable houses. From thence to Vicksburg, where he was due January 3d. Three railroad accidents en route (though not serious), caused detention, and rendered his arrival on time impossible. The longest delay occurred at Meriden, Miss., and involved the necessity of remaining over night in that uncomfortable locality. The hotel was a barn-like, cheerless place, with accomodations even worse than its appearance. Poor food badly cooked, unrestful beds, broken window-panes and uncleanliness were among the

12

discomforts. The only alleviation being that the endurance of these ills was temporary.

When Mr. Owens was paying his bill the following dialogue took place: "How much do I owe you?" Gazing at the opposite wall, the landlord mumbled, "Nine dollars." "What did you say?" "Nine dollars," reiterated the man. "Look me in the face, and tell me your charge." Staring up to the ceiling, the fellow repeated, "Nine dollars." "Come now, *look me in the face*, and say *for what* I owe you nine dollars." The man ejaculated spasmodically, "Nine dollars—dinner—supper and lodging;" but looked steadily on the floor. "Ah, my friend," said Owens, "I see it is impossible for you to meet my eye, and make a charge like that for the tortures of this hostelry. As you are not entirely lost to shame, I have some hope of your reformation. I present you with nine dollars, and enlighten you gratuitously. *The civil conflict is over; war prices are out of date.* You don't seem to know that fact. Bye-bye; I shall remember Meriden, and beware of a return to your hospitality."

The landlord was angry, but bewildered too, not understanding the mock gravity which Mr. Owens maintained while speaking. It was one of his peculiarities to always extract a "bit of fun" out of not only pleasant, but disagreeable surroundings. A keen sense of the ludicrous enabled him to find amusement where most people would discern only annoyance. These railroad detentions were so prolonged that Owens did not arrive in Vicksburg until Tuesday, 8.30 P. M. He hurried to the Opera House, where a large audience was patiently waiting for him. The curtain rose at nine o'clock. Lack of rehearsal, the inebriation of the leading man and much confusion behind the scenes rendered the performance anything but smooth; and at the fall of the curtain the star felt that the evening had been exhaustive both to his patience and physical strength.

The reaction after vexatious excitement and fatigue, made him thankful to get back to the hotel for supper and a night's rest. An uncouth and stupid boy brought supper to the room, and while he was placing it on the table, Mr. Owens remarked: "You have forgotten the ale I ordered." "Well, so I have," was the non-chalant reply. "Go bring it." "Can't get it this late; bar is closed," stolidly spoke the boy; "but," brightening up, "you can have it *first thing* in the morning." "Thank you," said Mr. Owens, ironically. "Tell you what I'll do," continued the imperturbable youth, "I'll bring it to your room myself, at six o'clock!" "No, you won't; not if you value your life. The person who knocks at my door at that early hour surely dies," responded Mr. Owens in solemn tones. The boy being impervious to a joke, looked puzzled; then, in a frightened way, turned to me, and lowering his voice, asked in all seriousness, "What's he mean? Is he crazy?" The question was never answered, except by hearty laughter; and the boy precipitately left the room. "It appears," said Mr. Owens, "my fun comes *after* the play, for an appetizer."

A thorough rehearsal on Wednesday rendered the performance creditable, and the remainder of the week was an experience of like nature, to crowded houses. Another engagement in Mobile followed, with an entire change of plays from those given the previous fortnight. Closing in Mobile, he returned to New Orleans for a visit of pleasure to enjoy the society of his friends.

Only one theatrical appearance was made by Mr. Owens during this holiday, and that was for the "Benefit of W. R. Floyd." A very strong bill was presented— "*Arrah na Pogue*," with Floyd in his famous part of "*Shaun the Post*," Owens in "*Solon Shingle*," and Jefferson in "*A Regular Fix.*" Of course the house was crowded. It was not the first time that Jefferson and Owens had played in the same bill, or in the same cast. Long ago the public had been favored with this double attraction in "*A Comedy of Errors*," "*Two Gregories*," "*Wags of Windsor*," "*Village Lawyer*," "*Money*," and other plays.

I remember the little piece, "*To Parents and Guardians*," being given with Mr. Owens as *Waddilove*, and Mr. Jefferson as *Tourbillon*, a French tutor. The parts were not especially strong or important, but they were made so by capital acting. Both artists being conscientious, believed that whatever they did was worth doing well. Mr. Jefferson's quaint punctilious picture of the old Frenchman was a fine characterization. In the more important triumphs of later years, the remembrance of this part may not linger with Mr. Jefferson; but it will never be forgotten by those who enjoyed it.

Mr. Owens was ever an appreciative admirer of Mr. Jefferson's genius, and highly prized the life-long friendship which existed between them. Late in February we left the Crescent city, returning home per steamer by way of Havana.

A few days quiet enjoyment on the farm preceded an engagement in Washington, commencing March 14th; after which he closed his season, that he might have a good long vacation at home. Many buildings and other improvements were added to his estate during this summer. Superintending this work and enjoying the society of guests at Aigburth Vale made the time pass pleasantly and swiftly.

One of Mr. Owens' stories of the happenings of this summer was in regard to a call he had from Mr. S——, a theatrical agent, and an old friend. The gentleman came out in the York Road car; sauntering up the avenue, he reached the house just as Mr. Owens was about stepping into his buggy to drive to the city. After salutations, Mr. Owens said: "I haven't time to talk business, I am late for an engagement in town *now*; jump in, we will chat as we go along, and I'll bring you back with me." Mr. S—— declined, and made an appointment for later on. Casting his eyes up to a large tree, beneath which the horses had been hitched, he remarked, "What magnificent mulberries; I haven't seen such large ones since I was a boy." "Go up to the house," said Mr. Owens, "and my wife will send one of the men to shake the tree, and you can have full enjoyment of the berries." "No," said Mr. S——, "but 1 would like to climb the tree and help myself." "Do so, and welcome," cried Mr. Owens, hurriedly jumping into the buggy and driving off.

With agility Mr. S—— reached the dense branches of the tree, and regaled himself plentifully; but when ready to descend, he saw at the base of the tree several dogs intently watching him. Here was a perplexing dilemma! It was dangerous for him to come down; and if he called for help he risked being regarded as a marauder, as no one had seen him in conversation with the master of the place. His only hope was that the dogs would become weary and go away, but they were too vigilant for that. One or two of them would leave for awhile, but never all at a time.

When Mr. Owens returned from the city (some five hours later), as he was walking his horses slowly beneath the shade of the mulberry tree, he heard a voice from its recesses calling piteously: "Owens, for mercy sake, get me out of this; I'm nearly dead." Looking up, he saw Mr. S—— peering through the foliage with woe-begone and fruit-stained face. "Great Scott! you haven't been there ever since I left!" "Indeed but I have; and now drive away those dogs, and let me come down."

The "sentinels" were dispersed, and the weary prisoner released. An explanation, amidst much laughter, ensued; and Owens insisted on Mr. S—— going to the house for refreshment and rest. The hero of this adventure, seemingly mindful only of its ludicrous side, gave it extensive publicity. Mr. Owens used to tell the story with gusto, in his own droll way. No one was fonder of a joke, but there was never any animus in his raillery.

When he indulged in satire, wit and humor, so tempered its edge that however keen it never wounded or humiliated. He had a facetious way of replying to questions. One day (in New York) I heard a gentleman ask him about a member of the company: "Where does G—— live now?" and receive the reply, "He *thinks* he lives in Harlem; but in reality his life is passed in the theatre, rehearsing and playing, with the prelude and finale of hanging on to a strap in a crowded car, to and from Harlem." A friend mentioning some contemptibly mean act of a man they both knew, indignantly concluded by saying: "He is a hog!" "Try to be just," said Owens; "the comparison is unfair." "I maintain it is *not*," was the vehement rejoinder. "Oh, yes, it is," persisted Owens; "unfair *to the hog*."

The season of 1870–71 opened September 19th; and from that date until November 26th the tour was under the management of George F. Fuller, who furnished a competent supporting company. Albany, Buffalo, Rochester and other New York cities were included in the route, which also extended through Pennsylvania's most important towns. This tour was a pleasurable success, with no especial event to mark it different from its predecessors.

# CHAPTER VIII.



NOVEMBER 28th, 1870, Owens appeared at Wood's Theatre, Cincinnati, then under the management of Barney Macauley. After a fortnight there, he proceeded to Cleveland to fill a week for which he was booked with John Ellsler. It was during the latter engagement that the lady cast for *Mary Apex* was taken suddenly ill, and there being no understudy, the withdrawal of "*Self*" seemed inevitable. Fully aware that Owens was averse to changing the bill, Mr. Ellsler suggested his little daughter for *Mary Apex*, saying: "She has not ventured a speaking part beyond a few lines; but her voice is good, and she has a quick memory. If you can rehearse

the scenes with her, she may possibly get through."
Owens was quite willing to run the risk. Miss Effie
(not yet grown) undertook the part with much trepida-
tion ; but made such a sweet ingenuous *Mary Apex* as to
score a triumph.  Mr. Owens praised and congratulated
her at the close of the performance; and the audience
had already, by unstinted plaudits, assured her of their
approval.  This was the first mark made by Effie
Ellsler, in the profession she has since won distinguished
position.

While in Cincinnati a flattering offer was received to
inaugurate the new Opera House in Terre-Haute.  He
hesitated about accepting it,·as he was wistfully looking
towards home, having arranged to give himself two or
three weeks' vacation at Christmas time.  However, he
finally telegraphed an affirmative for the four nights
requested.  The management offered as an additional
inducement, relief from rehearsals ; the company engaged
having recently played as Mr. Owens' support.

He left Cleveland in ample time to reach Terre-Haute
Monday afternoon ; but en route detention occurred,
the road being blocked by the debris from a collision
of freight trains, in consequence he did not arrive in
Indianapolis until 7.30, some while after the hour he
was due in Terre-Haute—seventy-eight miles further
on.  Much annoyed, he gave up all hope of fulfilling
his promise to inaugurate the new Opera House ; but

nevertheless continued his journey, having telegraphed the manager about the dilemma. At the first station after leaving Indianapolis, a telegram was brought on the train to him (a response to his own) which read : "The audience will wait for you." At every succeeding station was received a telegram to the same effect, variously worded. The entire ride of seventy-eight miles was made while the audience were waiting for the star of the evening. Upon arriving at Terre-Haute he drove rapidly to the Opera House, and exceeded even his own record for quick dressing. The curtain arose at eleven o'clock, and when "*Major DeBoots*" stepped on the stage, a deafening shout of welcome arose. The whole performance went off with éclat; the *Major* and *Solon* being applauded to the echo until the fall of the curtain at *two o'clock* in the morning, when the crowd dispersed in jolly good humor.

Previous to Owens' arrival, telegrams had been read to the audience, from time to time, giving information that "Owens was within seventy miles of Terre-Haute," then "fifty miles," then "thirty-three miles," and so on. The entire episode made quite a talk, and was dilated on in the various newspapers. A contributor to the *Cincinnati Enquirer* gave a descriptive rhyme of the incident—a parody on "Sheridan's Ride"—of which I quote a portion :

### "OWENS' RIDE."

Up from the ground a magnificent pile
Of granite and marble and Terra-Haute tile,
Arose with a grandeur terrific, sublime,
As if wrought by the touch of a magical mind;
A Temple where Thespeus sports in his play,
West of the Capital, seventy-eight miles away.

Like a herald in haste the news spread away,
That *"Owens,"* the invincible King of the play,
Was engaged to be here on opening day,
And tell unto all what *"Solon"* would say;
And the news seemed to strike us all with dismay,
That *"Owens"* was seventy-eight miles away.

The first snow was falling in dreary December,
When this house of the muses, in all its splendor,
Was opened to the gaze of admiring legions,
Who came from the nearest and remotest regions;
Well represented was fashion's array,
To see *"Owens"* who was seventy-eight miles away.

The crowd grew impatient, smiles yielded to frowns,
Nowhere could either of the managers be found;
But a man always *"Early,"* with kindness abounding,
Suggested the play should begin by refunding
The greenbacks to those who no longer could stay
To see *"Owens,"* seventy-eight miles away.

"But stay," said a voice—all was attention—
"While the contents of a telegram I'll mention."
There is a road from Indianapolis town,
A broad-guage railroad leading down;
And there, through the flash of a brilliant head-light,
An engine passed with an eagle's flight.

As if it knew the terrible need,
It stretched away with the utmost speed;
Bridges came and passed away,
With "*Owens*" only thirty-three miles away.

Under its iron hoof the road,
Like an angry Wabash river, flowed;
And the landscape sped away behind,
Like an ocean flying before the wind.
And the engine, with its wild eyes full of fire,
Is nearing unto our heart's desire;
It is snuffing the scent of "Lubin's" spray,
With "*Owens*" only fifteen miles away.

The first thing that "*Owens*" did, I think,
Was to get on the outside of a healthy drink.
That was done; what to do next he knew well,
For the audience set up a terrible yell,
So he rushed on the stage 'mid a storm of huzzas,
And checked the wave of impatience, because
The sight of John Owens compelled it to pause.
With frost and with snow the engine was gray;
It seemed most eloquently to say,
"I have brought you *Owens*, all the way
From Indianapolis, to begin the play."

The ladies now, all impatience forgetting,
Begin their old habits with lovers coquetting.
All were well pleased, and expressed it en masse,
That Owens was there to dispense "apple sass."
And now, Mr. Owens, "how dew you dew?"
We hope you will like us as we like you;
And should you by chance again happen this way,
Don't begin the play—seventy-eight miles away!

The exciting success of the first night extended through the remaining three performances; and the Opera House was prosperously launched on its dramatic career. Leaving Terre-Haute, Mr. Owens played a week in Louisville, then took a rest at home. He resumed his professional work January 16th, at the Park Theatre, Brooklyn, Mrs. F. B. Conway being manageress—"*Victims*" and "*Solon Shingle*" for the first week, "*Solon Shingle*" and "*The Live Indian,*" the second week. Snow, sleet, rain and bitter cold was the weather record of the fortnight; but inclemency did not seem to interfere with amusement seekers, as the theatre was nightly crowded with old "*Solon's*" admirers.

After closing in Brooklyn, dates of a New England tour were filled, with Clifton Tayleure as manager. This included all of the eastern cities as far northward as Portland, Maine; after which he played a week in Baltimore, another in Washington, thence to McVicker's Theatre, Chicago. These were, in detail, a recurrence of others I have already dwelt upon. From the west Owens came direct home, having completed his season 1870–71. Scarcely had he begun to be settled in rural pursuits when he received an offer to play in Montreal, which he decided to accept, and after its fulfilment make a pleasure tour up the St. Lawrence, visiting Quebec and other places.

An additional inducement to draw Mr. Owens to Montreal was the fact that the *Theatre Royal* was managed for the summer season by Mr. John W. Albaugh, who was a favorite and companionable friend. He also played the leading business of his theatre, which was an important matter to the comedian, who remembered the able support rendered him by Mr. Albaugh in previous engagements, prominently so during the season of 1864, in New York, where he distinguished himself by polished and conscientious work in " *Uncle Solon Shingle*," " *Victims*" and other plays.

After the Montreal engagement, and the ensuing pleasure trip, Owens returned to the farm; resting and enjoying the society of his friends during his vacation. In July some changes were made in employees on the place, and the position of head gardener was difficult to fill. Among the applicants came an Englishman, whose language was obscure from the wild and promiscuous disposal of the letter h. Not being able to understand his name, Mr. Owens (considerately desiring to spare the man the embarrassment of a third interrogation) asked, " how do you *spell* your name?" And the reply was given thus: " A he—a double hell—a hi—a hess—a ho and a hen—'*Ellison*.'" Mentally, Mr. Owens decided, " if this man's reference is fairly good, I'll engage him. I foresee a fund of amusement which I must not lose." For the three years that Ellison was employed at Aigburth Vale, he was an inexhaustible source of entertainment to Mr. Owens—not in the way of ridicule, but as a study of character.  The white cliffs of Albion were suggested by his every utterance; and combined with this was stolid wit and shrewd good sense.  To hear Mr. Owens relate some of their interviews, was as good a bit of character-acting as one could have.  He liked this head gardener personally, for the sterling integrity and mental ability which entitled him to general respect.

The summer weeks flew swiftly by until Mr. Owens again returned to theatrical life.  This occurred September 5th, at the Globe Theatre, Boston, Arthur Cheney being proprietor, and W. R. Floyd, manager.  The ranks of the stock company were filled by F. F. Mackey, W. E. Sheridan, D. Harkins, H. L. Daly, J. Jennings, Peakes, Miss Josie Orton, Miss Ada Gilman, Mrs. Barry, Mrs. Hunter and others.  Mr. Owens was the first star of the season; he opened in *Victims* and *Forty Winks*, and was received with overwhelming cordiality.

"*The Heir at Law,*" "*The Rivals*" and other comedies followed successfully; but the salient feature of the engagement was "*Grimaldi.*"  It set critical Boston wild with admiration, and packed the theatre for six consecutive weeks.  Owens' personation of *Grimaldi* was pronounced an unexcelled characterization—a carefully studied, yet thoroughly natural piece of acting.  He graphically pictured the old French emigré struggling with want and hunger—proud, tender, shrewd, and withal a gentleman.  Every intonation of the voice, the raising of the eyebrow, the glance of the eye, was perfect ; and in delicate shading vitalized " *Grimaldi.*" Owens had disappeared as completely as if swept from the face of the earth ; the old Frenchman stood in his place, and bore the audience with him through poverty, sorrow, pathetic affection— changing with prosperity to the volatility of supreme happiness. Boston audiences are ever discriminating; and they realized that this rôle was worthy of the artist's great reputation, and regarded it as a cluster of dramatic jewels.

It was at this time in Boston that Mr. Owens made inquiry relative to the author of " The People's Lawyer." The play had never been copyrighted, and in its originality widely differed from the " *Solon Shingle* " which Mr. Owens had made famous. Though only indebted to the author for the skeleton upon which he had formed " *Solon Shingle,*" he desired, in view of his success, to tender a complimentary recognition to Dr. Jones. Having obtained his address in Boston, he wrote a pleasant letter, and enclosed a substantial souvenir. To this he received the following acknowledgment :

" Boston, *September* 23d, 1871.

" John E. Owens, Esq :

" *My Dear Sir,*—Your favor enclosing a check drawn by you and payable to my order, for 'Five hundred dollars,' was duly received. 'The Souvenir,' so gracefully tendered, I accept with peculiar gratification in consequence of its relation to one of my earliest efforts as a dramatist, 'The People's Lawyer,' written nearly two-score years ago.

13

"You, sir, have made Solon Shingle famous, prolonged his stage-existence, and preserved to this time this relic of the dramatic past.

"My inclination would lead me to thank you, in presence of the public, for your novel recognition of my claim to the authorship of the drama in which Mr. Shingle was first introduced. I have not considered it proper, without your approval, to reply to your note through the press.

"I wish, however, that your gratuitous manifestation should be known to all who have interest in the success of plays and players.

"Let me again repeat my appreciation of the gift, and the generous motive that suggested it.

"Very truly yours,

"Jos. S. Jones."

Mr. Owens replied by assuring Dr. Jones how deeply he valued such kind sentiments, but positively declined to have their correspondence published; concluding to this effect: "The pleasure you express at the reception of the souvenir is not one-tenth of that which I experience in knowing that I have rendered to your gratification. Let that content us." This graceful act was never mentioned to anyone by Mr. Owens. Whether Dr. Jones was equally reticent, I do not know. They have both passed into the spirit land, and I do not think it amiss *now* to relate an incident which was creditable to both, evincing as it did the best feelings of human nature.

Owens next played at the Walnut Street Theatre, Philadelphia, to excellent business, and afterwards at Booth's Theatre, New York—opening November 6th,

1871, as "*Caleb Plummer*," in "*Dot*." That the characterization met with appreciative welcome, was a foregone conclusion. Never had this peerless performance elicited warmer praises; but the cast (though comprising much talent) lacked adaptability to the parts assigned, and the ensemble was unsatisfactory. Two weeks of *Caleb Plummer;* and then *Victims* and *Solon Shingle* held the boards for the same length of time.

To the details of setting pieces the management gave every attention; but nothing could counteract the fact that it was not a theatre for comedy. The company had been selected for tragedy, and a serious element lingered depressingly in the atmosphere. The immensity of the theatre was more suitable for declamatory acting than for the subtlety of humor, where the play of the features, or neatness of action intensifies points. The month at Booth's Theatre was chronicled by the press as an artistic success; but this meed of praise, and the large pecuniary results were insufficient to reconcile the comedian to the solemnity of his surroundings. "It is the home of classic tragedy, and unfit for comedy," said he. "Lotta," who was the next star, was similarly impressed. Some of her friends described the theatre as so antagonistic to fun as to render the merry little sprite entirely out of her element.

On the 11th of December Owens appeared, as the first star of the season, at the Varieties Theatre, New Orleans, Lawrence Barrett being manager. During the previous

year the old theatre had been destroyed by fire, and a
more magnificent structure reared in its stead.  Under
the supervision of Mr. Barrett the new theatre gave
evidence of the excellent judgment and refined taste so
inseparable from that gentleman.  The stock company
was efficient in talent, and full in numbers.

Mr. Barrett delivered the opening address in a polished
manner.    Then followed "*Everybody's  Friend*" and
"*Solon Shingle;*" and the vast audience, already in a
good humor, became exuberantly mirthful.  This bill,
announced for two nights, was by request continued the
entire week, thus deferring "*The Rivals*" until Monday,
18th inst.  Sheridan's witty comedy was strongly cast,
with *Bob Acres* as the central light;  and that character
was played by Owens with dash and spirit.  Rollicking
merriment contrasted forcibly with the abject fear of
"fighting Bob," when his cowardice became uncon-
trollable.  In every phase artistic, he evoked laughter
and won unanimous approval.

On Christmas night "*Dot*" was produced with Owens
as "*Caleb Plummer.*"  The old toy-maker was ever welcome in New Orleans, but especially at this season of the
year, from the memory of many other Christmas times
that he had held the hearts of his auditors.  This
retrospection went back as far as 1860, when Caleb's
timid tap at John Peerybingle's door was answered by
the hearty "come in!" of the carrier.  Entering irreso-

lutely, and meekly responding, "It's only me," there stood old Caleb with his patient manner. As he paused inside the door, wistfully gazing at the home circle, he was such a pathetic figure—meagre, cold and simply humble, that one felt like joining in the cordial greeting of Dot and John, that cheerily bid the old man "come close to the fire."

Long before Christmas time many New Orleans people would appeal to the manager: "Give us '*Dot*'; the holidays are incomplete without *Caleb Plummer* and his humanizing tenderness. The play is Christmaslike, and every one is better for having heard the cricket's merry chirping."

The New Orleans engagement having terminated, Mr. Owens returned home by steamer, *via* Havana, and indulged in a brief respite from professional duties by enjoying country life; for since home and farm had become synonymes, he had grown to love the country at all seasons. He claimed that he had always *innately* had that taste; but I remember a long-ago incident when this liking was somewhat modified.

Before removing from the city to Aigburth Vale, Mr. Owens and myself accepted an invitation to visit some friends in the country—driving out Sunday morning and remaining until next day. The hospitality, cordial welcome and genial conversation that marked this visit was exceedingly enjoyable. The winter landscape, beautiful with its garment of snow and jewels of prismatic icicles, was a novelty to us city people, and greatly admired. Indoors the ruddy warmth and cheerful blaze from the big open fire-place, with its huge hickory logs, sent a glow on the Christmas evergreens and holly which decorated the room, making a charming picture.

The bed-rooms of this home were of cottage style; and though exquisitely appointed, not comfortable as the wood fires died out. Narrow blankets increased the danger of taking cold. In the morning Mr. Owens remarked to me, " I fear I have contracted an influenza; if so, I hereafter veto the country *in winter time*—it is at the best in summer, and ought only to be visited *then.*"

While breakfasting, our friends with attentive solicitude, "hoped that a good night's rest had refreshed us." Replying with conventional courtesy, Mr. Owens was about to change the topic; when he was interrupted by our host observing: "I will tell you something very remarkable about those blankets you slept under. They belonged to Napoleon Bonaparte. I have authentic proof of this relic; they came into my possession," &c., &c. Of course, we listened with interested attention, and made the natural ejaculations of wonder and admiration.

As we drove to the city in a jaded and sneezing condition, Mr. Owens suddenly remarked: "I have made a discovery which will be valuable to history. The *true* cause of the divorce between Napoleon and Josephine is now clear to me—*Narrow blankets!* A lifetime of harmony together was impossible!"

Owens played in Washington and Baltimore during February and March, 1872, with the same pleasant results that had heretofore attended his engagements in those cities. In addition to his popularity with the general public, he had hosts of friends who loved to chat with him, and for these he always had a pleasant word, and ofttimes a merry story. To chance acquaintances he was ever affable; but sometimes his patience became sorely tried by a class of individuals who think they have a right (unintroduced) to intrude upon the time of an actor, even to the interruption of business or his social intercourse with personal friends. The usual introductory sentence "you don't know me, Mr. Owens," was met serenely at most times; but occasionally it became unbearable, and merited the reply, "No; and I don't want to know you"—especially if followed by prosy reminiscence and many questions.

One of the penalties of prominence is to be a target for bores, who sometimes have more imagination than memory. A case in point occurred one day as Owens was walking up Baltimore street with a friend. He was effusively accosted by a tottering senile individual: "I declare if that aint Jack Owens! I'm real glad to see you. I've been away from this city these many years. How do you do, Jack?" extending a tremulous hand.

"Oh, I'm quite well," replied the comedian; "but I don't remember you." "Now, that's hard," mumbled the octogenarian. "*I* never forgot *you*. Always would go to see Jack Owens play—'*old* Jack Owens,' as we boys used to call you. Never shall forget the first time I saw you. It was in the Baltimore Museum; my nurse took me when I was about six years old, and—" "Oh, that was my grandfather you saw," interrupted Owens. "No, no, no," insisted the mendacious bore; "it was *you*, I remember I—" "It couldn't have been my father, for *he* would be about your own age if he was alive—Ta! ta!" laughingly rejoined Owens, as he turned away and walked off, leaving the retrospective humbug uncertain whether he had been snubbed or misunderstood.

After the engagement in Baltimore, Owens made a brief southern tour; commencing in Augusta, Ga., and closing in Richmond, Va. On his arrival in the latter city (where he had not played since 1857), a committee of leading citizens waited upon him to request that he would favor the public with the performance of "*John Unit.*" He cheerfully complied, remembering with pleasure the long-ago success of "*Self,*" and the episode of the snow storm which delayed his first night in Richmond. Many of the persons who witnessed it then were among the audience of May 10th, 1872. The Richmond papers became reminiscent, and printed the original cast and criticisms. After the curtain fell on

"*Self*," Mr. Owens received warm congratulations on his success, and ultra perfection as *John Unit.* Strenuous efforts were made to induce him to prolong his engagement; but to these flattering appeals he was unable to respond affirmatively, though tendering his regrets at his inability to do so. The warm days had prematurely commenced in springtime, and Mr. Owens was desirous of entering upon his summer vacation at home.

I don't know whether, on this occasion, it was rest he was impatient to attain, as the fact that he had in prospect sundry improvements on the farm, in the way of fencing, ditching, &c., which he was eager to set going. Nothing delighted him more than to have the place pervaded with laborers; and to give occupation to those who asked for it was his constant rule. The invariable direction to his farm manager being: "Never refuse an application for employment. Don't turn a man away; *make* work for him." On one occasion he had a long line of fence moved a few feet back, and six months later returned to its original position. I always believed it was done for the sole purpose of giving employment to Tom B——, who by the way, was a favorite with Mr. Owens. He often said, that Diogenes' lantern-hunt for an honest man would have come to a speedy termination had he met B——.

Away from home once, Mr. Owens had occasion to write to B——, relative to some fencing; and as many of the same name lived in Baltimore County, he was puzzled about directing the letter so as to insure its being received. Jocosely, he said : "I'll indicate him by a quotation ;" and wrote "Thomas B——, 'a man skilled in fence.'" The letter was delivered to the right man ; though B—— was serenely unconscious of the witty address.

Having enjoyed a delightful summer at home, Owens began his next season in Brooklyn at the Park Theatre, September 2d, 1872. During the vacation he had organized a company to support him in a starring tour of thirty-seven weeks ; playing in one hundred and thirty-seven towns. The perfection of this undertaking was *then* a laborious task ; for it was in the early days of such continuous travel, and unattended with the present facilities. The result, however, was eminently satisfactory. A well selected company of marked ability rendered the various plays admirably. The leading lady, Mrs. John T. Raymond (known professionally as "Marie Gordon"), proved an immense favorite everywhere. After a fortnight in Brooklyn, the cities of Albany, Utica, and others in New York state came in rotation ; from thence a tour of the western towns en route for Cincinnati. There at Pike's Opera House he played the most brilliant engagement of his many great ones in the Queen city. *The Heir at Law, Poor Gentleman, The Rivals, Sweethearts and Wives* and other

popular comedies from his extensive repertoire filled the time with varied attractions; and the public rendered hearty tribute to his versatility.

By especial request he played "*Paul Pry*," that having been a favorite during his early engagements in Cincinnati. Owens was regarded as one of the best *Paul Prys*. He gave a piquant delineation of that eccentric character, rendering the full quota of dry humor without the slightest shade of buffoonery. The play of features, so expressive, testified his marvellous mobility of countenance—his magnetic eye-power was wonderful; and the artistic judgment with which he used these gifts, rendered the effect charmingly natural. His laugh was so hearty and genuine that it was echoed by all who heard it. The blunders unwittingly committed by *Paul Pry* were intensified in ludicrousness by the surprise he evinced at the resentment of those for whom he persisted "he was doing a kind act." No description can do justice to Owens' portrayal of this character, or to the manner in which he vividly brought out the idea of the play, that *Paul Pry* was not the *mar*-plot of the piece but rather the *make*-plot; for on his meddling hinges the working out of events.

While in Cincinnati, going to rehearsal one morning, the comedian encountered a brisk little man, who greeted him with the stereotyped salutation, "You don't remember me, Mr. Owens?" Scarcely waiting for response, he continued, "I was in your company when you managed the Charles Street Theatre, Baltimore. Don't you recollect when we made that big hit with the '*Comedy of Errors?*' I played the officer." "Oh, it's C——," said Owens, laughing; for he at last recognized a whilom factotum who, on the occasion referred to, had been entrusted with one line to speak. Breaking down hopelessly the first night, a tap on the shoulder was thereafter substituted for the few words (and *that* was how *we* made the hit). "Well, C——," inquired Mr. Owens, "at which of the theatres are you now?" "Oh, I've cut the the-ay-ters," disdainfully replied the youth, "I am in the book business; that is our establishment, across the street."

The large and handsome store indicated betokened wealth incompatible with C——'s costume. Making a margin for eccentricity, Owens congratulated his former employé on this rapid advancement in prosperity. "Yes, indeed, Mr. Owens, I am indeed much better off; I'm doing *fust* rate. The-ay-ters are low, except for stars like you. Well, good-by, sir, I have to be on the Hamilton & Dayton train by schedule time, and I've got to call for my books, peanuts and other things." The *train-boy* hurried away, all unconscious of the amusement he had afforded Mr. Owens by the denouement of his real occupation, so entirely at variance with his assumption of mercantile importance.

From Cincinnati Owens went to Lexington for two nights, thence to Louisville; and in the latter city he played at the Masonic Temple, the large auditorium being crowded all the week. He was the recipient of much complimentary congratulation, both from his old friends and from strangers; the latter often using the mail only, as a medium to convey expression of their commendation. Among the many letters received from unknown admirers was an eminently piquant one, whose envelope bore the following doggerel address:

> "To Mr. Solon Shingle,
>     A dealer in Produce;
>   'Tis apple sass, *he* calls it
>     (That's apples biled in juice).
>   His alias, '*John E. Owen,*'
>     An actor rare, all know.
>   He plays *De Boots* and *Solon,*
>     And I play—this for low!
>   Please leave this at the Temple,
>     Where Masons congregate,
>   In Louisville (Fall city),
>     In old Kentucky State."

# CHAPTER IX.



AFTER Louisville the tour was westward, and became fraught with much fatiguing travel. The weather was unusually severe, even for that inclement locality. Heavy snow-storms often prolonged the journeys; and though Mr. Owens endeavored by frequent use of special trains, and in many other ways, to insure the comfort of his combination, it was impossible to entirely obviate great fatigue. His sturdy health and buoyant nature rendered him equal to emergencies, and many a jest and laugh arose from taking a mishap in its ludicrous aspect. The flagging spirits of the company revived to a pleasant degree; and at night, before a brilliant audience, they forgot the discomforts of travel.

Snow-bound trains made many delays. The afternoon before Christmas the combination, overdue at B——, arrived just as the official in charge of the baggage-room was preparing to leave the station. Hurriedly approaching him, Owens said : " Please check my baggage quickly as possible; it is important for me to make connection to Milwaukee." Gruffly inquiring "Where is it?" the baggage master had the stack of over fifty trunks pointed out to him, with the information that "it was the 'Owens Combination' luggage." "You'll have to pay extra baggage," snarled the man. "I don't think so, because—" began Owens, mildly. "Tell you, *yes;* tell you that baggage is far over weight." " But," suggested Owens, "if you will listen to —" " No, I won't listen. Aint here to listen to nonsense. I'll *weigh* that baggage." " You are giving yourself needless trouble, I can show you—" "Don't want you to show me anything;" and the official savagely began to wrestle with the trunks, throwing them one by one viciously on the scales. " Well, if you insist on fatiguing yourself, I'll leave you," said Owens, retiring to the waiting-room.

After having remained there awhile, and becoming partially thawed, he returned to the scene of baggage weighing; and again endeavored to expostulate on the subject, but could not obtain a hearing. When the last trunk was crashed down, the official made a memorandum of the aggregate weight, and calling to Mr. Owens, said : "Now, I'll talk to you; you owe $38.98 for extra baggage. Got anything to say, eh?" "Yes, I have; and I wish you had permitted me to say it sooner. This," handing him a note, "is an order from the Superintendent of the road, to pass all of my baggage free of *extra* charge."

Inspecting the document, and finding it genuine, the man became voluble in expletives; and indignantly demanded, "Why didn't you tell me you had this paper?" "Because you wouldn't allow me to speak," was the reply, in a comically meek voice. A sense of his self-inflicted labor seemed to impress the baggage master as rather a grim joke. After a pause, he broke into a laugh, and said : "It's a big sell; *you* come out ahead. Good night."

The snow continued to fall, and all trains being belated, there was no prospect of reaching the next town for performance. Hope was now limited to arriving there, in time to secure a night's rest.

At nine P. M. the officials returned to the station to be on duty, in event of arrival of trains; though the violence of the storm rendered that occurrence improbable. At midnight, the baggage master, whose incipient dislike to Owens had changed to reverse feeling, came to him, saying : "There will be no travel to-night; I want you to come up to my house; I can make you comfortable, and it will give me pleasure to do so."

Thanking him cordially, Mr. Owens declined the proffered hospitality, preferring to remain with his company in this mishap of travel—a most disagreeable experience it was, as they passed the entire night in the dreary waiting room. On every subsequent tour, when a change was made at this station, the baggage master would facetiously salute Owens with the query: "Any *extra* baggage to be weighed to-day? I am not in as great a hurry to get home as I was on Christmas eve," &c., &c. It was a chronic joke between them; and the acquaintance, which began in a wrangle, was afterwards fraught with many a pleasant encounter.

The westward travel continued as far as Omaha, and despite some personal discomfort, was satisfactory. In the small towns at this time the advent of a prominent theatrical star was a novelty which was variously responded to; appreciatively by some, whilst others, accustomed only to a circus, stereopticon, or moral lecture, were puzzled as to the nature of the coming entertainment. Numerous and diverse were the interrogations, but none more absurd than that propounded to one of the ladies of the company. As she was leaving the dining room, the landlord's wife intercepted her, and the following dialogue ensued: "I am going to the show to-night; what feats does you perform? I should

14

say you was rayther stout to jump through hoops, and just a *leetle* too old." "Think so?" "Yes, I guess you hev to take a back seat and let the youngsters do them tricks now?" "Oh, no, it is as easy to me as when I was younger. Couldn't go through hoops and over ribbons a bit better then." "Well, well, I shouldn't 'a thought it; I mean to see you to-night for certain." "I hope you will be pleased," was the merry rejoinder.

At one of the hotels a citizen, who was lounging in the office, inquired: "Mister, do you belong to the show that's just got here?" "No," said Owens, "the show belongs to me." "Well, where's your horses; where's your brass band?" Eyeing the man quizzically, the comedian remarked: "This is not a circus, my friend, and there is nothing brazen about the company; as for myself I pose as the most modest individual and rely upon the public to discern my merit." Chaffing seemed to irritate the questioner, as he rejoinded: "I don't know what stuff you are talking, but I can tell you we expect a brass band; no show catches on in this town without it; make no mistake, mister." The auditorium at night proved the individual a false prophet. Retracing the route from Omaha, Owens played in Kansas City and other towns until he arrived at St. Louis, where he opened at De Bar's Theatre, January 20th, 1873. The seven performances here were eminently satisfactory,

which was peculiarly gratifying in view of the unpro-
pitious weather—cold, sleet, and snow prevailing.

The day before we left St. Louis, Mr. Owens received
a letter, the superscription of which was in a boyish
hand-writing. It contained a small photograph of a
handsome lad and these lines:

"DEAR MR. OWENS,—

"I want you to see a boy you have made happy. Father says
I'd be a bother to you if I went to the hotel; so I send my
picture, and tell you I've seen you play ever so often. I laughed
and laughed—why, I just hollered. Now, Mr. Owens, some time
when I'm bigger—I'm going on twelve now—will you give me
your picture? I'd be so glad to get it. No more at present from
Andrew L——,
"who lives at No. — Olive St."

The naiveté and earnestness of the boy was charming.
I don't know when Mr. Owens was more pleased with a
letter. His photograph and a few genial words were
speedily sent in response.

After six nights at Memphis, Tenn., Owens proceeded
to New Orleans, where he appeared at the Varieties
Theatre, February 3d, as "*Major DeBoots*" and "*Solon
Shingle.*" The transition from the rigor of winter
(endured for so many weeks) to this genial climate was
delightful; and the entire fortnight was an epitome of
pleasant hours to the comedian, his personal friends and
many admirers. Until March the time was filled with

southern travel from Mobile to Richmond. The tour then extended through the states of Pennsylvania and New York; thence playing the New England circuit as far north as Portland and Bangor, Maine.

Mr. Owens always inspected the setting of the stage before the curtain went up, so as to be sure that the properties, &c., were in place. In one of the small eastern towns, after the customary precaution, he called to a friend who was standing at the wing: "Come here; I have something to tell you. This theatre is remarkable; the management intends to make a horse piece of *Solon Shingle*. I have played old Solon many hundred times, and under various circumstances; but I never thought the part would lead me to the equestrian drama!" "What *do* you mean?" asked the puzzled listener. Crossing over to the witness-box, Owens threw up the drapery, and disclosed a wooden *clothes-horse* which had been utilized to improvise the witness-stand. "There, look at the fiery steed! Doesn't it suggest the circus ring and the odor of sawdust?" They both laughed at the "sell," and Owens rejoined, "The entire vamped set is so outrageously dismal, that I either had to fly into a rage, or make a joke; and I chose the latter alternative, even though I had but feeble foundation."

The route recently spoken of brought to Owens and his company the singular experience of two winters in nine months, with a summer intervening. In January

they left the western cities, where the extreme cold tested
the limit of thermometers; proceeding southward, they
basked in summer temperature for two months, and then
journeyed northward to Maine, where winter reigned
supreme—no vehicles but sleighs being available. Later
on, in the state of New York, this season drew to a close.
The last performance was given in Troy, terminating a
tour of thirty-six weeks.

An abridgment of one week was caused by illness at
Aigburth Vale—illness unto death of Mr. Frederick
Pinkney, a near and dear friend who was visiting there.
When we were apprised by telegram that Mr. Pinkney's
case was hopeless, and liable at any moment to terminate
fatally, Mr. Owens arranged to close the season, and
speedily return home. So desperate was this illness
that he feared Mr. Pinkney might not survive many
hours. Fortunately he rallied, and was sufficiently
conscious to affectionately recognize Mr. Owens on his
arrival.

He continued to fluctuate in strength, sometimes equal
to conversing, but often oblivious of those around. It
was a mournful satisfaction for Mr. Owens to be near
him for the three weeks of his survival; at the end of
which time he passed away, surrounded by his devoted
family and friends.

Frederick Pinkney held so prominent and exalted a
position in life, that not only was he mourned by his

bereaved family, but his death was an irreparable loss to his own city. He was one of Maryland's representative men. A son of the Hon. William Pinkney, the illustrious statesman; he had inherited his father's acute and comprehensive intellect, and early distinguished himself in legal lore. Being of a retiring nature, he did not share the ambition of his father for public life, but confined himself to the practice of law, in addition to the office he held as Deputy State's Attorney.

His scholarly attainment in all branches of science was great, his erudition unsurpassed; as a poet, he was unusually gifted. But beyond wisdom, learning and talent, he left even a more precious heritage of remembrance to his family in the record of his personal character, which was manly, pure and unimpeachable. The devoted affection of his domestic life was equal in force to the acumen evinced with sagacious jurisdiction in discharge of his public duties.

Mr. Owens passed the remainder of the summer at Aigburth Vale. His presence at home was always a delight, not only to his family, but most welcome to those employed on the farm. They were pleased by the interest he manifested in the work which had been done during his absence; and the fact that he listened to every detail, increased their satisfaction. Moreover, from the farm manager down to the herding boy each held the firm belief that "the master" cared for their personal joys and sorrows; and they came to him for advice, sure of ready sympathy and (if needed) assistance.

A marked trait in his nature was consideration for the feelings of his inferiors. I remember one day when he had been in the city since early morn; as he drove up to the house one of the farm hands met him when he alighted from the carriage and said: "Oh, Mr. Owens, I'm thankful you've gotten back. Please come to see my boy Dave, and tell me what to do for him. He has had a fall, and I'm afeared his leg is interrogated. I've rubbed it with merriment, but it's no good—he cries all the time." Some one standing by broke into laughter at these malapropisms. Mr. Owens rebuked this sharply, adding: "There's nothing amusing in a man's distress, or the boy having dislocated his leg. Go for a doctor instead of grinning over suffering." Then turning to the anxious father, he said: "Come, we will go to Dave and stay with him till the doctor arrives."

There was an old colored man on the farm who had been a servant in our family for many years. He was devoted to Mr. Owens, not only for the kindness he received, but under the fancied impression that the bond of free masonry existed between them; the latter delusion Mr. Owens encouraged, because it amused him to hear Luther talk, and gratified the old man to know that he could come to "Marse John" with his troubles and ask advice. I have heard him say to the other farm people: "We just passes the signs and 'Marse John' knows almost before I axes what I wants. Dat's de good of being brudder masons."

The old fellow, years before, had a legacy of a piece of land with a little house on it; but his title was disputed by the heirs-at-law, and litigation ensued. The dignity of "a lawsuit" was a matter of great pride to him, and rendered him somewhat important with his associates; but still he was anxious to come in possession of his land. Mr. Owens tried to arrange matters for him, but "the law's delays" seemed insurmountable. One day he came from town (where he had asked permission to go "to look after my lawsuit"), and, radiant with delight, he sought Mr. Owens, exclaiming: "Marse John, I've seed my lawyer, and sure as you is bawn he'll fix things for me now."

"Tell me all about it, Luther." "Well, sah, I went to Lawyer B——'s office; thar' was a gemlan thar' with him; and he 'scused hisself so as to talk to me, cos he knowed I had to ketch a car. Then he talked to me; same old story; wot 'he wos sorry, but my case would have to be put off agin.' I just said, werry respectful but werry positive: 'It's done been put off too many times a'ready; if there aint something done soon I'll fling de papers among de jury.' I tell you he was skeered! He got werry red in de face, and made believe to laugh. The other gemlan come over to him and says: ' For mercy sake, B——, hurry up that case; if the old man does what he *says* he will the court will be broken up! then what's to become of the country?' Yes, Marse John, I skeered 'em awful, and they das'sent keep me out of my rights now."

"Marse John" had almost as much difficulty to control his amusement as had the lawyer, but took care not to wound Luther's feelings by rendering it perceptible. He gave him words of good cheer, but cautioned him not to be too hopeful of settlement.

When the summer rest of 1873 was over, Owens resumed his professional work, supported by his own company; opening at the Arch Street Theatre, Philadelphia, in " *Victims*" and "*Solon Shingle.*" The delicious humor of the comedian was never more thoroughly enjoyed. To render *Joshua Butterby* and *Solon Shingle* salient creations, could only be possible with a man of absolute genius. In less competent hands, *Butterby* might have degenerated into buffoonery. To elaborate the coxcomb's peculiarities, and present the character with all its unconscious idiosyncrasies, was a triumph of art. The presentation to Minerva Crane was one of the best comic situations ever seen, and ably handled; or in other words, " Owens was *Butterby* throughout the entire play."

Possibly, but few reflected how much had been achieved in making " *Victims*" a success. The comedy

me to instruct this man in regard to costumes, &c., so that he could be utilized in event of my absence through sickness, or other contingency.

At the close of the week I was called home to remain over Sunday. Having thoroughly drilled De R—— about the dress and properties for "*Butterby*" and "*Solon*," I hoped that all would be right. Returning on Monday, I went direct to the theatre to arrange costumes for change of bill. I found the Frenchman in the dressing-room, and asked: "Did you have everything right Saturday evening?" "Parfaitement, Madame. True, I forget to give Monsieur ze *spectacle* for So-lon; but of himself he remember, before ze entrez, and did return for zem. Not, Madame, dat ze leetle zing like unto such trifle would make differance to so great actor. He would say somesing to turn him off." I could not repress a smile at this blissful ignorance of the importance of properties evolving the action of the play. I quietly remarked: "You are right; he would have said something"—mentally adding, "something that would have startled you."

As weeks rolled on the factotum grew to be such an ardent admirer of Mr. Owens' acting that he hung about the wings of the stage and was a chronic hindrance to everyone behind the scenes; he, moreover, became stage-struck, purchased play-books, and grew absorbed in them to the exclusion of all occupation. Worse yet, he took to drink, and assigned as an excuse that "he didn't care to live if he couldn't be an actor." After much patient endurance he was discharged.

A few days afterwards a package was received, and with it a note from De R——, the latter written in broken English, and of the wildest tenor. Depths of grief to begin with; followed by a request for the loan of five dollars, to take him to his dying son; followed up with the matter-of-fact statement: "I present to you a patent boot-jack; in ze future I will explain him. P. S.—I wait below for ze money, and ze train leave in an hour."

For a moment after reading this effusion Mr. Owens hesitated between anger and amusement, but finally laughed at the absurdity and sangfroid of the writer, saying: "I think the fellow is either crazy or a fraud; but I may as well give him the money; perhaps he really has a dying son." So he went down stairs and sent De R—— to the alleged train, and no more was ever heard of him.

After the conclusion of the engagement in Philadelphia, two prosperous weeks were filled at Pike's Opera House, Cincinnati, with "*The Heir at Law*," "*The Poor Gentleman*," "*Sweethearts and Wives*," and other comedies, together with "*Solon Shingle*" and several farces. Among the latter "*Toodles*" was in great favor. In the character of "*Timothy Toodles*" Owens was *sui generis*. Long ago he had received the high commendation of comparing favorably with William E. Burton (who was the original Toodles in this country). Avoiding the broadness which marred the effect of that great actor's rendition of the part, he adhered to his own conception. His drunken scene was original, and excruciatingly funny, but devoid of coarseness. With the finest instinct for humor, he never permitted anything coarse or vulgar to find place in language or situations of the parts he played.

Returning to Baltimore, he appeared at Ford's Grand Opera House for a week, thence to Washington, duplicating the performances and success; after which he made a tour through the State of New York. In the cities business was excellent, and audiences appreciative; but in the smaller towns the houses were not uniformly good. In one of these places (where expectations of manager and star were unfulfilled) the weather was dismally rainy, the hotel unbearable; aggregating a feeling of general dissatisfaction. Mr. Owens, while changing to his street costume, said: "Well, it is a one-night stand, let it go and be forgotten." He never dwelt on disagreeable matters, and did not like to have them discussed. As we were quitting the theatre his agent came forward to meet him, saying: "Mr. H——, a prominent citizen of this town, requests to be introduced to you." I knew that Mr. Owens was not in a mood for conversation; but the gentleman had advanced, and the inevitable introduction took place. Of course, Mr. Owens (though annoyed) was polite; but the coolness of his courtesy increased as, with mistaken zeal, Mr. H——

indulged in stupid retrospection and fulsome praise of the comedian's acting, adding that " he himself once had an idea of going on the stage." By and by Mr. Owens began to extract amusement from the interview, and became sarcastic in a humorous way. Utterly unconscious of the shafts aimed against him, Mr. H—— continued his meandering remarks, verging into regrets that the house had not been crowded, and lamenting that the engagement had occurred at such an inauspicious time.

"Ah ! I begin to understand," said Owens, "Mr. Brown raffles a turkey to-night?" "Oh, no," was the eager response. "Well, then, Mrs. Robinson gives a party; I am sure there must be some counter-attraction in town." "That's just it," innocently rejoined Mr. H——. " Local election excitement; that is what interferes with amusement, but please don't give us the go by; try us another time." This imperturbable earnestness of manner quite conquered the irritability of the comedian; he merged into a genial mood, and made himself so agreeable that the interview terminated pleasantly.

A successful fortnight at the Park Theatre, Brooklyn, was followed by a tour westward through Ohio, Indiana and Illinois, arriving in Chicago for an engagement beginning January 18th, during which time he presented many of his famous characters. All were appreciated, but none received greater praise than his portrayal of " *Caleb Plummer*." In Chicago, as elsewhere, this was a favorite part, and so closely associated with Owens, that in its consistency and fidelity to nature, he was recognized as peerless and inimitable. Through Wisconsin, Minnesota and Kentucky, the principal towns were visited, and though the travel proved tiresome at times, it had its bright side of pleasant happenings, and good business results. Inevitable discomforts are easily borne, when one has a light heart and good health; and the happy faculty of brightening the tedium by a good laugh at amusing or absurd occurrences of daily life.

Arriving at midnight in one of the towns, Owens had the gratification of finding that the small hotel was, at least, clean and neat. Next morning, he went out for a drive, the surrounding country being picturesque and beautiful. Before leaving the hotel, instructions were given to have the room put in order during his absence. At one P. M. he returned, much exhilarated by the drive, and proceeded to his room to write important letters, but found the place still in disorder. Having no bell, the only resource was a loud call for the chambermaid, who lazily sauntered down the hall, inquiring, "wot's up?"

When the situation was explained to her, she rejoined: "Oh, *that's* the fuss. Well, I'll do the room after awhile." "But," remonstrated Mr. Owens, "the day is half gone; I wish to write, and I can't sit down in such disorder!" This appeal was met by a burst of tears, with loud wailing and, between sobs, ejaculations of:

"I can't a-bear to be scolded; I ain't used to work. My pah, he got burnt out, or I shouldn't be here now. *I* ain't no common chambermaid." "I believe you; you are a very *uncommon* one," and sotto voce, "I hope there are none like you." "Don't cry any more." Suddenly drying her tears, she said: "Say, Mister, *now* you're talking straight; and if you'll give me two passes for the show, I'll fix these things in a jiffy." "All right," said Mr. Owens, beating a hasty retreat to escape details of how "pah got burnt out of house and home; and we gals had to go to work," &c.

In another town a new hotel had just been completed, the size, furnishing and appointments of which were many years in advance of the locality. No famous star had yet appeared in this town; and the announcement of Owens created a great excitement, not only in the town, but the country around it. The proprietor of the hotel (a former citizen of New York) was delighted to have him for a guest, and assigned to his use the best room in the house; remarking, as he handed the key: "I want you to notice the chandelier; I am rather proud of it."

When the porter brought the trunks to the room, he paused a moment, and with upward gaze, exclaimed: "I don't suppose New York City has a chandelier equal to that." The chambermaid seemed awe-stricken that anyone should occupy a room decorated with such a chandelier; and when her attention was called to the lack of towels and the scarcity of blankets, she failed to recognize the possibility of discomfort where that chandelier could be contemplated. The dinner was unsatisfactory; but request for food more palatable was ignored by the waiter remarking: "You is in 39, I believe, wid de big chandelier. Reckon you never seed anything like it before!" The fireman failing to start the fire properly, thought he apologized fully by the assertion: "I was just looking at that chandelier."

In fine, it was considered an adequate recompense for all manner of discomforts. This pertinacity grew so ludicrous as to be amusing to Mr. Owens; but preferring comfort to splendor, he asked to have his room changed. The amazement of the proprietor cannot be described—he exclaimed: "What! don't like that room with the big chandelier? I *am* surprised." "My friend, its magnificence demoralizes all who approach it. I need towels, fire and other every-day comforts, and to secure these, will gladly dispense with any amount of crystal and gas." The proprietor, with a puzzled manner, said: "You're always getting off some joke; all the same I'll change your room to 42—but," with a sigh, "I gave you the best in the house, and I did think you'd appreciate the big chandelier."

Proceeding southward, Owens played a week at Memphis giving a change of bill nightly, thence to Mobile for

15

seven performances.  Many "theatre parties" came over from New Orleans, thus bringing pleasant intercourse with old friends.  Bright skies and summer temperature prevailed until Saturday, when a heavy rain set in.  The company, under the charge of Theodore Hamilton (business manager), left the city after the final performance; taking the midnight train for Selma, Alabama, where performance was announced for Monday following.  During the afternoon telegrams had been received, stating that all reserved seats were sold, and a jammed house would greet the star on his first appearance in Selma.

Mr. Owens had promised some friends to remain in Mobile until Sunday evening.  The rain increased in violence throughout the day, flooding the streets, so that it was with difficulty we could drive to the station at eight P. M.  Arriving there, the prospect for the journey was discouraging.  All through the night the train made frequent stoppages, owing to inundation.  At seven A. M. the difficulty of progress culminated with a crash.  The engine had passed over a submerged culvert, but the tender jumped the track, and all the cars except the two sleepers were smashed to fragments.  Fortunately most of the passengers had, an hour earlier, exchanged to the Pullman cars, as the water was pouring in the windows of the day coaches.

With insecure bridges on either side, to advance or proceed was equally dangerous.  After remaining twenty-four hours in this stranded condition, the passengers piloted by the conductor, braved the rain, and walked back to Greenville, Alabama. The disagreeableness of this four miles' tramp through mud and over dilapidated bridges, from which the flooring had been partly washed away, required nerve and strength. But anything was better than sitting by the roadside. When the weary pedestrians arrived at Greenville, the plain hotel seemed to them a palatial refuge from temporary hardship and fatigue. Three days' delay ensued, telegraphic wires being down, communication with the outer world was impossible.

Among the passengers was an Alsacian priest, whose knowledge of the English language was limited. He attached himself to Mr. Owens, courteously requesting to be seated by him at the table—gently explaining: "I can receive ze word zat you speak; but I no comprenez ze rapide talk wiz ze mutter." Ways and means of proceeding on the journey, of course led all conversation; and theories were advanced, more or less impracticable. When the opinion of the Alsacian priest was asked, he invariably looked at Mr. Owens with a beaming smile, and replied: "I sall do whatever zis gentleman do." Mr. Owens afterwards laughingly said "he had never expected to attain the high position of mentor to a holy Father."

On the fourth day conductor Howard gave the welcome tidings that a resumption of our journey was possible for those who were willing to encounter rough travel. Most of the passengers declined, preferring to wait until comfortable transit could be had. The Alsacian priest, a Hebrew drummer, Mr. Owens and myself were all who bore the conductor company an hour later. A wagon drawn by oxen jolted the party over seven miles to a junction; there exchanging to a hand-car, propelled by relays of laborers on the railroad, they crossed the cribbing and trestles of the dilapidated road until a station was reached, where travel was resumed with all the comforts of a well-appointed train.

All this time Mr. Owens was in ignorance of the movements of his company; knowing only that his detention had entailed upon him heavy pecuniary loss. Arriving in Montgomery, he found the company waiting there, and learned that the immense audience in Selma had been dismissed, after which the company proceeded to Montgomery, where they gave two performances with meagre results. He never fretted over mishaps, or allowed them to dwell in his memory. Quickly relegating the Greenville disaster to the past, it was not spoken of again, save to mention some amusing occurrence of the four days' isolation.

A continuance of the southern trip extended to Atlanta, Augusta, Savannah, Macon and Columbus, Ga.; and then the season of thirty weeks terminated. During the final performance, a card was brought to the dressing-room, bearing the name of an old acquaintance, and a pencilled line: "Can I see you, just for a moment?" To which query Owens appended the reply, "Yes, if the moment (?) is limited to sixty seconds." The gentleman was ushered in, and after a cordial greeting, he said: "I've been trying to come up with you for three days. Misinformed as to your route, I went to the wrong towns; but here I am at last, and bent on accomplishing my mission. My dear boy, I am ambassador, committee or aught else you may term it from the powers that be— Charles Howard, lessee of the Varieties Theatre, New Orleans, and the public of the same city; all being desirous to prevail on John E. Owens to manage the theatre next season."

"Why this pilgrimage? I have already giving a negative reply to Howard's letter offering me that position." "Yes, I know that, but I am freighted with many arguments and much eloquence to change your decision." "Can't talk to you *now*. Your sixty seconds have vanished long ago. That's my cue— see you after the play—good-bye," said Owens, hurriedly leaving the room. The interview was resumed, and subject discussed at supper. Urgent persuasion finally gained hearing so far as consent to go on to New Orleans for a visit, and meanwhile, reflect, before utterly rejecting the managerial proposition. A fortnight was delightfully passed in the Crescent city, and the final decision was made to accept the alluring terms to become manager of the Varieties Theatre for the season of 1874–75.

Leaving New Orleans, by steamer for New York, Mr. Owens remained in the latter city several days, partly for recreation, but more especially that he might take preliminary steps towards forming a first class company. The summer vacation at Aigburth Vale was broken by frequent trips to New York on the same business; nevertheless, much delightful home rest and intercourse with friends was enjoyed.

# CHAPTER X.



THE dramatic company organized for the season of
1874–75, included E. F. Thorne, Chippendale,
Laura Don, Ada Gilman and many other talented
artists. Before proceeding to New Orleans, Owens
supported by this company, played at Mrs. Drew's
Arch Street Theatre, Philadelphia, opening August 29th
with "*Victims*" and "*Solon Shingle*," the same bill in
which he had appeared at this theatre the first night of
the previous season. The satisfactory results were equally
coincident. A varied programme filled the second week.

231

In this preliminary season, Brooklyn, Boston, Washington and Baltimore were also included, and in each city the personations of the great comedian were appreciatively enjoyed.

"*The School for Scandal*," was the comedy selected for the opening of the New Orleans theatre. Close attention having been paid to accurate costumes, stage setting, and thorough rehearsals, the initial performance took place November 4th. Owens' name being a tower of strength, led the cast as "*Sir Peter Teazle*," that the full force of the company might be utilized to fill the other characters. He assumed the part of "*Sir Peter*" for this reason only; not being drawn to it with a feeling of inspiration or desiring to achieve a triumph in its representation.

Possessing keenness as well as quickness of perception, he could not fail to bring into prominence any character he assumed; therefore his "*Sir Peter Teazle*" was an excellent performance. It did not reach the brilliancy of his famous characters, but came quite up to his expectation. Having attained its object in successfully inaugurating the season with a comedy which included the entire company, Owens, after the week allotted to the "*School for Scandal*," resumed his especial repertoire, and as usual found the public appreciative. Later on he indulged in a rest, and announced "*Clancarty*," which had for weeks been in process of preparation; then came

"*Belle Lamar*," by Dion Boucicault, and several of Bartley Campbell's comedies.

Guided by managerial experience and good judgment, he had purchased the rights to these and other plays. All through his life he bought many original plays, absolutely; some with a view of adding them to his personal repertoire, others to be available in his managerial capacity. After reading a play, if he deemed it possessed merit, he purchased it for possible future use; not narrowed down by the pressure of needing something new at the moment. Thus thousands of dollars were invested in manuscripts, which are now in my possession. Some of them he used, but even those not tested had the stamp of his approval.

In addition to the strongly attractive stock company which had been engaged for this New Orleans season, many prominent stars appeared. Lawrence Barrett, John McCullough, Emmett, and others, alternated with the stock performances. The theatre opened with every prospect of a great season; but its career was gradually overshadowed by much political excitement. A state of unrest had been brewing since the Pitt–Kellogg embroilment, and ultimately developed strong antagonistic parties. The influence on the theatres was slightly felt at first, but increased with various phases, and culminated when General Phil Sheridan and his staff were stationed in New Orleans, and martial law declared. This and the "armed banditti" accusation roused the indignation of southerners; whilst the northern element in the city were equally hot-headed in asserting their views of the situation.

The Rotunda of the St. Charles Hotel, and other public places, were thronged by those who excitedly discussed the political crisis. Amusements occupied but little thought. The floating population constituted the main attendance at the theatres; and the effects of political engrossment became increasedly apparent in the auditorium, and in the depleted receipts of the box-office. Adelaide Neilson arrived to fulfil her engagement at the St. Charles Theatre, but failed to appear. She speedily discovered that the climate (or the political atmosphere) made her ill; and cancelling the date left for less turbulent localities. At the Varieties Theatre attractions which, under usual circumstances, would have insured crowded houses, failed to draw even moderately well.

In January, Owens played in Galveston, Texas; and would have been entirely satisfied with his engagement there except for the intense cold weather, caused by a "norther," which prevailed during the latter part of the time; however, (as he remarked) "it is well to have experience of every peculiarity of one's country." This was his first professional visit to Galveston. The place had much improved since he stopped there en route to another town some years before. At that time he inquired of the proprietor: "Why don't you have bells in the rooms, and carpets on the floors?" "Good gracious! sir," responded the landlord, "we dare not do it. We should lose our custom. Even now we have complaints and discontent about 'putting on too much style.'"

This position seemed to define the general patronage as comprising a rough element; which was further verified by some of the rules on the printed placards in the bedrooms: "The proprietor will not be responsible for pistols or bowie knives, except when placed in the office safe. If left under the pillow, they are at the owner's risk. Guests are requested to remove their boots and spurs before retiring," &c. The town had made rapid strides since then; but, though dearly loved by native born citizens, it was not alluring as a permanent abode, in the view taken by a casual visitor.

Its magnificent beach, pre-eminent for great width, inspired admiration, and its enterprise commanded approbation; but the climate and other drawbacks deteriorated from its attractiveness to strangers. Viewing matters in this light, Owens unintentionally gave serious offence to a representative citizen of Galveston. Approaching the comedian in an effusive way, he said: "Mr. Owens, you've played a splendid engagement here. We like you, sir; yes, sir, we like you. I was born in this city, and here have I lived; and I can safely say that no star ever made a greater impression than yourself." Owens affably acknowledged the compliment tendered; and the gentleman continued: "You ought to settle here—we will build you a theatre. Make this your home!"

Involuntarily came the exclamation, "God forbid!" thereby invoking stormy indignation, and voluble assertions of the superiority of "cultured Galveston" to New York and all other cities. The peroration being: "All the world may concede eminence to an actor, but his position is not established until he has passed the ordeal of a Galveston audience, and gained their approval." Without discussing this point Mr. Owens quelled the storm of words by disclaiming intention of giving offence; explaining that his home was so entirely satisfactory that any suggestion to change it was objectionable.

The New Orleans season terminated April 3d; and immediately afterwards Owens, supported by the company, played in some of the smaller southern towns, as well as the more prominent ones—closing in Charleston, S. C., latter part of May. During such a tour it is always a desideratum to book Saturday where one can be comfortably lodged for the Sunday rest. The second week closed in a town where the best hotel was located in the railroad station; but the noise of incoming and outgoing trains was patiently endured for the sake of good fare and attention received. An unusually competent waiter served us at table, and eagerly recalled his identity by the reminder: "I waited on you at de ole Saint

Charles, in N'Orleans, sah!"    Mr. Owens responded
pleasantly, and for the sake of manifesting interest, asked :
"Do you have many trains to cater for on Sunday?"
"Kateyfow! Kateyfow!" replied the perplexed darkey,
"I really don't think dat town is on dis line of road, sah!"
"Perhaps not," said Mr. Owens, drily; "but I am glad
I asked you, because now I know my premises."

Business all through the southern circuit was excellent.
The perfect rendition of the plays by a strong and well
rehearsed company, giving additional zest to the enjoyment of the performances.

While Owens was playing in Charleston, S. C., Mr.
John Chadwick strongly urged him to purchase the
Academy of Music in that city.   Mr. Chadwick had
been owner of the property for several years.   He paid a
large sum for it, and subsequently spent many thousands
in alterations and improvements upon the building.   He
still considered it a good investment, but having extensive business interests in St. Petersburg, Russia, where
his family resided, he was desirous to place all his capital
there, and permanently locate in Russia.   Strong managerial proclivities inclined Owens favorably to becoming
the owner of the Academy of Music; but in view of the
magnitude and importance of the purchase, he required
time for reflection.   Mr. Chadwick was well content with
the promise given, "to think the matter over."

Homeward bound from Charleston, the comedian met a party of New York friends who had been passing the winter in Florida. They intended stopping over in Richmond, and were urgent to have him tarry with them; to this he said "nay"—but invited the party to spend a day at Aigburth Vale when they reached Baltimore. The suggestion was received with pleasure. "I'll meet you in the city; let me know when you are due there. My address is 'Towsontown, Baltimore County.'" "Quizzing again," remarked one of the party, "I never heard of Towsontown—don't believe there is such a place!" "Nor I!" "Nor I!" ejaculated a chorus of voices. "Oh, what dense ignorance!" was the retort, with an assumed injured manner, "Towsontown is famous! so well known that my letters to Baltimore are sometimes directed: 'Baltimore, *near* Towsontown!'" This was hailed with a shout of laughter and the reiteration of: "Don't believe there is such a place."

The car door opened at this juncture and a gentleman entered, who happily was known to the entire party; at once Owens seized him, and in imploring accents, said: "Major P——, come to my rescue, and the vindication of my veracity and hospitable intentions. Is there or is there not a village known as Towsontown?" "Certainly there is," attested Major P——, "I have relatives there; and can personally vouch for its being a beautiful and delightful town. But why am I thus abruptly questioned?"

An explanation, amid much laughter and joking, ensued. The name of our post-office town was often a source of fun with Mr. Owens' friends. He frequently received letters, addressed: Towzytown, Puseytown, Tansytown, Tollytown, &c., &c.

During the month of June, some correspondence was held with Mr. Chadwick, relative to the purchase of the Academy of Music; and in July, they met in Charleston, for the final settlement of the business. Investigation of title, drawing up of papers and every detail of purchase was entrusted by Mr. Owens to Messrs. Buist & Buist, a firm whose fame as counsellors is only equalled by their brilliant record as scholars and social magnates. On July 25th, 1875, Mr. Owens, by making a large cash payment, became owner of the valuable property that thenceforth was known as "Owens' Academy of Music." Immediate arrangements were made to have it thoroughly equipped for the following season. Sparing no expense, the work progressed rapidly; and when the theatre was opened in September, it well merited the encomiums lavished upon it.

From that time it has continued to rank as one of the handsomest theatres between Baltimore and New Orleans. Ably managed, the best attractions have been offered to the public of Charleston; thus meriting the position conceded to it as a standard theatre. For two seasons Mr. Frank Arthur was resident business manager of

Owens' Academy of Music. He possessed considerable energy and ability, but he proved to be a very undesirable employé; and his connection with the Academy terminated disastrously for Mr. Owens, even though the theatrical engagements had been largely successful.

In the autumn of 1877, Mr. John M. Barron was installed as business manager, and by excellent judgment and close attention, he maintained the first-class record of the theatre. Mr. Barron was thorough in everything he undertook. Comfort and neatness behind the scenes was as carefully considered as the completeness and effectiveness of the stage and auditorium, or aught else subject to public comment only. Mr. Barron previously held a similar position, for several years, with Mr. J. H. McVicker, at his famous theatre in Chicago. He left there to resume his profession as leading man in a dramatic company. Mr. Barron had charge of Owens' Academy of Music for seven years. The severance of his connection with it arose from the fact that (in 1884) the owner desired to rest from playing, and was yet unwilling to remain entirely idle; therefore assumed personal management of his theatre.

Mr. Barron kept the Academy in exquisite order, and was thoroughly conversant with every business detail. He spoke fluently of its antecedents. The drop-curtain of the Academy was painted by Maynard Lewis, with close attention to the beautiful perspective and atmos-

OWENS' ACADEMY OF MUSIC,

CHARLESTON, S. C.

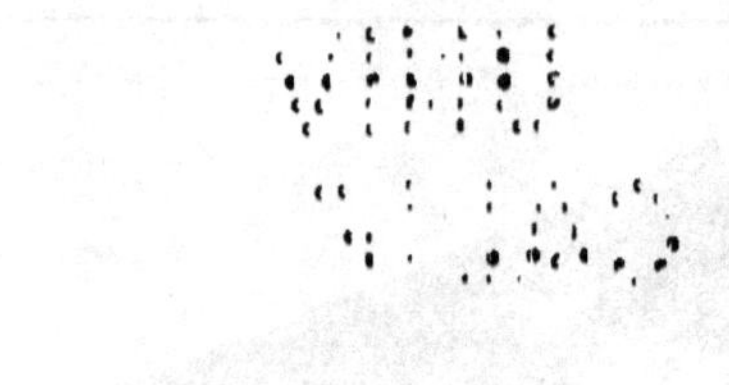

pheric effects, for which that great artist was famous. Mr. John Chadwick paid one thousand dollars for the curtain, delivered in New York, and received the worth of his money.

After returning from Charleston, Owens passed the summer at Aigburth Vale; prolonging his holiday for the October shooting. And to participate in this, he invited some friends who like himself were ardent sportsmen. It is hard to decide which was enjoyed most by the host and his guests—the outdoor excitement with guns and dogs, or the jovial chats at table and in smoking-room. From ten years of age, Mr. Owens had been fond of gunning and devoted to dogs. When a boy, a friend of his father often took him out gunning, and culminated his happiness by lending him an old gun. The day he was actually able to buy a new gun marked a proud moment in his life.

Owning fine hunting dogs was a passion with Mr. Owens, and the training of them a great pleasure. I recall a rather droll incident apropos of this taste. While playing in Grand Rapids, a gentleman of that city gave him a pointer puppy of pure pedigree. He appreciatively accepted the gift, thinking that the care of the dog would be satisfactory and brief, as the season was drawing to a close. The new acquisition was named after the town of his nativity, but abbreviated to " Raps." Mr. Owens' liking for him increased daily, and he was

16

eager to get home and train the puppy for a hunter. A few days before the close of the tour, an offer was received to play two weeks, further west, on good sharing terms or fifteen hundred dollars certainty per week. He remarked to me: " I'll have to think that over; I don't mind playing a fortnight longer, but what will I do about my dog? He ought to be at home and in training." "Postpone his education," I jokingly suggested, "if that is all interfering with signing the contract." The comic side of the objection seemed to strike him, and laughing heartily, he dictated a message accepting the offer.

All of Mr. Owens' dogs were fond of him, but some of them gave such wonderful evidences of affection and remembrance that it is with difficulty I refrain from mentioning a few of these remarkable proofs of canine intelligence. I am only restrained by the consciousness that dog stories, like fish stories, are apt to be incredulously received; and mine, though strictly true, might share the fate of those which are manufactured. Long before purchasing the farm Mr. Owens was a member of two ducking clubs on the Maryland shore. A capital shot, he cared more for the sport than he did for making a big game bag. The few days spared now and again from business were inspiriting, and the recreation healthful; except, indeed, when by tarrying too long in the blinds, malarial influence asserted its sway in the form of chills and fever.

I remember a severe attack of this kind, which was treated with medicine containing much quinine, "to be given in small quantities." Mr. Owens concluded to use (or rather *mis*-use) his own judgment by trebling the doses and lessening the interval between them; consequently, he became flighty during the night; being aware of the cause I was not alarmed, but quietly agreed to any assertion he made. In the morning, standing beside him, inquiring what I should order for his breakfast, he suddenly remarked: "There is a mouse in this bed." Deeming this a vagary from the lingering effects of quinine, I soothingly replied: "Yes, so there is." He indignantly exclaimed: "I am not delirious; I tell you there *is* a mouse in this bed." "Yes," continued I (intent on humoring the fancy), "there *was* a mouse there, but it has gone." Becoming quite angry, he said: "It is here now; I've caught it, and I'll convince you." Meeting my indulgent manner with a glance of triumphant merriment, he took my hand and placed in it—a live mouse!

With a shriek, I rushed to the middle of the floor and sprang on a chair. Mr. Owens laughed until he cried; and presently I joined in the hilarity. Later in the day he said to me: "The excitement about the mouse, and the hearty laugh it evoked, threw me into a perspiration, and broke my fever; and now I am quite well. 'Throw physic to the dogs'—but no; don't distress the good beasts with quinine."

November 15th, 1875, Mr. Owens began his next season, opening in "*Self*" at the National Theatre, Washington. The succeeding week was filled with the same bill at the Academy of Music, Baltimore; Mr. John T. Ford having engaged that theatre for six nights, his own Opera House having other attraction. At the latter house Owens appeared, November 29th, in "*Our Boys*," this being the first time he had essayed the part of *Perkyn Middlewick*. At once the character pleased him, and the jolly butterman never found a better representative.

His supporting cast had strong points; noticeably, Mrs. Jane Germon, as *Aunt Clarissa;* Harry Lee, as *Charles Middlewick;* M. Lannegan, as the *Baronet*, and Miss Eugenia Paul, as *Belinda*. The witty, crisp dialogue and the strong situations were fully developed, thus scoring a triumph for the play. Owens conceived *Middlewick* as a man of intelligence and sensitive feelings, with bluntness and vulgarity held in check on the right side of coarseness. His blunders in polite society (the inevitable sequence of ignorance) transpired without apparent acting. Wounded pride, anger and that tenderness which was a fibre of Middlewick's really great nature, were portrayed with touching effect. In this intermingled the shading of racy humor, inseparable from the naturalness of the good-hearted English parvenu.

"*Our Boys*" filled the week (and the theatre) satisfactorily; closing the engagement with John T. Ford,

MR. OWENS as PERKYN MIDDLEWICK

In "Our Boys."

December 4th. After which Mr. Owens remained at home through the Christmas holidays, enjoying the rest and the society of some invited friends—friends whose visits to Aigburth Vale were to them and their cordial host something to look forward to and remember as red letter records in the calendar. The humorous stories, jolly laughter and witty repartee lingered long in their memory.

Resuming professional work January 3d, 1876, at the Brooklyn Theatre, the opening bill was "*Our Boys.*" Shook and Palmer, managers, furnished an excellent supporting company, among whom were Miss Maud Harrison, Mrs. Farren, Claude Burroughs, Harry Murdoch and other favorites. The Brooklyn public unanimously pronounced the character of *Perkyn Middlewick* to be especially suited to Owens' style of eccentric comedy; and decided that it was destined to be associated with his name. This opinion became firmly established not only in Brooklyn, but wherever he played *Perkyn Middlewick.* The clear-cut personation bore evidence of infinite artistic ability and careful study.

"*Our Boys,*" in prosperous run, was intended to fill the fortnight in Brooklyn, but so many requests were made for "*Caleb Plummer*" that the manager, in compliance with general desire, announced "*Dot*" for the last two nights of the engagement. Said a gentleman, in Brooklyn, "Owens, whenever your name is heard, we begin to hunger for dear old Caleb. The thought of that part is inseparably linked with you, and it holds exalted rank among the perfect things which have been accomplished by dramatic art and impulse."

March 21st inaugurated an engagement at McVicker's Theatre, Chicago; thence to St. Louis for two weeks, and next, a like period at the Walnut Street Theatre, Philadelphia. The Centennial was in its incipiency during the latter engagement, and Mr. Owens anticipated recreation from the inspection of wonders from many lands. Unfortunately, the announcement of the opening of Centennial Hall was premature, and early respondents were disgusted by the commercial aspect of numerous packing boxes, with their contents hidden away; the din of hammers, and the incompleteness of the entire affair. However, after the summer vacation the disagreeableness of this experience was obliterated by spending several days of September on the Centennial grounds, and fully investigating its wonderful resources; and thus overcoming prejudices of the first unfavorable impressions, he came away fully imbued with patriotic pride in the "Great Centennial Fair."

A western tour inaugurated the season of 1876–77—the financial success making amends for trivial discomfort. It was not always possible to "see the players well bestowed" in the hotels where they must abide awhile. From the rural districts adjacent numbers flocked to enjoy "a good show;" and though less appreciative than the denizens of the town, they were loud in praise and applause. Many ludicrous happenings came within one's notice. I remember an inexperienced rustic entering the box-office with his dulcinea (both uncomfortably conscious of wearing best clothes); with a "good mornin'" to the ticket agent, he continued: "Me and Sarah wants to see the show to-night; can you keep good places for us if I pays for them now?" Giving an affirmative reply, the agent presented the box-sheet, asking: "What seats do you prefer?" "Isaiah, get the best," interrupted Sarah. Orchestra seats being suggested, they were marked off and paid for, but still the couple lingered; the young man nervously fingering the coupons which had been given him. "Can I do anything else for you?" blandly inquired the agent, as he noticed embarrassed whisperings passing between the two. "Well, yes," said Isaiah, "we've got to go round right smart number of places to-day, and we can't carry this big ticket with us handy (pointing to the box-sheet). Will you please take care of it for us till we come to-night?" With well-assumed gravity the agent assented; and furthermore promised that he would give instruction whereby the small tickets alone would secure their seats. Isaiah and Sarah, with many "thank 'ees," retired; much relieved that they were not obliged to "tote" that big ticket round town while they did their shopping.

The small western towns have one great charm; their vicinity abounds in lovely drives, and good horses can usually be had at the livery stables. The exhilarating autumn air adds additional enjoyment to this healthful recreation, and gives to a professional tour the flavor of a pleasure trip. In October Owens played at St. Louis, then Louisville, presenting *"Our Boys"* in addition to his usual plays. The piece took firm hold on the public, and the comedian was unanimously congratulated on his splendid characterization of *Perkyn Middlewick*. His method was as delightful as his personality, and each were of the highest order. He next filled two weeks at the Brooklyn Theatre; for the three concluding performances of which *"Our Boys"* was given with a strong cast, and this being a return engagement, its brilliancy was all the more complimentary to the star.

After six weeks embracing Elmira, Syracuse and other New York towns, supported by the stock company of "J. Clinton Hall," Owens began an engagement at the Opera House of that manager in Rochester, N. Y., December 4th. This was destined to be interrupted by a terrible calamity, the burning of the Brooklyn Theatre. Unlike the usual rumor of disaster, news of this conflagration was, at first, reported as mainly destructive to property. While reading of it, a thankful feeling arose in every heart that human life had not been sacrificed. Hence, the shock was all the greater, when the startling

[illegible]

[illegible]

[illegible]

Returning home, Owens signed a contract with John T. Ford for a southern tour; pursuing which, he arrived in Charleston, S. C., March 9th. This was his first appearance in that city since he had become owner of the Academy of Music. When, as *Perkyn Middlewick*, he stepped upon the stage, he was received with deafening applause and cheers. Modestly expecting a mildly cordial recognition, he was quite taken by surprise at such an overwhelming manifestation of the kindly feeling of the Charlestonians. Beyond his gratification was a deeper sense, which led him to understand that the enthusiasm indicated that he was now regarded as being identified with Charleston; to this he rendered responsive feeling, and increasingly regarded "the city by the sea" with a home feeling.

The plays given at this time were "*The Rivals*," "*Married Life*," "*Heir at Law*," "*Poor Gentleman*," together with sundry after-pieces, "*Happiest Day of My Life*," "*The Spitfire*," "*Solon Shingle*," &c. The entire engagement was an ovation of which the comedian had cause to feel proud. Savannah, Macon, Atlanta and other southern towns came in pleasant sequence; and turning northward again, the route lay through Tennessee, Indiana and Ohio. Owens having renewed his engagement with John T. Ford, played in Michigan and Canada; closing at Hamilton, Ontario, late in April.

However much one delights in the fascination of the theatrical profession and the plaudits of the public, a respite from excitement and mental and physical strain is ofttimes an agreeable change. The repose of home was a delightful transition from the bustling life of the previous eight months.

One of the most enjoyable events of this vacation was a visit to Lawrence Barrett, at Cohasset. The ten days passed at this ideal home were charming beyond expression. Mr. Barrett and his family contributed to the enjoyment of their guests in every way, without *seeming* effort of entertaining. Resources were endless—yachting, fishing, driving, and last, but not least, conversation. Thus condensing in our brief visit more genuine pleasure than could be reasonably expected in thrice the time. A strong attachment existed between Barrett and Owens, and it was of life-long duration.

In addidition to personal regard, Mr. Owens greatly admired Barrett's talent, indomitable energy and moral qualities. He considered the exalted position which this conscientious artist had attained, fairly won; and his untiring and liberal efforts to promote the advancement of the stage, something that entitled him to the admiration and gratitude of the entire theatrical profession. Whenever Barrett essayed a new part, the interest of Owens as to the result was second only to that of the tragedian. I remember when Barrett produced "*Pendragon*" in New York, he incidentally mentioned in a letter, his nervousness at the approaching event. We were at home then, and Mr. Owens consulting a New York paper, said: "It is to-night that Barrett brings out his new play. I thought it was to be later, and intended writing to him; however, I will telegraph." He then dictated to me (his amanuensis) the following message:

"LAWRENCE BARRETT, *New York City,*—

"May your success to-night be as instantaneous as the lightning which flashes the good wishes of your friends from Aigburth Vale.

"JOHN E. OWENS."

I kept a copy of this impromptu telegram, for it impressed me as being a concentration of earnest good wishes, unaffectedly expressed. Mr. Owens thought of his friends from the heart, and if he thought aloud, the words were just such as endeared him to them.

The season of 1877–78 began in Pittsburg with "*Barncastle and Reform,*" a five-act comedy by a Chicago journalist. If I remember right, his original authorship of this piece was in the form of a story which appeared in the Chicago *Inter-Ocean.* Afterwards he dramatized it, and sent the manuscript to Mr. Owens, requesting a careful reading, as the play had been written especially with a view of his creating the leading part.

"*Barncastle and Reform*" had good points, which decided Mr. Owens to give it a trial. The character he assumed, *Ebenezer Barncastle,* was that of an impecunious individual known in slang term as "a dead beat." On the basis of affected familiarity with distinguished people, he imposed upon the credulous by borrowing money, and in various ways utilizing them to his own advantage. Unscrupulous, untruthful, but with quick wit maintaining the semblance of a gentleman, this impostor was a strongly drawn character.

The action of the play transpires in Washington, and some of the situations gave Barncastle, in his pretended position of political influence, scope for humorous effects. Owens gave an admirable portrayal of this adventurer. The pomposity and brazen effrontery were clever bits of acting, and the Virginia dialect assumed, was perfect. Roars of laughter and much applause evinced the keen enjoyment of the audience. Owens carried the piece through, but even his efforts could not compass its success. Five acts of *"Barncastle and Reform"* proved tedious. Condensation and reconstruction might have saved it, but the author would not take this view of his play; so, after a further trial in Brooklyn and Louisville, the piece was shelved, much to the author's disappointment, who said to Owens: "I firmly believed that your superb conception and acting of the leading part of my play was destined to make me a famous dramatist,"—receiving the reply: "The comedy cannot survive unless a free use of the pruning knife vitalizes it."

Closing in Brooklyn October 13th, Owens indulged in a holiday, part of the time in New York and the remainder at home. November 26th he opened in *"Self"* at Robinson's Opera House, Cincinnati, Barney Macauley, manager. The weather was bitterly cold, and a chronic record of snow and sleet; and except Thanksgiving matinee and night the attendance was not large. Whether this was owing to the unpopularity of the theatre or the inclemency of the weather, he could not determine; but that the public were not alienated from him was clearly demonstrated by subsequent big engagements in Cincinnati—on a scale with all prior ones in that city.

Newark, Trenton and sundry New England towns were next visited with agreeable results; concluding in Fall River, January 5th. Two weeks later Mr. Owens, supported by his own company (which he had meanwhile organized), played return engagements in all of these towns; the repertoire being limited to *"Dot"* (Cricket on the Hearth) and *"Our Boys."* The dramatic corps was selected with a view to making a strong cast for these especial pieces. An admirable performance was given of both plays. *Caleb Plummer* and *Perkyn Middlewick* were most enthusiastically received. The former seemed in each city to meet with increased favor.

The character of Caleb was never obtruded, but Owens' personation of it was none the less a conspicuous creation. The return trip, including towns recently visited, terminated with six nights in Brooklyn. On March 11th he began an engagement of two weeks at the Standard

Theatre, New York; the brilliancy of which made an appropriate finale of a successful tour.

Since Owens' visit to California in 1869, he had frequently received offers to play in San Francisco; but other contracts prevented his acceptance. Having pleasant remembrance of California, he determined to make a brief visit there before settling at home for the summer. He therefore booked for a fortnight at the California Theatre, San Francisco, which was then under the management of John McCullough, opening April 1st, 1878, as " *Caleb Plummer.*" Admirable talent distinguished the stock company; but the performances of some of the characters was unmistakably mechanical. Apparently, they were unsuited to the ability or taste of those in the cast. The effect of the play as an entirety was marred; but no adverse surroundings could chill old Caleb's hold upon the emotions of the audience. This masterpiece of the artist, standing midway between the tragic and comic confines, evoked the unanimous tribute that, "of all his histrionic triumphs, *Caleb Plummer* was the crowning glory."

The second week was filled with "*Self*," "*Our Boys*" and "*Heir at Law.*" All were well received; but especial commendation was rendered to *Dr. Pangloss*, that personation being in sharp contrast with the other characters. This human encyclopedia of learning, with his apt quotations and the facial expression that gave them point, was a polished performance. The pedantic and obsequious tutor was depicted with subtlety of humor which delightfully developed his peculiarities. Said a gentleman who witnessed it for the first time, "I have seen Owens in many parts, but in none of them is he alike. There is a different voice in each play, a different face, a different laugh, a different pair of legs; in fact, a different man altogether." A few nights in Virginia City, Nev., one or two nights in Sacramento and the smaller towns completed this professional visit to the Occident. Afterwards six weeks of recreative travel were enjoyed.

Though fraught with enjoyment, this excursion lacked the keen zest of his first visit to California. The progressive spirit through the intervening decade, though valuable in consummating improvements, had in its rapid strides obliterated the attractive peculiarities of various sections of the state. Characteristics were merged into commonplacedness, and stage-coaches were only a reminiscence. Whilst this was a matter of self-gratulation to the residents, transient visitors selfishly regretted the change that rendered California less unique. But no march of improvement could alter the perfect climate and beautiful fairy-land of flowers. These, together with the grand scenery, formed an inexhaustible source of delight to Owens on his pleasure tour, for as such he regarded this visit to California; the professional engagement being an interlude of secondary importance.

MR. OWENS as DR. PANGLOSS, LL. D. and A.S.S.

In "The Heir at Law."

# CHAPTER XI.



RETURNING from California in July, the remainder
of the summer was passed at Aigburth Vale, in
home rest. Among the guests during this vacation was
a gentleman whom Mr. Owens had met some years previous in Indianapolis; subsequent visits to that city had
ripened the acquaintance into friendship. Their first
meeting had its origin in an absurd occurrence. The
Bates House long ago was noted for its execrable table
of unpalatable viands, uninvitingly served. Mr. Owens
by liberally feeing the waiter impressed upon him the
necessity of obtaining the best the hostelry afforded, and

17

above all things inveighed against the bad butter.  As a pleasant result of this exhortation we were served with delicious butter for two days, and then the rank article again appeared.  "Sam," said Mr. Owens, "I can't stand this axle-grease; you gave us good butter for two days, why can't you continue to do so?"  "Well, Massa, dat was de Captain's butter."  "What do you mean?"  "Just dis heah, de Captain live here all de time, and he buys butter for his own self.  I bin a just cuttin' off a bit for you; but now de Captain done locked it up, and I can't find whar he's hid it."

The serene simplicity of the darkey while making this explanation cannot be described; nor yet can Mr. Owens' consternation when informed that his waiter had been stealing butter for him.  Ascertaining "de Captain's" full name, he immediately sought him to make amends for having been the unconscious instigator of petty theft.  The interview was a success, if one might judge from the hearty laughter which pervaded it.  "De Captain" proved to be a whole-souled and companionable man.  During his visit to Aigburth Vale he insisted on his host telling the origin of their acquaintance to a party of gentlemen; supplementing the story with the jocose remark: "But I have had my revenge here, enjoying free run of the dairy; and many pleasant hours have come to me through peculation of 'de Captain's butter.'"

While narrating this, or any of Mr. Owens' stories, I instinctively wish that I could reproduce his manner of telling an occurrence. Clearly, in thought, I can see the twinkle of the eye, the merry twitching of the mobile, sensitive mouth, even before he began to speak. These, and the vivid character with which he invested the most trivial point, no description can convey. My hope is that those who knew him in private and professional life will, by what I write, grasp an outline, and recall something of his method and manner. My pen and ink picture must needs be far inferior to the reality. I strive to give the likeness from life; but my mental camera is, I fear, a diminutive Kodak in size and force.

I am conscious of the same inefficiency when I attempt to delineate the traits of Mr. Owens' character. They were naturally and unreservedly manifested to me in daily life, and increasedly evoked my admiration and reverence. But I hesitate even now to dilate upon his grand nature, knowing that he shrank from praise and the publicity of kindness extended to others. After he passed into the spirit-land, I received from many persons letters expressive of gratitude to *John Owens*, for helpful service rendered in time of need. I was cognizant of some of these kind acts; but the knowledge of many of them came to me thus, in letters from strangers.

The attributes of Mr. Owens' character were noble and well balanced. His celebrity as an actor and popularity as a man, he prized with honest pride; but fame and adulation did not evolve the slightest tendency to vanity. Unostentatious by nature, the greatest of his manifold theatrical successes never inspired conceit or self-assertion of manner, for he was as unpretentious then as when roaming over the farm and talking to the laborers about rural affairs. His judgment was clear, and attempted imposition was always manifest to him; but a generous disposition rendered it impossible for him to withhold kindness from those in trouble, even though their misconduct had brought them to dire straits. At the risk of his own interest, he extended a helping hand to save the reckless. Often it has been said to him: "Don't waste time and money on that fellow, he is incorrigible;" but disregarding this caution, he would quietly endeavor to give aid and incite a desire for the recovery of self-respect.

A strong case in point occurs to me. A young man made application for a position, unaware that Mr. Owens had the slightest knowledge of his antecedents. The request was met with the candid response: "I know your record. How can I trust a dishonest man?" "Try me, sir," said the suppliant; "I was only a boy at the time I went astray, and was sorely tempted. I have repented, and am striving to earn an honest livelihood." "I will give you chance to reclaim yourself," replied Mr. Owens. "You shall have the situation you ask for; and I put you on your honor to do justice to yourself and me." A few months afterwards, an old acquaintance said : " Why do you keep that man in your employ? He is a born thief, and an ingrate. I know it from personal experience." " I am aware of what he *has* been," was the reply, " but he is trying to live it down. It seems hard that a man's life should be blighted if he strives to retrieve the past." " Chimerical Owens !" laughingly ejaculated his friend. " You will find you are handling bad material for reform."

Unfortunately, the result was discouraging to philanthropy. The protegé, after two years of apparently irreproachable conduct, embezzled several thousand dollars, and decamped. Mr. Owens was indignant at this abuse of his confidence; but whilst the dishonesty and ingratitude led him to be more cautious, it did not prevent extension of kind acts subsequently, to others.

The season of 1878–79 began September 23d, at Ford's Opera House, Baltimore. "*Our Boys*" and other pronounced successes were admirably cast, and thoroughly enjoyed by large audiences. On Saturday, in compliance with much solicitation, "*The Serious Family*" was produced. Owens, as *Aminidab Sleek*, revived the delight of his admirers, who a score of years previous had applauded this performance, then in the zenith of popularity. To the young people it was new, and their appreciation of its merits was equally evident.

When it was underlined and in preparation, the comedian hurrying home from a lengthy rehearsal was hailed by an acquaintance (a physician of the city), who driving up to the sidewalk, said: "I want to tell you how glad I am that you are to play *Aminidab Sleek*. It was the first part I ever saw you in, and I shall delight in renewing the recollection of the old Museum days. Baltimore is your debtor for many happy hours. I tell you, Owens, you are a public benefactor." The recipient of this compliment made brief recognition, and endeavored to terminate the interview; but the M. D. exclaimed: "Hold on a bit. You have often brightened my life and dispelled depression by your matchless humor. I want to testify my gratitude by some special attention." "That is quite unnecessary," was the response. "But I insist. Jump in my carriage and drive with me to the Alms House, and I'll show you some remarkable small-pox cases out there; a most interesting study, I assure you."

Declining this invitation, Owens mildly suggested that "his dinner was more attractive to him just now, and less dangerous than medical investigation." "Ah, I'm sorry you won't go. I know you have scientific tendencies; and I'm really afraid you're not likely to have another opportunity of seeing such a variety of small-pox cases." With surprise and disappointment, the doctor drove off; leaving Owens quizzically amused at this idea of "complimentary attention."

The Baltimore engagement being ended, it was dupli-
cated in Washington under the same management. After
a few days' rest at home, his tour was resumed with a
supporting company organized by J. W. Norton and
T. Davey. Detroit was the initial town of this route;
from thence through Michigan, Minnesota, Wisconsin
and Iowa—arriving at Omaha, Neb., November 11th.
Three nights there, a week in St. Louis, and another in
Louisville, Ky., completed this engagement.

An incident in one of the Wisconsin towns where Mr.
Owens played, so truly reflects his chronic good humor
and dry wit, that I cannot refrain from mentioning it,
even though it was a trivial occurrence. The first-
class (?) hotel of the town was situated about a block from
the station. The morning we were leaving, Mr. Owens
remarked to me: "I am thankful we are turning our
faces towards Chicago and plenty, and so escaping starva-
tion in this house." Just as we had descended the long
flight of steps from the hotel, a cabman approached,
eagerly asking: "Have a cab, sir?" "What for?"
queried Mr. Owens, assuming a perplexed expression of
countenance. "Take you to the depot, sir." "Oh! no,
thank you," was the response in an innocently simple
manner. "We have only been two days in this hotel,
and are still strong enough to walk half a block—don't
we look so?" "Sir, I—" stammered the cabman.
"Now, that gentleman," confidentially, indicating a

feeble old man coming out of the door, "looks as if he had been a guest here for two or three weeks; he needs your cab, and will be glad to have it, I am sure. Good morning."

During the western tour, Owens gave a varied repertoire, and received the usual laudations. His artistic methods, mercurial temperament and inexhaustible fund of humor made each and every one of his personations acceptable. One of his admirers remarked: "It is not only that I like to have a good laugh; but I believe a town is better after a visit from Owens. His magnetic mirth smooths asperities, and puts life in a bright aspect." Concluding in Louisville, with *"A Double Knot,"* on Saturday, November 29th, the next date was Toronto, Canada, December 2d. Rather a long jump, even now; but then, travel had not been perfected to the degree of such rapid transit as at present. It still means a fatiguing journey when we say "the star closed in Louisville, Kentucky, on Saturday, and conducted rehearsal Monday morning in Toronto." *"The Heir at Law"* and *"Toodles"* inaugurated the week—*Dr. Pangloss* and *Timothy Toodles* winning golden opinions. Other comedies making a change of bill nightly, gave scope for versatility.

Returning home, after a brief rest he played a week in Baltimore, another in Philadelphia. January 20th, 1879, he opened at the Park Theatre, New York, in

fulfilment of a contract for one month with H. C. Abbey,
"*Dot*" (*Cricket on the Hearth*) the attraction. The
manager staged the play appropriately and beautifully,
new scenery having been especially and elaborately prepared. The original fairy prologue of this (Boucicault's)
adaptation was effectively presented. The stock company
included C. W. Couldock, Sara Stevens, Minnie Palmer,
Ada Gilman and other noted artists. The two first-
mentioned names will be recognized as connected with
"*Dot*" in its earliest triumphs.

Such auxiliaries with Owens' *Caleb Plummer*, rendered
the success of the piece a foregone conclusion. The old
toy-maker was, as heretofore, tenderly and perfectly
delineated. The eloquence of many pens, the loving
admiration of many hearts have rendered tribute to this
soulful and artistic picture far in excess of my power
of description. "*Victims*" and "*Solon Shingle*" were given
towards the close of this engagement, with the full quota
of rollicking merriment of *Butterby*, and quaint eccentricity of *Solon Shingle*. The entire month was a record
of brilliant performances, largely appreciated. A week
in Brooklyn concluded the comedian's season of 1878–79.

While in New York, Mr. Owens received an offer to
play in Australia for six months, commencing the ensuing
summer. Taking this offer into consideration, the terms,
&c., inclined him to give a favorable reply; but, before
signing the contract, circumstances transpired which

caused him to alter his views. He therefore declined the offer for the time specified; but by no means relinquished the idea of playing in Australia. The usual happy summer vacation began, but was pervaded with an unsettled feeling, as correspondence, relative to the Australian tour, continued, and decision might at any time be made to start on the journey.

An interlude occurred in July, when some of the leading citizens of Baltimore interested themselves to get up a benefit for a charitable and patriotic cause; the attraction to be the (then craze) comic opera of Pinafore; provided Mr. Owens would be the star of the evening, as *Sir Joseph Porter.* When the request was made of the comedian, he laughingly replied: "Like Fusbus, 'I haven't got a singing face'—Opera is not in my line." "Ah! but your voice is good, and your name a sure drawing card. Remember this is for charity, and the musical critics will not be ultra exacting." "All right, I am ready to help the cause; I will play Sir Joseph, and as to the musical score—do the best I can with it." July 11th, was the date appointed for the benefit.

Mr. Owens studied the character thoroughly, but had only two rehearsals. The Academy of Music was densely packed by an audience in holiday mood; but I doubt if they enjoyed the Opera more than Mr. Owens did. From the first furore in New York, when Pinafore was played at five theatres simultaneously, he was enthused with its satirical humor. He played Sir Joseph Porter with a keen relish, and from his tremendous reception until the fall of the curtain, the entire house was en rapport with him, taking all the points instantaneously. He rendered the music fairly well; not of course on the plane of the perfect vocalization of Miss Annis Montague, Mrs. C. Richings Bernard, and others of professed lyric ability, in the cast. The receipts of the entertainment, yielded two thousand dollars to the charity for which it was given.

In August, Mr. Owens decided to go to Australia, and also to combine with that expedition a pleasure trip around the world. Preparations at once began, to put business and home affairs in such shape as to insure their smooth running during our absence; the length of which was intended to be one or two years. A state-room was engaged in the steamer to sail from San Francisco, September 29th, and arrangements for our departure were rapidly completed. September 19th, 1879, we left Baltimore; everything was auspicious for the undertaking. Mr. Owens seemed even brighter in spirits than his usual cheery mood.

Arriving at Sacramento, two telegrams were delivered to him—offers to play in San Francisco en route. Negative replies were returned. At another station, three hours later, reiterated importunities were wired him, meeting the same response. Two managers awaited his arrival at Oakland, and accompanied him to 'Frisco, but he declined to discuss their propositions; merely stating that "in two days he should start for Australia, and at present, he was weary with a long railroad journey," and so dismissing the matter, proceeded to the Palace Hotel for a comfortable rest.

In the evening, the subject was urgently renewed; and finally, Mr. Owens consented to remain over, if his state-room could be exchanged for one in the steamer sailing a month later. Unfortunately, this was arranged, and subsequent developments merged the month's postponement of the Australian voyage into its abandonment. Owens began an engagement at the Standard Theatre, San Francisco, October 6th, and played his usual round of characters. He also produced the comedy of "*Dr. Clyde*," for which he had secured rights from the author, Sidney Rosenfeld; and afterwards he purchased the play for his sole ownership.

The comedy made a favorable impression, and the part of *Higgins* enacted by Owens, was pronounced a great creation. His conception of the Doctor's factotum (or office-boy) ever eager to display (fancied) medical knowledge, was full of humor and neat points. It was replete with good situations; and in managing a ludicrous position, he was without a rival. So much was conveyed by a glance of the eye, quaintness of delivery, and yet with repose of manner that accentuated the naturalness of the mirth-inspiring words.

Soon after Mr. Owens arrived in San Francisco, efforts were made to interest him in a gold mine (already incorporated) which was situated in Arizona. Not being of a speculative disposition, he at first gave but little attention to the subject; but gradually became sufficiently interested to make investigation. Appearances indicated to him, and to those who were more experienced in such matters, that the investment was desirable. But not content to rest on evidence of reliable testimony and specimen ore, he went to Arizona, accompanied by two friends who were celebrated mining experts. The trio thoroughly inspected the mine, and found that it equalled the representation given of it.

Mr. Owens personally chipped off several large pieces of the ore, and immediately sealed them up in a box, which remained in his posession until he placed it on the assayer's table in San Francisco. These specimens being tested, ranked with the richest ore ever assayed in California. On this encouraging basis, he purchased stock, and finally became owner of two-thirds of the mine.

The Australian engagement and tour around the world was indefinitely postponed, and a temporary residence in San Francisco substituted, with a view of exercising a personal supervision to expedite development of the mine. For awhile everything indicated fulfilment of sanguine hopes; but adverse fate brought a change. Delay in the arrival of the mill and machinery at the mine, culpable neglect of employés, and other unforeseen circumstances gradually involved the enterprise. In fact, so great were the complications that Mr. Owens concluded to withdraw from the business, being unwilling to lose further time and money in pursuing the speculation.

Even while thus deciding, he continued in the belief that a fortune could be realized from the mine, if ample means were judiciously rendered for its development. His opinion proved to be correct four years later, when a syndicate of wealthy capitalists put the mine in running order, and realized from it millions annually.

I have spoken at length on this subject that I may remove an impression resting with some persons that Mr. Owens was duped by salted ore and mining sharpers. He was by far too level-headed to have been thus victimized. Though he never profited by his investment, much satisfaction accrues from the fact that his judgment of its value was corroborated by the golden harvest reaped by others.

In the spring of 1881 Owens returned east. I have omitted to say that, during the winter of that year, he filled another theatrical engagement at the Standard Theatre, San Francisco, the salient feature of which was the production of a new comedy, "*That Man from Cattaraugus.*" This play, from the German of "The Cattle Dealer of Upper Austria," was translated and adapted for Mr. Owens by a prominent member of the San Francisco press. The star part was that of the cattle dealer, an honest, ingenuous, warm-hearted countryman, of vigorous intellect and marked business methods. An old man, but diametrically opposite to garrulous *Solon Shingle*, or tender, self-effacing *Caleb Plummer*. The character was replete with bluff humor, and yet had its affectionate side. In light and shade it was an exquisite creation; and general opinion gave the verdict that "it fitted Owens like a glove," and was to him another leaf of laurel.

The comedy entire, made a hit, necessitating the use of that agreeable notice—"Standing room only." The supporting cast was excellent, especial praise being awarded to Mr. Joseph Arthur, who as *Stockman*, the broker, achieved prominence for the individuality of character with which a small, but strong, part was invested.

In February, Owens commenced an engagement in Portland, Oregon; "*That Man from Cattaraugus*," was the opening bill. An immense and enthusiastic audience greeted the star on his first appearance, and never was an actor more generously, courteously, and warmly welcomed. The new comedy made a sensation; "*Dr. Clyde*," "*Self*," "*Our Boys*," and other plays followed, and were applauded to the echo. These personations marked a series of triumphs. Every available seat was engaged long in advance. The excitement and enthusiasm was unparalleled in the record of dramatic engagements in Portland. The fame thereof, spread to the neighboring towns. Managers near by came to arrange dates with Owens for their theatres, and from more distant places telegrams and letters arrived proposing terms.

A tour was suggested onward to British Columbia, and returning by a different route. This would have proved lucrative and also afforded delightful travel; but Mr. Owens did not feel free to accept, as he had, before leaving San Francisco, signed contract with C. R. Gardner to appear at the Fifth Avenue Theatre, New York, in March. He, however, telegraphed requesting a postponement of his New York engagement, but was refused; being strictly honorable, it never occurred to him to cancel, and thus he sacrificed thousands of dollars to keep faith where honor was non-responsive.

The Portland engagement closed on the 10th of February; its financial results were great, and the pleasant visit to Oregon, fraught with social reminiscence ever prized. Returning to San Francisco, Mr. Owens remained there a few days, and then proceeded to meet his New York date. "*That Man from Cattaraugus*" was the piece for which he was booked.

Of this New York episode I have little to say. Many details arise in my memory, but I refrain from putting them into words. Difficulties at once began in regard to the company which Mr. Gardner had engaged, and also about other matters for which he was responsible, thus engendering his animosity. A play, which elsewhere had packed theatres and turned people away, was here a failure.

After three weeks in New York, Mr. Owens played in the adjacent towns; next in Philadelphia, where he received a cordial welcome; thence to Baltimore. The ovation on his return home, after an absence of eighteen months, was simply indescribable. His reception lasted for several minutes, and was mingled with cheers. This seemed likely to be of indefinite duration, had he not broken it up by insisting on speaking the first lines of his part. He afterwards said to me: "If I had permitted my reception to keep on a second longer I should have been unable to speak, I was so deeply touched by this welcome home."

At the fall of the curtain the applause was uproariously renewed, and continued until Owens appeared and spoke a few words of heartfelt appreciation for the cordial good will manifested towards him. "*That Man from Catta-raugus*" was the opening bill, and at once became a favorite. "*Dr. Clyde*" and some of the old pieces filled the week, which as an entirety was marked with brilliant éclat. The summer at home was ideal in happiness and restful enjoyment. Old friends gathered around us at Aigburth Vale, and content reigned supreme.

On the 29th of August Mr. Owens began the season of 1881–82, at Ford's Opera House, Baltimore; thence a southern tour of many cities, extending to Pensacola,

18

Florida. After leaving Baltimore the September weather
was unusually warm, and unfortunately the time was
filled in theatres where the dressing-rooms were small.
In one situated on the ground floor, Mr. Owens requested
me to leave the shutters partially open, thinking he was
secluded from observation. But he quickly perceived
male and female figures sitting on a fence, gazing into the
room. Indignantly closing the shutters, he remarked :
" To be stifled seems inevitable ; " and calling the janitor,
directed him to " order those people to go away," wrath-
fully adding : " It is the most impertinently low-bred
conduct I ever saw—bad enough for men and boys, but
even worse for women." " Well, now, see here, Mr.
Owens," remonstrated the janitor, " I don't want you to
say that, 'cause them ladies is some of the first ladies in
Norfolk."

# CHAPTER XII.



THE southern tour of 1881 was a counterpart of many previous ones in the same localities, where Owens was ever a superlative favorite. No adverse comment occurred except at Talladega, Ala., where he was booked for the first time. After inspecting the so-called theatre, he declined to play; assuring the owner of the building that "he never played in halls, destitute of scenery, gas, and other indispensable appliances for theatrical performances;" but, at the same time signified his willingness to pay the rent and other expenses that had been agreed upon.

This arrangement was entirely satisfactory to the proprietor, but some of the inhabitants were not so easily propitiated; their disappointment at not seeing "*Solon Shingle*" merged into indignation, and they threateningly asserted that "Owens would be sorry for the day he put such an insult on Talladega—he'd rue it, that he would! When shows was printed in papers, and their picters stuck up on walls, the people had a right to them—perhaps the law might have something to say, &c." These impulsive words were probably the safety valve for chagrin, and did not arise from ill feeling to the star, as most of the speakers thereof, went on the train next day to see him play in Selma. An extension of this engagement with Mr. John T. Ford included a return trip through Tennessee, Ohio, and other states, and terminated November 26th, 1881.

The following month was passed at home, and the Christmas season fully enjoyed. During this interval he organized a company for four weeks' travel through the Pennsylvania towns. An inefficient business agent and the illness of the stage manager trebled Mr. Owens' labors. At the end of the month he felt the effect of these combined duties to have been severely exhausting in mental and physical stress; and therefore determined to rest for the remainder of the season.

A little while after his return home, some theatrical friends, from New York, said to him: "Owens, that play of "*Esmeralda*," now on the Madison Square Theatre boards, has an old man in it who would be something wonderful in your hands. You ought to secure the right of that play outside of New York." Later on others said to him: "You are the man for that part;" and the same suggestion met him in sundry newspaper articles. He concluded to run on to New York and see the piece.

He was by no means enthused with the play of "*Esmeralda*" nor with *Elbert Rogers*, but thought he could make the latter prominent. He regarded it as a desirable acquisition in the light of an easy part that would be a restful change from his usual comedy characters and double bills. The proposition to purchase rights for "*Esmeralda*" was refused by the management; but they eulogistically descanted upon Mr. Owens' adaptability for the part, and made him an offer to join the company and play *Elbert Rogers* in New York. This was promptly declined; but after considerable discussion he consented to reflect upon the matter.

The Madison Square Theatre was conducted with a stock company which included several stars. Mr. Owens, weary with the fatigue and responsibility of managing, finally concluded to accept the desirable terms submitted to him, and signed a contract for the remainder of the season. He began in February, making an immense hit as *Elbert Rogers*. So thorough an artist could not fail to turn any character into something quaint, beautiful or mirthful, and bring it into prominence by his assumption of it. The popularity his personation of Elbert Rogers attained, grew and strengthened with the public.

His engagement at the Madison Square Theatre was pleasant and non-laborious. Being within easy access of home, sundry happy Sundays were passed there; ofttimes accompanied by a party of friends, who were his guests from the time they left New York until their return to that city. Mr. Owens' hospitality was lavish, and to the minutest detail he delicately and thoroughly attended to the enjoyment of his guests. "A prince of good fellows" in social life at large, he was also a perfect host at home. His position at the Madison Square, being free from care, gave him much leisure, as well as relieving the strain of hard work which heretofore had devolved upon him. He was so comfortably situated that he yielded to the pleading of the management, and continued another season with the company.

This was a year of travel, but not of fatigue. The route was through the usual cities of Owens' former tours, and everywhere he was greeted with enthusiasm. Perhaps in New Orleans the greatest ovation was rendered to him, being manifested, not only by applause and cheers at the theatre, but by myriads of friends in private life, eagerly competing who should shower the most attention upon him. Though he was deeply touched

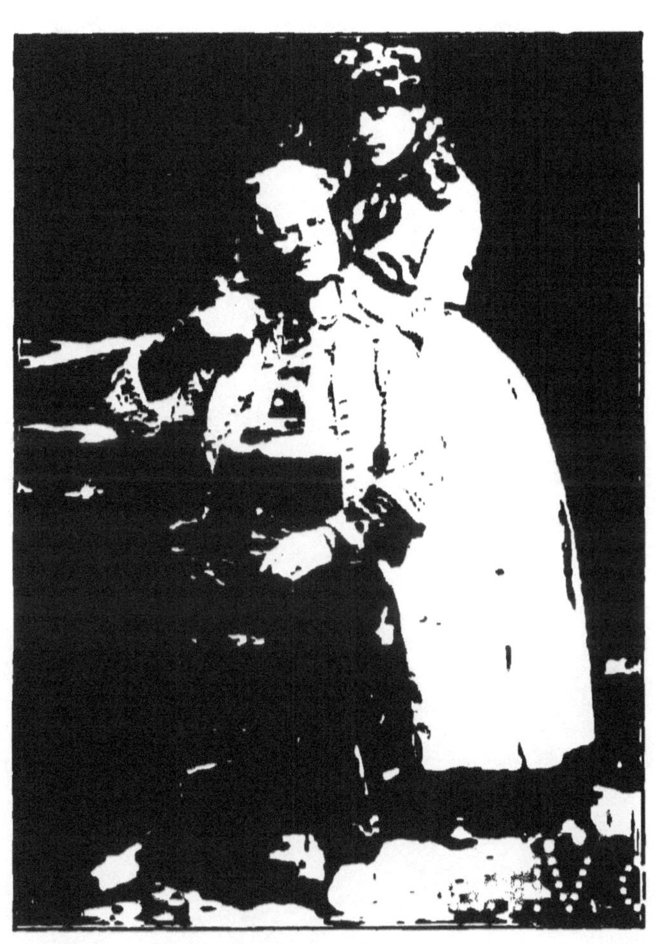

MR. OWENS as ELBERT ROGERS

In "Esmeralda."

by the evidence of such enduring attachment, he persistently declined feasting and fêtes, and enjoyed the society of his friends in a quiet way.

The daily offering of many flowers, which brightened his rooms in the hotel, also spoke of old associations, and was pleasant incense to the heart, and lovely to the sight. New Orleans people thought of Mr. Owens as their own comedian. Many of his masterpieces were perfected there, during his former years of management of the "Varieties." At that time his genial humor, sparkling wit, and noble nature, drew to him a large circle of friends. Essentially cordial, he was the centre of an extensive and intelligent coterie, and time intensified the impression then made; this was evinced by the spontaneous welcome now extended to him.

He visited all the haunts of former days—the "Chalmette," "Pickwick," and other clubs; there enjoying much pleasant intercourse with friends of yore. The Pickwick Club sent an exquisitely beautiful stand of flowers of immense size, symbolically arranged; accompanying this testimonial was the following note:

PICKWICK CLUB, NEW ORLEANS, *December* 14th, 1882.

"JOHN E. OWENS, ESQ.:

"*Dear Sir,*—We desire to show you how kindly we appreciate your presence here among your old friends, who have witnessed your great triumphs in characters, which have been living ideals, through your eminent ability as an actor.

"We recognize the same powers now exhibited in your personation of Elbert Rogers, and we are glad that your heart is as warm, your eye as bright, and your wit as keen as in the days of 'Auld Lang Syne.'

"With the best wishes of all your old friends composing this Club,

"I am yours very truly,

"JAMES G. CLARK,

*President.*"

A copy of the reply to this note has been furnished me by a prominent member of the "Pickwick Club." For this favor, I am indebted to Mr. T. L. Bayne, of New Orleans, a renowned lawyer and courtly gentleman, whom Mr. Owens regarded with esteem and friendship. I subjoin the letter, and am strongly tempted to give Mr. Bayne's eloquent lines which accompanied it.

"ST. CHARLES HOTEL, NEW ORLEANS, *December* 15th, 1882.

"JAMES G. CLARK, ESQ.:

"*Dear Sir*,—How shall I express my thanks for the kind note and beautiful flowers, conveying as they do a cordial welcome from the 'Pickwick Club,' and the remembrance of 'Auld Lang Syne.'

"Your assurances of esteem and friendship, and your good opinion of me, both personally and professionally, touch my heart, and are very precious to me.

"I will not attempt to put in words how deeply I feel your kindness; but as long as I live, I will ever remember my warm-hearted friends of the 'Pickwick Club.'

"Hoping that there are many bright days of social intercourse for us in the future,

"I am, regardfully yours,

"JOHN E. OWENS."

MR. OWENS as HEZEKIAH PERKINS

In "Cooke's Corners."—Act 1.

This visit to New Orleans was not only charming at the time, but remained so as a treasure of memory. It was, alas! a final adieu to that city and its people.

The "*Esmeralda*" season concluded June 10th, at Rockville, Ind. Mr. Owens deferred his return home, proceeding at once, with his wife, to Hot Springs, Arkansas, that she might be relieved from the suffering of rheumatism. The stay at these springs was prolonged until August, thus rendering the summer at home very brief. Mr. Owens had positively declined urgent persuasion to remain another season with the "*Esmeralda*" company; and no inducement offered could shake his determination. The separation transpired amicably; and though much disappointment was expressed by the management, friendly feeling existed ever afterwards.

Some months previous, a new play had been submitted to Mr. Owens, but did not entirely meet his approval. Later on the author altered the piece, and solicited a second reading. An appointment was made, and the play had another hearing. After suggesting some further improvements to which the author acceded, he consented to personate the leading part. This with the understanding that a first-class supporting company was to be provided, and all details of business attended to by the manager; for in that capacity the author purposed to act. In this way it was agreed that the star should be entirely relieved of every responsibility save that of playing.

Rehearsals began in November, and the comedy of
"*Cooke's Corners*" was produced first at Wilmington,
Del., thence, Newark, and through the state of New
York. The play was unsatisfactory when staged; the
effect did not equal expectation made from reading the
manuscript; and the company falling far short of the
"first-class" standard promised by the manager. Liking
the part of *Hezekiah Perkins*, and reflecting that the play
could be built up and the company strengthened, Mr.
Owens continued to fulfil his engagement. All of this
might have been accomplished in the hands of a competent manager; but weakness and inexperience were
incapable of carrying out the ideas suggested.

The inevitable result was, that though Owens received
highest commendation for his creation of "*Hezekiah Perkins*," he declined to be burdened with the weight of
incompetency attending "*Cooke's Corners;*" therefore,
shelved the piece and returned to his former repertoire.
With a reorganized company, he appeared at the Arch
Street Theatre, Philadelphia, in "*Everybody's Friend*,"
and "*Solon Shingle*," playing with his accustomed vim
to a responsive house. Two nights in New Brunswick,
and four in Providence filled the ensuing week.

At the matinée Mr. Owens was sick, but no evidence
thereof was apparent to the audience; nor at night, when
the plays went off gloriously. After performance he
continued very sick, but decided to leave for New York

MR. OWENS as HEZEKIAH PERKINS

In "Cooke's Corners."— Act 2.

by the midnight train, that he might have a full day's rest on Sunday before commencing in Harlem, which was the next booking. Arriving at the Sturtevant House early Sunday morning, we were comfortably located in the rooms we had occupied the previous winter; thus adding a home feeling to a restful one. Mr. Owens refused to see a physician until he had tried repose, and simple remedies for relief. After a quiet sleep of several hours he felt much better, and so continued through the day; retiring at night in the full belief that his indisposition was rapidly vanishing. But towards morning he grew ill, and a hemorrhage from the stomach supervened. Dr. Quackenboss, who was immediately summoned, greatly lessened my anxiety by the assurance, that this, in all probability, would relieve the liver and avert congestion. He strictly interdicted resumption of professional engagements; impressively dwelling upon the necessity of perfect rest for a fortnight, and the danger of exertion at this critical juncture.

Mr. Owens acquiesced in the mandate, but later in the day suggested the possibility of playing a portion of the week. I implored him not to think of doing so; but on Tuesday he decided to fill the remaining nights of the Harlem booking, saying to me: "I never broke faith with the public, and will keep that record, if I can." With superhuman effort he went through the performance, and under excitement played "*Major De-Boots*" and "*Solon Shingle*" with his usual brilliant humor and perfection in those personations, but the reaction next day was severe.  Dr. Quackenboss was indignant, and alarmed at Mr. Owens' persistence; but he used every means to build up his strength in response to the appeal—"Get me through this week, and I will be an obedient patient; go home and rest for a month."

The Harlem Theatre was well filled each night, and on Saturday there was an overflowing house; as the shouts of laughter penetrated the dressing-room, they jarred upon me, in my great distress lest my husband should suffer from the exertion he was making.  At the fall of the curtain he responded to a vociferous call, but merely bowed in acknowledgment of the compliment; some friends who were among the audience called to see us next day, and were surprised to find Mr. Owens ill. They said it was the general comment as the audience dispersed—"Owens is in fine spirits, he never played that bill better."  This was his last theatrical appearance; and it was "made in a golden set," as brilliant as the noontide of his fame.

His place in the drama, is not likely to be filled. Seldom does an actor possess his power to run the entire gamut of the passions, combining with it the richness and variety of intonations to vividly convey every emotion. · Thoroughly in love with his art, experience gave him a deeper insight into the philosophy of humor; and time, mellowing mirth, intensified its raciness.

Mr. Owens had booked for a season to continue until May; he cancelled two weeks of it, pending his expected recuperation. After his return home, though acute illness lessened, chronic liver trouble continued, and rendered the renewal of professional work impossible. In a few months he had improved very much; and the baths and water of White Sulphur Springs, Va., (where he passed the summer) completed his restoration to health. Returning home in September, he concluded to decline all offers for the ensuing theatrical season, having decided to fulfil an intention he had deferred from year to year—that of personally managing his own theatre in Charleston.

This arrangement enabled him to spend the winter in a southern climate, and combine pleasurable restfulness with moderate occupation. He engaged Will. T. Keogh, a resident of Charleston, as assistant manager. Mr. Keogh had been connected with the Academy of Music when a mere lad, being nightly employed as a distributer of programmes. After his school days finished, he was given a situation in the box-office, while Mr. John M. Barron was business manager. Energetic, industrious, and quick of apprehension, he attracted Mr. Owens' favorable attention; but no promotion being possible at that time, young Keogh associated himself with the " Hess Opera Co." for advance work.   Remaining in that capacity for two seasons, he returned to the Academy of Music in 1884—being selected from many applicants for the position of assistant manager; Mr. Owens discerningly foreseeing that Keogh's aptness and conscientiousness would render justice to the duties required, and stand him in good stead for the lack of experience in one so young.

The result fully justified this confidence.   Under Mr. Owens' guidance Will. Keogh developed intelligent executive ability, which formed the basis for excellent business habits.   This pleased Mr. Owens; and with his approbation was combined personal esteem and regard for his protégé, who warmly reciprocated the sentiment.   The position of "Assistant Manager" continued to be filled by Mr. Keogh during Mr. Owens' lifetime; after which he became lessee of "Owens' Academy of Music," and has ably maintained its record as a first-class theatre.

The theatrical season 1884-85 of the Academy, with the owner at the helm, was a magnificent success; unequalled in financial and other respects.   The delightful climate of Charleston admirably suited Mr. Owens; and the charming winter and spring, with pleasant associations, were so attractive that we lingered there until late in May.   The weather grew very warm, and it was decided that our return should be by steamer, via New York; stopping over in the latter city a few days before settling at home for the summer.

A sea voyage had ever been enjoyable and invigorating; but on this occasion an attack of dyspepsia interfered with the usual experience, and for the first time in Mr. Owens' life he was sea-sick. So extremely was he depleted that, on arriving in New York, he felt unequal to the few days' recreation he had planned. Resting a day, he proceeded home; but deeming his indisposition transient, did not call in medical aid. Probably he would have done so, had our family physician, Dr. T. H. Wingfield, been alive; but that dear friend had passed into the spirit-land some months before our return. Mr. Owens mourned this loss of a personal friend, and felt the need of his professional skill as sickness continued. At length an acquaintance persuaded him to consult a new physician, represented to be a specialist in dyspepsia. This step proved to be a fatal mistake; for under the treatment of this alleged proficient, he gradually grew worse, until he became alarmingly ill.

Finally the case was pronounced to be "internal cancer—incurable." Having faith in the physician, his decision was believed by me, and received as a death knell. After four months of this agonizing delusion, something occurred which caused me to doubt the infallibility of the attending M. D. I requested a consultation, and selected Dr. W. C. Van Bibber. The result was total annihilation of the cancer diagnosis. Like the glory of sudden sunshine and warmth breaking through total darkness came Dr. Van Bibber's assurance that "Mr. Owens' illness was curable." Not the slightest symptom of cancer existed. Liver and stomach trouble had been the cause of sickness; this was the true diagnosis, and subsequently substantiated.

Mr. Owens' strength had been seriously impaired by four months' lavish administration of anæsthetics; but his iron constitution enabled him to survive this treatment, which would have proved fatal to a less vigorous man. Under the care of Dr. W. C. Van Bibber, he steadily improved, and by the spring was quite well. A happy summer was passed at Aigburth Vale, and the dreadful past relegated to oblivion, or only remembered as a horrid nightmare, where suffering contrasted darkly with the present brightness of thankful hearts.

The glory of the summer was on the wane. Mr. Owens having received propositions to play during the coming season, was considering the same, when all business engagements were set aside by the tidings of the earthquake in Charleston; it was a shock in every sense of the word, involving monetary loss in addition to solicitude for friends in Charleston. As soon as access was attainable to the city, he proceeded there to make personal inspection. His impressions were given in the following telegram which I received from him: "Calamity more serious than pen or picture has described. No words can depict the desolation."

At once he set about having the Academy of Music repaired. Its massive strength had rendered it better able to meet the shock than many of the other public buildings; but still it was greatly defaced. The repairs, frescoing, &c., were immediately put in hand; and regardless of expense the theatre was speedily restored to its condition of safety and beauty. The early bookings could not be met; but before the renovation was completely finished, the season began, and Mr. Owens arranged to have the receipts of the first entertainment given to the earthquake sufferers. He had previously offered the ball-room (a portion of the Academy that was uninjured) as a hospital for the disabled, or a refuge for the houseless otherwise unprovided for.

After his return home, he estimated the pecuniary involvement that had accrued from the earthquake; and then, to the utmost dollar he could spare, sent a check to Mayor Courtenay for the "earthquake fund," with a few lines expressive of sympathy, and regretting that his own losses from the calamity prevented the sum being as large as his inclination dictated. In reply came this graceful acknowledgment from Mayor Courtenay:

"CITY OF CHARLESTON,
"EXECUTIVE DEPARTMENT, *October* 1, 1886.

"DEAR MR. OWENS,—

"There is before me, as I write, a little slip of paper, with numerals and an autograph which will convert it into currency;

19

and this will ultimately tighten the roof, strengthen the foundation and restore to comfortable use some needy sufferer's home wrecked by the earthquake. This is your offering, which is accepted with thanks and appreciation.

"In an extensive reading, I have this distinctive recollection—that, be it fire or pestilence, or the elements that causes destruction to life and property; the profession to which you belong always lead in the offerings of kindness and charity, and old ocean does not bound their benefactions. In many places dramatic entertainments have been most successfully given, and large sums realized for the sufferings caused by our mysterious calamity. The gifted Irving signals from London, and the renowned Booth sends his check to a stricken family here.

"And so the record runs through all the years, and so it will continue to be made in the years to come; and with it too we have received something above currency value—it is the felt pulsations of warm hearts, which cheers and strengthens all.

"In accepting your offering, our people will at once recognize the kindly voice and the goodness of heart of "*Farmer Shingle*," and will wish that all good fortune attend him in life.

"Very truly yours,

"WILLIAM A. COURTENAY,

"*Mayor*.

"JOHN E. OWENS, ESQ."

The visit to Charleston, with its inevitable excitement and agitation, the over-exertion of every hour of his stay there, had injurious effect upon Mr. Owens' health. When, months before, Dr. Van Bibber rescued him from imminent peril, an unusually strong constitution enabled him to rally, and respond to medical skill; but the effects of treatment arising from the former mistaken diagnosis, had impaired the organs of life, and rendered him less resistant to fatigue and harassment. As a sequence, he was extremely ill in October. Strong will power aided him to overcome this attack, and be up and about assuming direction of daily matters.

Whatever sickness afflicted Mr. Owens, was borne, not only heroically, but with a gentle patience perfectly marvellous. His own suffering was never so hard for him to bear, as the thought of the anguish it caused. A noble and unselfish nature was evinced in this, as well as every other phase of his life. Recuperating from illness, he took up the various threads of business, and the propositions for professional engagements were again under consideration. Once more we were encouraged to believe that he had thoroughly and firmly regained his health. This blessed experience of happiness soon vanished.

On the morning of December 4th, 1886, he arose early, in the happiest mood, and after breakfast took a walk about the farm, preparatory to going to the city. The extreme coldness of the weather decided him to defer his drive until midday. Like a thunder-clap in a clear sky came a terrible change. A sudden hemorrhage from the stomach occurred. For many hours life was in jeopardy ; but gradually improvement gave hope—almost certainty of recovery.

Thus the symptoms continued until the morning of the 7th inst., when he fell into a calm sleep which it was thought would refresh him. From that sleep he never awoke. His spirit passed into the other land, leaving its bright reflex on the tranquil and smiling face of its earthly tabernacle.

Of this time I am unequal to speak in detail. The mortal remains of John E. Owens rest in Greenmount Cemetery beside those of the dear mother he loved so devotedly. His genius and talent have given him enduring fame; but even more effulgent are his deeds of humanity, sympathetic kindness and tender helpfulness that are recorded in many hearts. They may not be blazoned forth to the world in trumpet tones; but they rise as fragrant incense to the shrine of his memory, and from them are distilled heavenly dew that keeps fresh and pure the remembrance of his life on earth.